"H
WELCOME TO DEATH . . ."

said the young punk in the yellow T-shirt, as he reached into his pocket and came out with a sliver of bright metal. The click of his switchblade was the loudest sound I'd heard in some time. I backed up, both hands on the chair I'd been sitting in, and the smiler with the switchblade moved closer in small steps, turning his wrist in tiny circles like a man who knew how to carve.

My instincts said *survive*, and I swung the chair as hard as I could, hitting him in the left hip and spinning him around. The chair slipped from my hands, flying between yellow T-shirt and his buddy, who was between me and the door. And then I was heading for that door like it was eternal salvation. I almost made it, but suddenly I was moving backwards instead, with a forearm across my windpipe making air hard to come by. Somebody also had my right arm and leg, and my throat hurt like hell as the room started turning red around me.

Then the front door slammed open and through the hot red-darkness that had swollen my head up to the size of a house, I heard somebody yell "Freeze!" *The cavalry had arrived just in time, and now it was my turn for revenge. . . .*

THE HARKER FILE

NATHAN HOLLANDER

LYNX BOOKS
New York

For my father,
Georg Elliot Olden,
with love

THE HARKER FILE

ISBN: 1-55802-196-5

First Printing/April 1976
Lynx Edition/January 1989

Published by special arrangement with the author.
Originally published in 1976 by Signet/New American Library.

Printed in the United States of America
0 9 8 7 6 5 4 3 2 1

1.

Trotman said, "Once is an accident. *Twice* is queer."

"Not when you're in love," I said.

"Yes, sireee. Twice is pretty damn fucking queer. Two dead people. Not one but two."

I watched him slowly stroke his flat nose, using a thumb the size of a knockwurst. Large thumbs go with a man two hundred and forty pounds and barely six feet tall. We sat in darkness, in the front seat of Trotman's Chevrolet parked in an apartment-house garage just off 15th and F Streets in Washington, D.C. The June night was Washington summer weather at its worst: hot and humid, hard to breathe, and thick enough to kick a hole in.

A mosquito whined near my ear. In the darkness, I felt it brush the back of my hand, its touch as light as an old man's whisper. I smacked myself quickly, zapping the mosquito. Rubbing my palm against my thigh, I blended the remains of the little bastard into my new tan summer gabardine.

Trotman's eyes closed to slits as though in prayer. Trotman praying? Now there's a thought. Trotman on his knees at night, head bowed, thick hands folded, praying to God to please send him a dog to kick. Trotman worked for the CIA.

Trotman cared about America, about what was being done to it by some of the people he worked for. That's why we were talking.

"These people shouldn't have died," he said, his voice hard to hear. "No reason for it."

I started playing investigative reporter. "Did you know them?"

He nodded yes.

I lifted an eyebrow, eyes on the big man. He'd shown me local newspaper clippings of the funerals. One funeral had been in Madison, Wisconsin, involving an ordinary dairy farmer named Rankin who had died of a heart attack four days ago. Nothing unusual. No police inquiry, no insurance company tearing his life apart to avoid payment.

The other clipping, dated six days ago, was from a small town in Iowa. A sixty-two-year-old man named Conway had been killed in an automobile accident involving three cars.

But it did seem a little out of place to me that a CIA man like Trotman would have known two ordinary citizens living in the boondocks.

"What's your connection with them?"

He sighed, large hands gripping the steering wheel as though he wanted to yank it loose and hit somebody with it. Trotman's hands were big enough to juggle typewriters as though they were oranges.

"I used to work with them." He said it so low that I almost didn't hear him. A CIA man working with two men whose lives and deaths should have been ignored by most of the world.

"When?" I said.

"Long time ago." His hands were still on the wheel, large hands made ugly by his line of work. Twice he'd been unlucky enough to be captured by the other side, and on at least one of those occasions, things had been done to his hands.

What they had done to his hands had stayed with him

long after the pain had pulled back to some small corner of his mind. Today the hands were stiff, thick at the joints, and he would never be able to stretch them entirely open. It was my guess that he couldn't deal a deck of cards.

"Long time ago," he said, still looking through the windshield into darkness. "Knew them before they were born."

"*Before* they were born?"

"Yeah. When I knew them they had other names. The names on their tombstones ain't what they came into the world with."

Trotman's telephone call to me in New York this morning said get down to D.C., that what he had for me couldn't be said over the phone. And he wasn't going to break the habits of a lifetime and start putting anything down on paper. Nobody in the Company puts anything on paper. Rule #1 and don't you forget it.

Trotman was one of six sources I had in the Company. Like the others, he was nobody's revolutionary or leftist. The big man was a Republican; Caucasian in thought, word, and deed; Episcopalian; and as far left as Julie Nixon. For all I knew, he wore, red, white, and blue underwear and his idea of fun was arresting blacks for being niggers on a sunny day.

America was being hurt by men with power who hadn't been elected to power, men with a free hand, lots of public money, and the morals of a child molester. Washington was full of them. Men appointed, hired, and brought in by friends and acquaintances. Putting these people in charge of anything amounted to taking a 747 up ten thousand feet and turning the controls over to Daffy Duck.

That was the trouble with the CIA today. The CIA was a bunch of sinister adolescents with tire irons, roaming the world and crushing skulls in the name of the American way of life. And these bloodstained cretins didn't have to account to anyone for their private little body count.

This didn't bother Trotman much. It bugged some of my other Company sources, but not the big man. After all, he'd gone forth more than once in his forty-eight years with a tire iron of his own. "Terminate with extreme prejudice'' was the way they put it. Having your brains smeared across your face was extreme.

No, what bothered Trotman was the practice of terminating *agents* when they weren't needed anymore. Agents who'd put their lives on the line for America. When you weren't useful anymore, the Company turned its face away and you were terminated, Jack. Killed, betrayed, left to be eaten by large rats in foreign jails. God help your ass when the Company looked the other way.

That's what Trotman didn't like. And I had the feeling it had something to do with what had happened to his hands and what might be happening right now in dark corners of the world to the hands of other agents. When you've been there, like Trotman, you *knew*.

That's what brought us together tonight.

I started to ask him about dead men with two sets of names. Trotman didn't give me the chance to open my mouth.

"Don't want to make this an all-night affair, Harker, so just listen. You'll understand why I couldn't go into this on the phone. We're losin' 'em. Givin' them up . . . and that's what disgusts me. Somebody, one of us, is givin' up names. And somebody else is looking up these people and terminating them. It's that simple.''

Not to me it wasn't. But I had the feeling now was the time to start taking notes in the dark. I swiveled around in my seat, feeling my underwear crawl up around my scrotum. It wasn't a nice feeling, but I couldn't think of another way to get my notebook out of my jacket.

"Specifics, Trotman. Something to go on.'' The heat wasn't bothering me anymore.

He was different now. His eyes burned into me, nailing me in place.

"Those two dead people I told you about aren't Americans. They're defectors. One's Russian, the other's Cuban. Both worked together in Cuba 'bout ten, twelve years ago. Worked for the Russian mission in Havana. I helped 'em cross over. Got 'em set up with new names, backgrounds, the works. I brought 'em over.'' He pounded his chest with an open hand and I listened for the sound of cracking bones. Nothing happened.

I went back to writing. Fast. I had the feeling, that funny feeling, that this trip was worth it. Can't explain . . . I never could. It's something a reporter knows or doesn't. And I know it was starting to happen now, right here, in the front seat of a cheap Chevrolet that Trotman had either stolen or borrowed for this meeting.

I wasn't about to interrupt him. I scribbled words, half-words, scribbled fast and didn't worry whether or not I could read it back later.

"The defectors were given American names, and relocated. At the time, five defectors came in with that bunch, all of them part of the same operation. They were in Cuba during that missile crisis we had some years back. Combination Russian-Cuban team working between Havana and Moscow, setting up nuclear-type weapons and shit like that."

He paused to take a breath. I didn't.

"The Russians couldn't go back to Moscow because of that Cuban missile thing. The Russian leader got blamed for backing down, for making Mother Russia look bad. Almost got his ass burned permanently for that one. But he lived through it. Some of his buddies didn't. When the new premier came in, he kicked ass right and left. So some of the Russians in Cuba decided it was better to defect than return and maybe get killed 'cause their honcho fucked up. Naturally we were interested in getting our hands on them."

I interrupted. "You said something about losing them, giving them up. That sounds like, uh—" Shit, I wasn't sure what it sounded like.

Trotman was. He leaned closer, and I could see his big red face with its high cheekbones, flat nose, yellow eyes, and knife edge of a mouth. I held my breath, fingers in a white knuckle grip around my ballpoint pen. Trotman's face could curdle milk.

"I'm saying that somebody in the CIA is killing these people."

I listened and couldn't take my eyes off him. Then I
forced myself to look away and started writing again.

"I'm telling you, Harker, that we either got super patriots in the Company, to pass judgment on these people,
or information on where these people can be found is being passed to the KGB."

"Jesus." I exhaled the word, leaning back against the
front seat. Too fucking much. The CIA giving up defectors. No. Couldn't be. Impossible. Hell, didn't I know
better? *Nothing impossible in Washington these days*.

"Trotman, you're telling me—"

He was impatient now, a professional who knew how
his game was played.

"Harker, shut the fuck up. I'm telling *you*, you ain't
telling me. OK?"

I said OK. I wasn't that stupid.

"Harker, I'm telling you it ain't right. Two times is two
times too many. Man, I *know*. In my business, you learn
to distrust perfection. Perfection means somebody's
workin' too hard to make it look good. Perfection sucks,
let me tell you."

"So tell me."

"Harker, I been in 'Wet Operations.' I can smell one.
And this is a wet one, believe me. Blood's being spilled,
I'm tellin' you. I think you can do something with this
one."

I sighed. I could . . . but what? I was on a CIA story
already, a story about Thomas Merle DeBlase, a sixty-
nine-year-old right-wing Texas fanatic worth seven billion
dollars. T.M. DeBlase would set up legitimate businesses
in foreign lands to be used as fronts by CIA agents. I was
trying to find out if the Company gave him economic tips
not available to your average businessman, enabling T.M.
DeBlase to grow richer.

I also wanted to know if T.M. DeBlase had encouraged
the Company to meddle in foreign countries so he could
make a profit on everything from helicopters to guns to tin
mines.

I *had* my CIA story already, and it would be a goody
if I could put it all together. That's why I was working six

CIA sources. But Trotman's story. Now that was something, really something. The Company bringing defectors across, then zapping them. My, my.

"Want to show you something, Harker." His big hand came from beneath the seat with a brown manila envelope. He passed it to me, a corner of his wide, no-lipped mouth pulling up in what passed for a smile.

I took four photographs out of the envelope, and, beside me, Trotman flicked the cover off a lighter and thumbed it into flame.

The photographs were eight-by-ten blowups, glossy, grainy prints that reflected the flickering orange flame like a mirror. I got the surprise of my fucking life.

Trotman said, "The tall dude, the one with the white hair, long face, and nasty look is Walter Fragan. He works in the library at Winslow University out in Indiana. Fragan's real name is Viktor Mikhail Valentine. He used to be a KGB colonel in Havana. Mean, tough son of a bitch. Got to watch Fragan. And the other guy—"

Trotman was enjoying himself now. Somebody was hurting.

"Is me," I said.

I could practically hear myself sweating. I shivered, suddenly chilly in the heat, wondering just what the hell was going on with my life. I was scared.

"Yeah, *you*, Harker. *You*." Trotman was smiling, actually smiling.

"*You*, Harker, right beside a man who came into the country with them two dead people ten years ago. A man who will probably be killed next, if I'm right about this shit that's goin' down. And you're right next to him. You think my story's worth your time?"

I looked down at the photographs.

"Do I think this story's worth my time? Does the bear shit in the woods? Do birdies sing in the morning? Trotman, what the fuck are you asking me dumb questions for?"

But I didn't take my eyes from those four photographs for long, long seconds.

2.

Winslow, Indiana, was one of those small towns where the natives had long been in the habit of parking their cars and pickup trucks with the fronts facing the sidewalk. This means Winslow had a wide street running through the center of town called "Main Street." I knew there had to be at least two people in town making a good living teaching baton twirling.

Two weeks ago, when I was there, the booster club had stretched a banner across the width of Main Street announcing an upcoming county fair.

Today, as I drove through, I got the feeling the fair was still going strong. There were more pickup trucks around than I remembered from my last visit. Some had crates of live chickens stacked on the back.

At least half the population of seventy thousand appeared to be in overalls, and maybe it was my imagination, but the number of country-music stations seemed to have tripled since my last visit. I fingered the car radio until my wrist ached, but all I came up with was men and women singing in nasal voices about having a last cup of coffee in a lonely diner.

Driving through Winslow took me as long as it takes to unwrap a stick of gum. My rented Mercury carried local plates, so I didn't sweat a hometown sheriff leaning on me because I was a so-called big-time New York reporter. If they had a reason to do it, and if they knew who I was, they might. But I drove through town under thirty miles an hour, and when I was outside it with a clear road ahead, I put my foot down until the speedometer needle touched forty.

I'd stayed in Washington last night, spending a restless six hours at the Hilton with a lot of things on my mind. Trotman had shaken me up with those photographs, now in the mail on the way back to my office at the *New York World-Examiner*. We'd talked some more and I knew I wasn't gong back to New York without first making a quick trip to Winslow University in Indiana. Walter Fragan had a small house near there.

Chances were he wouldn't be around, not if he was as smart as Trotman said he was. I could still come up with something, though—his friends, his interests, women, little boys, favorite television shows, what he wanted to be when he grew up. Something.

Also, I figured to get there first before the line formed. If Trotman was right, then other people would be poking around. Good guys and bad guys. And these days, who the hell knew which was which? Anyway, get there first, I thought, and you won't have any trouble. That's what I thought. Shows you how wrong a thirty-three-year-old investigative reporter can be.

Just wait till the word got out that I was working on this one. The shit would hit the fan by the barrelful. I'd gone through it before.

My paper, the *New York World-Examiner*, would be getting telephone calls by the dozen. The Company, naturally, plus the Justice Department, the State Department, and, if I was lucky, the White House would get in on it, too. At first, everybody would be as sweet as Annette Funicello, asking me on a buddy basis to kill the story.

After I was my usual nasty, uncooperative self, they'd go over my head to my editors and probably my publisher, the grande dame Elizabeth Edith Evans herself.

Most of the time, I could count on Eddie—my nickname for Mrs. Evans—to be on my side. Hell, wasn't she paying me eight hundred dollars a week, with expenses? And didn't I deliver two Pulitzer Prizes and ten other journalism awards in five years? How's that for poking your nose in other people's business?

A sign on the left side of the highway came toward me: WINSLOW UNIVERSITY—FIVE MILES. On the car radio, a woman sang about a cheating man who was fooling around with her sister, her cousin Mae, and her grandmother.

My girl Eddie. Eddie for Edith. She'd go with me on a story until it looked like we might get sued because the other side had a case. Then she would call a meeting and have a little talk with me and I'd better be ready to back up my side of the story. Eddie didn't get rich by eating bonbons and watching daytime television.

So, I was driving out to Winslow University to get on Fragan in a hurry, to come up with something quickly and quietly. My story on Thomas Merle DeBlase and how he was using the CIA to make himself even richer would have to wait.

And yet . . .

I wouldn't be coming back here if I hadn't dropped in on Winslow University two weeks ago.

On either side of the highway, low green hills were in the distance. I inhaled. Smelled nice out here, with just a tinge of horseshit in the air . . . but what the hell, how are the crops going to come up without it?

I looked at the land around me. Unreal. Plowed with a neatness you only see in postcards. Green stalks of some kind—small ones, medium-sized ones, big ones—all in long, even rows like something out of a Rodgers and Hammerstein musical. It was enough to make you take up tap dancing. A couple of farmers sat high on huge pieces of machinery, tearing at the land with mechanical perfection. What they were doing looked easy from where I sat.

But then, I'd been wrong about a few things in my life.

Like my marriage. That had ended in divorce not long ago. I still loved Loni and I was probably wrong there, too.

Two weeks ago, I'd made the same trip I was making now. A plane to Indianapolis, a car to Winslow. Then I had wanted to see the dedication of the Thomas Merle DeBlase building, a fifteen-million-dollar ego trip for the rich man from Texas. He'd donated a chrome, glass, and concrete monstrosity, plus money to pay the salary of a professor of political science for the next ten years.

It was when I approached one of DeBlase's high-priced flacks for an interview that I'd got the word on how low I stood in his scheme of things. Back had come the reply: "Mr. DeBlase does not support your ideology, Mr. Harker. Your request for an interview is denied." La de da.

Did that stop me? Does VD stop the world from screwing?

I tried again. And again. And again. The old fart was consistent. *No*, every time.

But I learned a few things. Like I learned about people he'd done business with and screwed in both ears. I learned about people who'd once worked for him and still hadn't stopped shaking. These people were willing to talk. They did.

Our boy DeBlase was nobody's Mr. Nice Guy. You don't get seven billion dollars by passing the plate in church. You get it by leaving a lot of bodies behind you. T.M. had done his share of leaving. He was a tough dude, despite his shy, polite, down-home manner. Our friend was as ruthless as a hammerhead shark, except that he had more teeth and used them better.

All he wanted out of life was money. Seven billion apparently wasn't enough for him. He wanted more. Currently he was out there scratching for his second seven billion. Some people are just go-getters, I guess.

Two weeks ago I'd shown up at the dedication of the DeBlase building hoping to change somebody's mind and get next to the big man himself, to ask him about his romance with the CIA. DeBlase has got to be there, I thought. Got to.

He was. With enough security on hand to fight a war or handle a rock concert. His own men, plus goons from Winslow. They were everywhere: in the audience gathered in front of the building, around the building, even near the speaker's platform.

It happened so fast I almost missed it. Almost. One minute the college president, a sweating clown with a sleazy smile, was leaning forward and speaking into the microphone, thanking the honorable Thomas Merle De-Blase for his gift to higher education. The next minute some students were running onstage, holding placards, yelling, cursing, calling DeBlase a warmonger.

The students—anywhere from six to a dozen—were also spitting invectives in the direction of the university president for being a mercenary cocksucker out for a buck.

What happened next only went to show that the meek would not inherit the earth until T.M. DeBlase is good and finished with it. His security guards went into action and began pounding on the demonstrators. T.M.'s apes were pros. The demonstrators got on the platform, God knows how, but they didn't get close enough to T.M. to ruffle his pocket handkerchief.

The goons took them on, beat the pee out of them with factory-line efficiency, then, as a crowd-pleasing finale, tossed a couple of them onto us more restrained onlookers who were still sitting stunned in our seats. A kid in jeans and a short-sleeved sweatshirt had come flying at me with arms and legs churning like a toy out of control.

I moved in a hurry, me and those sitting on either side of me.

That's when somebody had taken those four photographs I'd dropped in the mail this morning. Pictures of me and a highly annoyed Walter Fragan, trying like hell not to get our skulls bashed in by flying students.

At the moment, all I could figure was that somebody eyeing Fragan had taken the pictures and I had been in the wrong spot at the wrong time. Somebody at the CIA. That's how Trotman had got his gigantic hands on them.

3.

Ahead of me, heat waves danced on the highway, shimmering on both sides of the yellow dividing line. It didn't make driving any easier. Looking at the heat waves was like trying to see through crumpled cellophane. Reaching up, I pulled down the sun visor and blinked to clear my eyes. My watch said 11:00. My stomach rumbled, rebelling against the nothing breakfast thrown at me on this morning's no-frills flight. One stale cheese danish that had tasted like a frisbee, washed down with a thimbleful of hot orange juice. Terrific.

There was no air-conditioning in the car, and rolling down the windows had only let in the heat. All of a sudden, it had become hot. Sweat rolled off me in cupfuls and breathing was hard work. Well, what the hell. I'd be in the Winslow suburbs soon, on my way to Fragan's house. Who knows what I'd find there.

Right now, not even the Company knew where Fragan had run to ground.

That's what investigative reporting was all about: getting your ass out on the street and doing your own bird-dogging. Not like television. "Electronic journalists." That's a laugh. Those TV clowns sat around air-conditioned studios smiling into the mirror at their capped teeth, waiting to be handed something to read on camera. You think a guy wearing makeup is going out to dig up his own stories? If these turkeys are reporters, then whores are social workers.

The car radio wasn't helping me. I'd heard "The Wabash Cannonball" twice on this drive. Need I say that was twice too much. And speaking of two . . .

In the rear mirror, I saw them behind me. Two pickup trucks, both covered with a coat of soft white dust. They didn't seem to be in a hurry. Neither made any attempt to pass me. We were a sun-roasted little convoy. Me in my rented Mercury, followed by Farmer Brown #1 and #2.

On the other side of the highway, traffic was light to nonexistent. A couple of cars, no more, came toward me on that side, passed, and kept heading behind me into the sun and heat. Other than that, the highway was bare on both sides. Something lonely about an empty highway. Nothing but black asphalt, tall green cornfields, and, far down the road, pale blue sky. So why didn't the two pickups behind me pull out and swing around the slow-driving, big-city reporter? Why didn't they hightail it to Winslow for fun and frolic at the fair? Yeah, why?

Seconds later, I found out why . . . and didn't like it at all.

Truck #1, the one directly behind me, sped up and pulled out with a roar. Whoever was behind the wheel moved out like he was on fire. When the roar from his motor punched my ears, I turned to see what was going on. By then, he'd eaten up almost all of the space between us. By a count of two he was inching up beside me in the next lane.

Drag-race time? No way! At this point, I still wasn't concerned with him or his friend. Shitkickers out on a spree. That's what I thought. Wrong, Harker.

For a pickup truck, Farmer #1 had a motor A.J. Foyt would have drooled over. For a second or two he was in the lane to my left, no cars coming toward him. Then with

a spurt that opened my eyes, he swung ahead of me into
my lane and kept on speeding. But not for long.

Suddenly he braked, swerving to his left, tires squealing
and leaving long white dusty skid marks on the bare black
asphalt. Oh, shit. The bastard was blocking the entire
highway, his pickup truck now parked sideways and strad-
dling both lanes. What the fuck was he trying to do? Drunk
out of his mind on mountain dew, probably.

I still had enough yards between us to slow down. But
before I could even touch the brake, I got hit from behind.
Clang! Truck #2. It smacked me hard, my head snapping
forward, then back. The seat belt across my chest bit into
my ribs and I guess my eyes must have been open wide
enough to see into tomorrow. Somehow my foot reached
the brake and I swerved into the next lane. Goddamn it! I
was going to get out and give these farmers some heated
words.

I wasn't happy at having shitkickers in dusty pickups
use me for a hockey puck. Man, I was going to park this
thing and do some yelling.

Bang! Behind me Truck #2 ramming into me again.
Twice from the rear. The son of a bitch must have been
Greek. My head jerked forward, then back again, like one
of those toy wooden birds that sit on the edge of a water
glass and go back and forth, back and forth. That did it.
That did it. I was good and pissed now, ready to step out
and start swinging at somebody.

I wasn't your barroom brawler, being more of a schemer
than a warrior. But twice? Shit, that was deliberate. That
was . . .

Suddenly, Trotman's words came back to me. *Once is
an accident. Twice is queer. Twice is queer.*

Harker, this is a setup. You are in the process of being
had, my man. Those farmers know what they're doing.
Two pickup trucks are playing volleyball with your entire
body on an Indiana highway. You are being double teamed,
sucker.

In a fraction of a second, my stomach felt as though it
were wrapped in crushed ice. My hands shook and I
breathed loudly, chest heaving up and down like a giant

piston. Fear paralyzes you if you let it. It was about to do that to me. If I let it.

Another quick look behind me. Truck #2, which I saw had two occupants, was backing up, getting ready for a good shot at me this time. No, I didn't have any idea who they were. I didn't care, either. At the moment, I had a gut feeling that it would have been a waste of time to get out of the car and tell them that they could get in trouble wasting a reporter.

Obviously I was doing something somebody didn't want me to do. Obviously it had something to do with Fragan. Obviously I had to get my ass out of there in a hurry.

My hands quickly tore at the seat belt. Bad time for a case of stone fingers. But I got the seat belt unhooked. Truck #2 was rolling now, speeding toward me with its tires scraping loudly against the highway. It was moving. So was I.

I looked front. Farmer #1 jumped out of his pickup and out onto the highway. A small man with faded blue jeans, boots, straw hat, mirrored sunglasses. And a gun. The little man was quick. He dropped to one knee, left hand cupping his right fist, which held the gun in the steadiest grip this side of *Kojak*.

His right arm was stiff, extended as far as it could go. He gave me the feeling he'd done this before.

Here I was, a lousy driver with a lousy car. No way around or over little-man-on-his-knee-with-a-gun, backed by his dusty little truck. And I definitely couldn't go backward.

I jerked the steering wheel left, turning it for all I was worth, turning off onto the dirt between highway and tall, green cornfield. Roller-coaster time. The Mercury bumped, jerked, and bounced. My teeth chattered like dice in a cup and not just from the poor shock absorbers. I bounced up and down, head jerking as though keeping time to a beat that was much too fast.

Behind me, the second pickup sped by, braked, and kept on sliding until it was out of sight in my rear-view mirror. Looking into that mirror wasn't easy when you were bouncing two feet off the seat every other second.

One minute, I had a fairly good view of the highway. The next, all I could see was blue sky as the Merc hit a patch of rough ground and took off.

The bad thing about going up is that you have to come down. I did. Hard.

A sharp pain jolted my ass, shot up to my spine, then stabbed my brain. I clenched my teeth and kept my foot down on the accelerator. Bump, bump, bump. Shake, rattle, and roll. The car tried, Lord, did it try. It bounced but kept on going. So did I. For me, it was like being inside a cement mixer. Under the Merc the ground was plowed, but plowed ground is not intended to sustain a Grand Prix.

In the rear-view mirror, the dust shifted enough for me to see the little man on the highway, jumping up and down like Rumpelstiltskin, waving to Truck #2 to get the hell on back and get after me. Rumpelstiltskin seemed frantic, as if in an intense hurry to catch up to me. His little arm sliced through the air in vicious signals, pointing me out, encouraging Truck #2. I cringed, expecting to feel a bullet any second.

I crashed into the tall stalks of green and pale gold, crushing them, sending them flying left and right with a series of sharp *snaps*, one after the other. *Whish, whish, whish.* Cornstalks brushed the car, reaching for me through the open windows and beating me in the face for being so goddamn destructive. It all smelled so nice and fresh, it was almost tempting to stop and enjoy nature's wonders. Almost, but not quite.

Snap-snap. The car ran into more corn as it rocked from side to side. It slid down one furrow, climbed out, and slid down another. Cornstalks continued to beat against the sides of the car, the opened window, the windshield. Bumpety-bump-bump. Just like riding a rocking horse down a flight of stairs while somebody swung at your head with a broom. Me, I could do without it. But the alternative was to let those homicidal farmers behind me get close enough to shove a gun up my nose.

Swish-swish-snap-snap-snap. I was totaling somebody's

cornfield, not that I meant to. My Merc was a four-wheel wrath of God, flattening corn every which way.

No telling how big this field was; no telling where I was headed. Nothing behind me except a cornfield that had been hit in a hurry by a man who had trouble driving well on concrete. . . . Then I saw them.

The bastards were in one truck, at least I assumed they were. Bouncing up and down, following my trail with no trouble at all. Shit. *That was the trouble*. I wasn't exactly the invisible man out here, with flattened cornstalks pointing the way and my car bouncing and grinding gears at three miles an hour. Time for a shift in tactics. My foot jammed down on the brake.

At the same time I opened the door on my left, grabbed my jacket with my notebooks in the inside pocket, and jumped out. I hit the ground running. Around the front of the Merc and heading right, crouched over like John Wayne hitting the beach at Iwo Jima. Across two, three rows, pushing cornstalks aside, sinking into soft brown earth up to my ankles. Then forward, between rows. More running room now, and I took it.

Jogging and fornication were my primary exercises. Some folk who didn't like what I wrote often said my only exercise was jumping to conclusions. What the hell did they know? In college I'd run track. Middle distances because I didn't have much speed. Four-forty, half-mile. At thirty-three, I wasn't what I'd been at twenty, but I could still move. Especially when I thought about what would happen to me if I didn't.

In the past, I'd had people dislike my stories. Jesus, had I ever. And their displeasure had been expressed in such ways as obscene phone calls, letters written in crayon, letters with shit smeared over them, dead snakes, live tarantulas, income-tax audits, death threats galore, and promises to beat the hell out of me as soon as possible.

So I have developed a nose for a displeased public. Those dudes behind me were displeased.

I stopped, crouching, sweating and breathing hard. My hands fumbled with my jacket, taking out the notebooks and putting them in my back pants pocket. Didn't want to lose them. No, sir. Didn't want to lose my wallet and credit cards either. That I shoved in my front pants pocket as best I could. Behind me and to my left, too soon if you ask me, I heard the truck pull up, stop, and somebody shout. I got up and started running.

4.

They didn't bother being quiet. They shouted and stomped around the cornfield as if they were in their own living rooms. The shouts said they were three. Three with guns against one with a ballpoint pen. Whoever wrote that the pen is mightier than the sword wasn't sitting in a cornfield when he wrote it. I was trying to be quiet, moving between rows rather than across them.

By now, I had enough dirt inside my shoes to start my own mountain. Running in a plowed field was a little better than driving in it. A little, but not much. I kept sinking down in the field to my ankles, which made running very tough. The tall corn still smelled sweet and fresh, and it kept a lot of the hot sun off my tired, sweating body.

A shout. Closer now. Another shout.

"Hey! Hey! Here 'tis, here 'tis!"

They had found my trail. Some loudmouth bastard shouting about me as though I were a possum. *It*. Is that what my life had come down to, an *it*? I thought of Loni, the way you always think of someone you love when you feel it's all over for you. She had always told me this job would kill me one way or another. I'd told her I'd rather die with her sitting on my face.

I held on to my jacket. No sense leaving clues for them to find me. The cornfield seemed endless. Like a bad dream. Row after row of tall green and no way out. Maybe I was lucky the cornfield was so big. Who the hell knew what was on the other side? Maybe a brick wall fifty feet high. Maybe open ground for thirty miles in every direction and me on foot. And them on foot, too. With guns. No. Calm yourself, Harker. Sit on your nerves and keep on running. Behind me, they ran too. And from the sounds they made, they were running faster than I was.

"Split up! Go 'round! Git on up ahead, git out in front of him!"

The mysterious drawler again. Shouting instructions. Nice to see somebody was organized in this chaotic world, even at my expense. *Get around me. Get out in front of me.* Fuck you, too, shitkickers, whoever you are.

My soaked shirt was as dirty as a coal miner's socks. My chest ached from sudden running. I was tired, jumpy, anxious to stay alive. Like I said, fighting's not my game. Scheming is, however. Time to do some. Be tricky, Harker. Be mean. Be yourself.

If they had split up as ordered, they'd be moving in on me one at a time. Cool. Let's hope it was going down that way. One at a time. Let's see.

First, I needed some ground that wasn't so level. Needed it in a hurry. I looked around, hating the sound of the three men thrashing through the cornfield and getting closer. Over there. A little dip between rows, where the ground dropped somewhat. Almost the size of a man. Almost enough to bury me in if I was wrong. OK, so much for that. Now, what's next? Yeah, over there.

I ran over to a stalk of corn six feet away from the dip in the ground. My hands shook as I hung my coat on the stalk. I was breathing too loud, I knew it. Tough shit. Can't worry 'bout that now. Nice, strong stalk of corn. America's finest. It bent and so did my hopes. But it held and my coat clung to it. I breathed out. Jesus. Thank God for high-class fertilizer. Makes for strong vegetation every

time. Watching that stalk of corn bend and hold made my
heart stop at least twice.

Over to the incline. And down in it. Flat on my stomach. Scooping dirt on myself like a child at play. Or a man
trying to bury himself alive. I was now at an angle to my
coat, six feet or so away and not to be noticed immediately
if you had your mind somewhere else and all you thought
you were chasing was a big-city reporter, a soft, easy
mark.

Sooner or later, whoever found the coat would look
around and find me there. But I wasn't about to hide forever. All I wanted was time . . . and one shot of my own.
As I frantically piled soft, dark brown dirt on my legs,
back, shirt, I heard them. Still thrashing around trying to
pick up the exact trail instead of the general direction.

That's where I'd been a little smarter than the drawlers.
I'd done my running between the rows, on the natural
path. I'd made less noise, broken almost no cornstalks,
left less behind me. They had to work to find my trail
now. It could be done. I'd be a fool to think differently.

The dirt was warm against my face and mouth. I
scooped like I had never scooped before. Some of it got
in my mouth. I didn't care. If my quickie idea didn't work,
I'd have dirt in my mouth for a lot longer time.

I stopped. Somebody was close. Damn. Real close. I
froze, lying in my semi-hole as stiff as if I belonged there
permanently. Mustn't think like that, Harker. Think pos-
itive.

I heard him. One man. To my left. I shifted my head
by inches, lifting it up and expecting a bullet in the ear
any second. My heart tried to jump out of my rib cage
and I was close to peeing in my pants.

He was the little dude. Mirrored sunglasses and all.
Face burned red by the sun, short-sleeved yellow shirt
with arms burned brown. A man who spent a lot of time
outdoors. Probably killing newborn birds.

Oh, God, he was taking his fucking time creeping
through the corn toward my coat. But he had his eyes on
it and nothing else. After he got close enough to it and
looked around, he'd spot me lying here and my dick would

be in the wringer thereafter. Closer, closer, then he was on the coat, reaching out for it with the hand that held the gun, poking gently at the sleeves. My new summer gabardine.

He was to my left, eyes on the coat. He'd be shouting soon. My hand fumbled around for a rock, something hard to throw over his head. I found it. It wasn't a rock. Farm youth called it horse apples. City folk called it dried horseshit. I threw it, arching it over the little man's head. Before it landed, I was up on my feet with two hands full of dirt. He turned from my jacket to the sound of the horseshit hitting a stalk of corn. When he snapped quickly around to me, I heaved the dirt in his face.

He stumbled backward, hands in front of his eyes. I kicked him in the balls, sending him flying backward into a row of corn, crashing into it and tearing some more of it loose.

Spinning around, I ran back toward the highway, pulling all the speed I could out of my tired body. Hell, I didn't smoke, didn't drink. Hadn't jogged in months, either. But I promised myself I would start tomorrow if I got out of here alive. I ran, Jesus, I ran. My lungs burned, my eyes watered, and lifting my feet up out of the dirt was an effort. But I ran.

I reached my car. Shit! The way it was stuck in the ground at an angle like that, I couldn't back that sucker out in time. The men with the drawl would be on me like white on rice before I had backed up two feet. I kept running.

I reached the highway.

Nothing. No cars coming either way. Shit. Then—

I saw it. Pickup truck #1. Still in the middle of the highway. In seconds I reached it, yanking the door open. Hallelujah. Little dude with mirrored sunglasses had come out of it in a hurry. I'd remembered that. He'd come out too fast to pay attention to the keys. They dangled on the ignition, with a rabbit's foot and a small pair of red plastic dice attached. I switched on the motor and didn't bother putting it into reverse.

I swung the truck around, bumping over dirt. I kept my

foot on the accelerator. Back on the highway, I looked in
the rear-view mirror. One man ran out of the cornfield,
across the dirt, and stopped in the middle of the highway.
He wore jeans, too, with a work shirt and dark sunglasses.
He kept getting smaller as I sped toward the Winslow suburbs.

I had the strong feeling that neither he nor his fellow
drawlers would forget what I'd just done to them. Fuck it.
I exhaled and kept driving. My hands didn't stop shaking
for much longer than that.

5.

Walter Fragan's house was on Willow Springs Lane, a name straight out of a Walt Disney movie or a Fire Island gay bar.

Me and the dusty pickup rolled slowly past it once. Circling around on the empty, quiet streets, I passed it again. Nothing moved in or around it. The Fragan residence appeared empty. Cool. The last thing I wanted was company. What's more, I was in a hurry. That trio behind me might get tired of stomping around the cornfield and decide to come for their truck. Along with my scrotum.

Having those three clowns play sandwich with me and my car back there on the highway weighed heavily on my mind. Had to be the Company. Who else had a strong interest in seeing me back off from this story?

The Company would be hurt by a public airing of its inability to protect defectors. No two ways about it. Tough. My job was reporting, not sympathizing with people who had made "dirty tricks" an art form and slept with tire irons under their pillows. So I was on the CIA's shit list. Wasn't I always?

However, this was the first time they'd ever got physical about it. Nasty phone calls, nasty looks when we met, but nothing more than that. Until now.

God, did the air around me smell. I reeked. In the small front seat of the pickup, the hot air trapped my body odor and held it in place. Sweat, horseshit, farm dirt. I looked rotten and smelled ripe.

Breakfast. Food was back on my mind. Maybe Fragan would have an apple or jelly beans or something I could rip off.

I played it cool, walked up to the front door and rang the bell. No answer. I rang it again, looking left and right to see if anybody was watching me. Clean windows, curtains drawn, and green grass looking like the top of a pool table. Fragan was neat.

Stepping off the tiny front porch and back into the sun, I shaded my eyes and blinked, looking up at the top floor. My sunglasses were in the cornfield and I wasn't going back to get them. No sign of anything or anybody. I was playing it straight. Just a friend come to call.

I tried the back door. *Open.* How about that? Unlocked. My heart started jumping around again. Son of a bitch. Was the open door something to worry about or ignore? Well, I'd come this far. No sense backing off now. I went in.

Two steps brought me into a small kitchen. Like everything else around Walter Fragan, it was neat. Not that it did me much good, but I opened cabinets and closets. Nothing. Nothing to eat either. A lot of spices, seven or eight different kinds of peppers, sauces. Not what you'd call gourmet eating.

The refrigerator was next. Well, well. A container of milk, half full and not sour. Your health, Colonel. I drank it all, letting the coolness slide down into my stomach. Putting the empty carton back, I pulled out some slices of cheddar cheese and a pineapple yogurt. Cramming the cheese in my mouth, I found a spoon and began walking.

I was in the living room, scraping the bottom of the yogurt container, loading up the spoon for that final trip to my mouth.

"Damn, Harker. Don't they pay you people enough money? Now you're down to breaking and entering and ripping off iceboxes. What *is* the world coming to?"

I froze. My heart hit my throat, then bounced back to where it belonged. I stopped breathing and stood there with the last spoon of yogurt poised in front of my opened mouth. My feelings swung from stone fear to feeling like an asshole as soon as I recognized the voice.

It came from behind me.

Roy Lupus.

Of the CIA.

A Company man like none other. Meaning trouble.

That voice. Precise as algebra, with enough malice in it to let you know that he meant business and took life seriously. And enough politeness to hide the meanness.

Better to face him while I was still breathing. "Mr. Roy Lupus," I said. "And friends. I recognize Kalter but the other gentleman's a stranger to me." Kalter was a small man with a long nose and thin, wet brown hair combed sideways. He chewed his bottom lip a lot and followed Roy Lupus everywhere. He followed Lupus so closely that if Lupus ever stopped suddenly, Kalter would be arrested for sodomy. The third man with them, the one I'd never seen before, was an unsmiling black man no bigger than a 747. Like other blacks in government service, he wore only a moderate Afro, along with a suit, tie, and expression of respectability. He could win the hearts of law-and-order-minded whites everywhere.

It's when you looked closer that you saw he could be a bad ass on wheels. His brown eyes picked at me like a hawk clawing at a dead deer. I got the feeling that if Lupus had pointed a finger at me and screamed, "Kill!" the black man would have pulled my leg from its socket and beat me to death with it.

"The other man?" Lupus said playfully. "Lamont, say hello to Harker, prize-winning reporter and house-breaker."

Lamont nodded once, dropping his square jaw a quarter of an inch. Blink your eyes and you would have missed it. As for words, Lamont wasn't wasting any. The stingy nod was it. All the time he watched me as though I were planning to run off with the silverware and he was being paid to see that I didn't.

I nodded back, a hell of a lot bigger nod than his. "Lamont. Well, you guys interested in why I called you all together?"

Kalter shook his head from side to side sadly, as though I were a child refusing to learn to pee the right way. Big, black Lamont gave me another one of his special nods, this one going the other way, his chin coming *up* a quarter of an inch and something like laughter brightening his eyes for a few seconds. Lamont was cool, contained, and not about to show anything. He'd learned that in the ghetto, where he'd long since decided that the best way to get along with whitey was to keep everything inside. Unless Lamont caught somebody in a dark alley one night and felt like having fun.

Lamont was close to six feet four, two hundred and forty plus, and no more fat on him than a brick. He was the kind of man you'd call "sir" at all times, if you were smart.

"Love that outfit, Harker." Lupus pointed to me, taking one step in my direction and grinning like a wolf hot after a job as chicken plucker. Behind me, Kalter snickered. Lamont's eyes grew brighter, then faded. His hilarity obviously had its limits.

"Yeah," I said, smoothing my filthy, stinking shirt. "Going to be all the rage next year. Thought I'd be the first on my block."

"You always were a man of vision, Harker. Want to tell me what you're doing here?"

"No, I don't want to tell you what I'm doing here. But I will. I'm here for the same reason you are."

"What's that?"

"Don't *you* know why *you're* here?"

Roy Lupus smiled, if you could call it that. He was average height, average looks, no moustache or beard, and all his clothes came right off the rack. A perfect CIA man. You wouldn't look at him twice. If you did, you couldn't describe him if somebody shoved a gun in your ear. His sense of ethics was about the same as Attila the Hun's.

We'd had run-ins before. As a result, we got along like oil and water. I'd once written a story about the CIA and something they'd done to an emerging African nation. Roy Lupus had been involved in that. Some people had died. Another of my stories had exposed the Company's hiring of homosexual male prostitutes to entice UN delegates. Lupus had his grimy fingers in that one, too.

When the stories broke, Congress did what it usually does. Nothing. Oh, a couple of Congressmen took time out from their lecture tours to come back to Washington and pose for new photographs with copies of my story waving in righteous indignation above their heads.

Nevertheless, the Company was shaking over that one. That's why Roy Lupus would love to wander by and see me hanging from a tall building by my fingertips, so he could tap-dance on my thumbs.

"Harker, you're in over your head this time. Playing cute won't cut it. It's show and tell. You're a long way from home, pilgrim." Lupus cupped his fingers in front of his crotch, then twiddled his thumbs.

I wasn't buying it. Not his half-assed threats, not his eyeball-to-eyeball bullshit.

"Nothing. You're getting nothing, Lupus, and if you want to make a case out of it, go ahead. You haven't learned yet?"

"Learned what?" He stopped twiddling his thumbs and began chewing a corner of his mouth, like a man starting to deal with a problem.

"Learned that I'm not some high-school reporter you can drag down to the principal's office and give five demerits."

I sounded like a hardass reporter who could topple empires. But I felt like a schmuck wearing dirty clothes and holding an empty yogurt container.

Lupus sighed. Maybe that was a sign some of his hard-nose approach was easing off. Maybe.

"OK, Harker, you can burn us. No two ways about it. You know it, we know it. I'm asking you to cooperate."

"You're not asking me to cooperate. You're asking me to bow my head and bend my knee. Don't come on wrapped in the flag like Kate Smith. Cooperate is one thing. Letting you fuck me over is another." I suddenly remembered those three clowns back in the cornfield.

Lupus turned both palms up, a sign of sincerity and openness in some people. Not in Roy Lupus. "OK, OK. You got power. You sit down at that typewriter of yours and ten minutes later somebody cries. Maybe we can work together."

"Like cobra and mongoose."

I was tired of standing. Let these three stand. Looking around, I saw a brown and yellow couch near a grand piano. I walked over to the couch, noticing Bach piano scores propped up on the piano. So the good Colonel liked to run his nimble fingers across the keyboard. We had that in common. I didn't play but I loved Bach. Great music to indulge in unnatural sex practices by. Somebody had dropped a Spanish newspaper on the couch. *La Luz Fuerte* out of Miami, Florida. There was a name in pencil on the outside: Enrique Estevez-Blanco.

"Cobra and mongoose? Shit, Harker, why the hell are you always coming on so strong?"

"Me? Me coming on strong?" The thought of that cornfield made me want to run across the room and drop-kick Lupus' nuts into Kentucky. It would have been a good idea had Lamont been up someplace in Harlem.

"Look," I said, "the Constitution and the Bill of Rights guarantee free speech. Which means I get my say no matter who doesn't like it. It doesn't say in either document that you have the right to run me off the road and chase me around some fucking cornfield in ninety-degree heat. Furthermore, I don't see where it says you got the right to wave guns around—"

"Harker? You out of your mind? You been in the sun too long?" Lupus looked at me as innocently as he could. He seemed confused. He frowned like a man with constipation.

Innocent, my ass. I was wound up now.

"Three goons, Lupus. Three of them. Playing bump the

reporter. Just ten miles out of town. Then ring-around-the-rosy out in a cornfield, and they had guns. Fucking guns. When I get back East, I'm going to drop this on somebody's head and you ain't gonna like it.'' Assuming they let me out of here alive. I was coming on strong, pushing like I had all the aces. I didn't. They had at least one. Big, black, mean-looking, unsmiling Lamont. The ace of spades.

Lamont was big enough to shot-put me into the Gulf of Mexico.

Lupus was all smiles. ''Harker, if we had tried, we'd have succeeded. You are not loved, not one little bit. Sending you to that big typewriter in the sky would have been a labor of love with us. And we would have made sure you made the *early* edition.''

I guess my mouth was opened because Kalter snickered again, like the mouse in those Tom and Jerry cartoons.

''Harker, there's no order to terminate you that I know of. Of course, I haven't phoned in, in the last ten minutes.''

''Very fucking funny.'' At least I had my power of speech back.

Kalter entered the we-hate-Harker sweepstakes. He said, ''Harker, I'd give a month's pay to piss on your grave. If they told me you had to go, you'd go. But nobody's told me yet.'' His voice was soft, like that of an old family friend. And he meant every word he'd just said. Lamont let a small smile touch his lips, as though enjoying the sight of us white folks tearing each other limb from limb.

My eyes went to Kalter. ''Can't wait until they develop the rest of those CIA fag films, Kalter. Like to see what you look like on your hands and knees with your mouth full.''

He didn't like that. His eyes grew round as saucers and he inhaled, the noise speeding across the room like a gunshot. His little head tilted back on small shoulders and he stared at me as though I were kicking his mother in the head and he couldn't wait to get at me.

Lupus snorted and went into his Henry Kissinger number. "OK, OK. Let's not make it any worse. We're not after you, Harker. At least not after you *that* way."

"*Somebody* came after me. Less than half an hour ago. Three men, two pickup trucks. I didn't like it."

Lupus leaned his neatly combed head to one side, connecting what I'd just told him with the way I was dressed. He nodded gently several times as though understanding. His sympathies appeared to be with the unknown threesome.

"Well, Harker, I guess a few people out there don't think you're the American Dream. Maybe they don't like what you write."

"I don't think these three can read. Anyway, strange as it seems, I believe you."

I did. Lupus and Kalter were the type to do it right the first time, especially if doing it right meant getting rid of a reporter they didn't like. What's more, Lamont looked perfectly capable of lending them a helping hand. Who was after my ass?

"Like I said, Lupus, I believe you're not after me. Which doesn't mean I'm your dearest friend. Far from it. So we trade. I show you yours, you show me mine."

"Harker, it's the other way 'round. You show me *yours*, I'll show you *mine*."

"OK, me first. My one and only act of good faith of the day. Tracking down a rumor that you're having trouble holding onto defectors. Specifically, they're getting killed and it's making you look bad."

Lupus filled his cheeks with air until he looked like a chipmunk. He blew the air out slowly, then scratched the back of his neck. When he spoke, he was looking at the floor.

"Who told you?"

"You got to be kidding, Lupus." I leaned back against the couch, glancing again at that Spanish newspaper beside me. It had come to Fragan in the mail. From Miami. Again I noted the Cuban name on the outside, then turned back to Lupus.

"Harker," he said, "I know you're not going to believe this—"

"You're right, I won't."

"—But it really is a matter of security. I can't play one on one with you. It's heavy this time. There's trouble with defectors, OK, you know that. But if anything gets out on this—"

"I know, I know. You won't have anybody to show off to Congressional committees, and without foreign bodies, live ones, Congress might cut back your oversized appropriations."

"It's more than that—"

"It usually is." I kept watching Lupus. He hid his anxiety well, but his eyes gave it away.

"Harker, I'm asking you to—"

"To give away my sources, to open up to you, to be a shitty reporter. No way. Look, Lupus, someday this story's gonna come out anyway. Six months or six years from now, it'll come out. So it might as well be *now* and it might as well be *me*."

Lupus licked his lips, filled his lungs with air, and said in a voice deceptively soft, "Why do you always have to do it the hard way? Other reporters—"

"Other reporters, my ass. Those clowns aren't reporters, they're typists. Washington's full of them, which is why I work out of New York. Washington reporters are party-goers, happy to be having lunch with Henry or Jerry or Nelson so they can call up Aunt Mae and squeal to her over the phone about what big men *they* are. Washington reporters socialize and make friends, the worst thing a reporter can do. You can't fuck over your friends. They suck, these reporters."

I stood up and yawned. I was still hungry. And I was sick of breathing my own clothes. Lupus sighed, patting his neat hair. "So that's it, you're not going to cooperate."

"Lupus, let's stop jerking each other off. You want to pick my brains and give me shit in return. No deal. Look, send me a press release. Washington's big on that. Press release, press kit, press conference." I looked around Fragan's living room. Nothing much. Clean, not a throw pillow out of place and enough books to start his own lending library. Mostly books in Spanish. One thing was certain: Lupus wasn't going to let me look around. He had the right to stop me from doing that. He also had Lamont.

But I had seen that newspaper. And that name.

"Guess that's it, huh, Harker? Power of the press and all that?" Lupus clapped his hands together, a signal that we'd come to the end of an unproductive get-together.

"Power of the press and all that, Lupus." It was all that stood between me and having my teeth knocked out. That's why I was still standing.

"Where you going now?" Lupus grinned, letting me know I was being dismissed without a chance to search Fragan's home.

I shrugged. I couldn't argue with them. Especially not with Lamont.

"Back East." Miami, where Estevez-Blanco was.

"What with those people you said tried to get you, maybe it would be better if Lamont here drove you back to town."

I frowned. Since when was Lupus being so good to me? Then it flashed across my slow brain, like a light bulb going on over Little Orphan Annie's head when she gets a brilliant idea. Lupus wanted to keep an eye on me, to keep me out of this area.

Funny thing. For once he and I agreed on something. With Lamont along, at least until I could get another car, I'd have a good chance of living until Thursday. Yeah, I liked that idea. My man Lamont.

"Yeah, OK, Lupus. Lamont here can keep an eye on me, make sure I leave the area."

Lamont's eyes lit up and again he started to smile, but changed his mind.

Conversation was over. Turning, I walked to the front door, opened it, and stepped out onto the front porch and into the summer heat and sun. Lamont was behind me. I hadn't even heard him.

"Nice day," I said, squinting up at the sun, my hands shading my eyes.

Lamont walked past me, saying nothing. A man of few words, Lamont.

6.

"Uggghhh!"

Belching into the telephone, I patted my full stomach. "Sorry about that, Mrs. Karakas. Let me have that name again, please?"

Belching into the telephone is a display of bad manners. The forty-eight-year-old Sarah Karakas, my pumpkin-faced secretary at the *World-Examiner*, wasn't going to let me get away with that. I should have known better.

Her disapproval exploded in my ear, a snort of air as sharp and as deadly as anything that ever speeded out of a Winchester. Wincing, I shifted the receiver to my right ear. I didn't have that many ears left.

"McClan," she said coolly.

"McClan." I scribbled fast.

"You'd have heard it the first time, if you weren't making such a pig of yourself. God, you sound like an Arab. *They* belch after meals. Compliment to the host, according to *them*." *They. Them.* Mrs. Karakas was an expert on the shortcomings of us all.

"Yeah, yeah. Who else?"

She rustled through sheets of paper. I was at the Indianapolis Airport. She was behind her desk at the *World-Examiner*, checking messages for me. Mrs. Karakas enjoyed being a puritan.

"Let's see. McClan. Oh, Perry and the Colonel."

All three names were sources on T.M. DeBlase and his money-making with the CIA. McClan was a lawyer who'd helped DeBlase set up small airlines abroad, for use as CIA covers. A few months ago, T.M. had dumped him. Six months' severance pay and nothing but a one-line note saying "Get out." Today, McClan was a bitter fifty-nine-year-old living in Vermont. He drank too much. He didn't practice law anymore either.

The Colonel was a code name for Malcolm Mullen, Lieutenant Colonel, U.S. Army, Retired. Another man with a grudge against T.M. The wily old Texan had once considered the sixty-eight-year-old Mullen his top security man. But that was several years ago.

Suddenly, DeBlase had formed a new security company. It now had the responsibility for protecting his person and property worldwide, from luxury hotels to oil fields in Iran. The Colonel was fired. The new man had been given a ten-year contract at one hundred and fifty thousand dollars a year plus expenses. You might say the Colonel was bitter.

Perry, code name for Regis Cooler, still worked for T.M. Perry, forty, was with a New York public-relations firm that had fallen into the currently popular and pretentious habit of referring to itself as an "image maker" and "communications consultant."

But the firm got five hundred thousand dollars a year to plant photographs showing T.M. plucking daisies and handing out Tootsie Rolls to handicapped children. Perry wanted to save his soul or some kind of moral horseshit like that. So when I'd been turned down by T.M.'s flacks for an interview with the old bastard himself, Perry had let a few days go by, then got in touch with me.

He'd given me McClan and the Colonel.

"Anything else, Mrs. K. ?"

"Letters. One looks like a ransom note."

"Open it and throw it away." It sounded like one of those letters in pencil that start out: *Fucking cocksucking jew lover you write shit why don't you go back to russia you asshole your mother is . . .*

Etc.

"I read it," she said. Efficient, loyal, nosy Mrs. Karakas.

"Any good?"

"If you like slime and sleaze, yes." Her voice was cast iron, the kind Pontius Pilate wished he'd had when giving Jesus the bad news. Tough, moody Sarah Karakas. Uncooperative and nasty with everybody, and called "Mrs. Karate" behind her back by some people. Me, I found her kind, as efficient as Julius Caesar, and, more important, loyal to me. She'd been my secretary for four years and not once had she ever told anybody what I was working on. Loyal Mrs. K., with her calf-length dresses covering her dumpy body, her space shoes that looked to be a foot *wide* at the tip, and the six-inch hat pin tucked in her fat, graying bun, a hair-style she'd worn since Franklin Delano Roosevelt's first term.

The hat pin was for "sneakers." "Sneakers" was her name for black and Puerto Rican youths who snatched purses and pawed at snatches.

"Anything else?"

"Mr. Ramey asked about you."

"La dee da."

Julius Ramey was the *World-Examiner*'s executive editor, meaning he didn't work too hard and got paid well for it. A tall, lean, well-tailored sixty-four-year-old with silver hair and a tendency to throw people to the wolves in order to keep his job. Julius stayed scared most of the time, covering it with a used-car dealer's grin I couldn't stomach. The grin stayed on until he knew for certain whether or not you could do him any good. In the scheme of things, he ranked just under Mrs. Evans, who owned the paper. In truth, he had no balls. He got sixty thousand dollars a year. Somebody else ran the paper, a man named Jack Sommers who I didn't like and wouldn't trust with a bag of dogshit.

Jack Sommers was managing editor, an egomaniac and the kind of bastard who'd set fire to a crowded church if he needed one more story to fill a page. Jack Sommers was a prick. Jack Sommers was the best editor at the *World-Examiner*. We didn't like each other.

I turned around in the telephone booth. Twenty feet away, Lamont sat reading Machiavelli's *The Prince*. Lamont seemed engrossed in sixteenth-century Italy's dirty tricks. Still, I had the strong feeling he was taking care of business. Meaning, he'd watch me until I got on a plane and away from Company doings in this area. Watching Lamont read and eye me at the same time brought that old black spiritual to mind—"His Eye Is on the Sparrow, but I Know He Watches Me." He sure do.

Machiavelli and Lamont. That brought a chuckle to my hard heart. Something told me that the boys at the Company would be wise to keep an eye on big, black, bad Lamont, if that was his name. Anybody who reads *The Prince* wants to get ahead in the world. Anybody who reads *The Prince* doesn't go to sleep at night dreaming about watermelons.

While talking to New York, I'd kept my back to Lamont. This way, he'd have to lip-read through the back of my head.

"Any other calls, Mrs. K. ?" I covered the phone with my hand and belched again. The lunch counter around the corner hadn't been four star, but I hadn't been particular either. Hot grease and additives in Indiana.

Mrs. Karakas hesitated before answering. She knew.

Her voice suddenly changed. It was understanding without condemning. She understood.

"No," she said softly. "She didn't call." There were a few seconds of silence and she added, "Sorry. I am so sorry."

She sounded as though she meant it. Loni hadn't called. That hurt.

We let my heartache hang in the air between us for a few seconds. I looked at the people in the airport, envying them for being happy in love, though when I stopped feeling sorry for myself, I'd realize that they were all bleeding in their own way. Loni. She was in me so deep, I must have been born with her inside. The heart doesn't know why, it only knows when. Loni was now and forever for me. And all I could do about it was bleed.

"When are you coming back?" Mrs. Karakas' very practical question pushed me back into the land of the living.

"Can't say." In the past, I'd stayed away from the paper as long as five months working on a story. I took as long as I had to, to put a story together. I was a star. As long as I kept on delivering.

"Fine. Any messages for anybody back here?" Mrs. K. never pressed me on anything. Except belching.

"No. I'll land in New York—" spinning around, I gave Lamont my back again, cupped a hand around the receiver and dropped my voice almost on the floor—"then go directly to Miami."

"Why can't you fly directly to Miami from where you are? And why are you whispering?"

I took a quick peek at Lamont. *The Prince* had him by the balls. He never looked up.

"Got a shadow," I whispered. Jesus, did I ever.

"Don't we all."

"Not like this one. This one stands in the middle of the road and lets speeding trucks come at him."

"Why?"

"It tickles. How the hell do I know why? He's big and I don't want him knowing what I'm up to. He saw me buy a ticket for New York and that's where he thinks I'm heading. When he finds out I've tricked him, I plan to be long gone twice over."

"If you say so. I'll wait to hear from you. Call me at home if you have to."

"Thanks, Mrs. K. Take care."

On the drive into Indianapolis, Lamont had said three words. Two had been, "Don't smoke." If I'd been a five-pack-a-day man, I'd have kicked the habit right then and there. When Lamont says don't smoke, you don't smoke.

Better to sweat and twitch than to have your skull toyed with like it was Silly Putty.

I'd got the third word when Lamont had reached out for the car radio's dial with a hand the size of a suitcase and learned the hard way that you don't get soul music in Indiana. You get country. Lamont's third word had been a whispered, "Sheeit." And that was it for conversation. Something about Lamont discouraged a man from idle chatter. Let's say it discouraged me.

Twenty more minutes and it was another no-frills flight for me. Indianapolis to New York to Miami to Estevez-Blanco to, I hoped, Fragan.

Since we were in a public place, I figured Lamont wouldn't beat up on me in front of witnesses. So I strolled over to him with the idea of a cultural exchange—a sentence or two—until the plane arrived. Thanks to my credit cards, which I had used to buy a new suit and shirt, and to the men's room, with its soap, water, and paper towels, I was now a lot more fun to be around. And breathe around.

"Any good?" I stood near him as he continued to read.

He shrugged his big shoulders. Muscles moved under his dark blue jacket like bowling balls rolling around under a sheet.

"Read it a few years ago," I said. So far this conversation was like playing with myself.

Lamont closed the paperback. His big hands reduced the book to the size of a dime. "Read it five times." His voice rumbled at me like boulders down a mountainside.

Encouraged by this desire for harmony, I said, "Oh? You must have found it a help over the years."

"Five times *this* year," rumbled Lamont. He didn't bother looking at me while he talked.

Five times *this* year. Jesus. Something told me Lamont had more going on in his African skull than he let anybody know about. Including the Company.

"Hey, uh, well, that's interesting, Lamont. You read a lot? I mean, you, uh . . . ?" That's all I needed. Lamont thinking I was being snotty. If he killed me here, where the fuck would they bury me? Probably in that potted plant over there.

I got lucky. Lamont didn't answer. Lamont obviously read a lot, and I don't mean Motown album covers.

His dark brown eyes swallowed me and he seemed to think about something before getting ready to speak. Then—

"Thin ice, man," he said. "That means you better work fast."

"I don't follow."

"Your father alive or dead?" he said.

My mind was wandering and I only half heard him.

He started to repeat the question.

"Your father—"

"Yeah, yeah, I heard you. Dead." My father had been shot to death in a Los Angeles bar during a holdup a couple of years ago. Stupid way to die. He'd stopped in the bar to lend a friend fifty dollars, but some coked-up Chicano who had come in to rip off the place got pissed when my father refused to take off his pants. So the Spic bastard killed him and three others. Dumb way to die. Just because you won't take off your pants. I loved the old man. All my life I had busted my ass for his approval.

"Too bad about him being dead," said Lamont.

"Why?" I was curious as hell about that remark.

"Herodotus. He said, 'In peace, sons bury their fathers; in war, fathers bury their sons.' You in a war, Jim, and you don't even know it."

For a long time I didn't say anything. Lamont was a surprise and a half. A big black superfly kind of cat stuffed into a suit. The CIA was going in heavily for ethnics, but whoever had recruited this "token" was in for a big surprise.

Lamont was telling me something. Lamont was telling me to watch my ass.

"And no father to bury me," I murmured.

Lamont gave me his biggest nod of the day. This one was a whole half-inch.

7.

Drummond McClan's voice had a permanent slur from drinking. The man who had once made good money setting up cover businesses for T.M. DeBlase and the CIA had now crawled into the bottle for the rest of his life. I doubt if he noticed it. While we were talking on the telephone, he dropped the receiver twice, sending ice picks into my ears.

T.M.'s pilots and mechanics always knew his whereabouts. McClan still kept in touch with them, several of whom he'd hired in the first place.

"Iran. Yeah, uh, Iran. That's where he's goin'." Drummond McClan's bitterness dripped into my ear. I was at Kennedy Airport in New York, waiting for a shuttle flight to Miami.

"Who's he meeting?"

"*Who? Who?*" McClan chuckled. A boozed-up owl with a sense of humor. "Who? Who, you say? Who else? The man hisself. Shit, what kind of reporter ish you?"

I ish sober, I thought, keeping my whimsy to myself.

"The Shah, right?"

"Riiiiiight." Drummond dragged the word out until I thought he'd take the rest of the day finishing it.

T.M. and the Shah of Iran. Impressive. Yes, indeed, that was something to jot down in my eighty-cent notebook in a hurry. And nobody knew about the meeting. Wonder why. Hell, that was an easy one to answer. T.M. and His Highness were undoubtedly wheeling and dealing in a manner less than honor bright. Nice to know that a man in his golden years, like T.M., didn't have to wait around airports like reporters had to. Me, I had thirty-five minutes to kill until the shuttle took me down to Florida, the land of shuffleboard. T.M. had only to snap his fingers and *poof*! A plane. He was a kid with a lot of toys. A rich kid. A rotten kid.

I switched ears. "What are they talking about?"

"Hell, wha' the fuck you think they're talkin' about, cream of wheat? Oil. Thash wha's goin' on. *Oil*." Booze made Drummond McClan as hostile as a middle line-backer on the Chicago Bears. If there was a way to reach through the phone and grab his scrawny neck, I would. I hate having drunks talk to me like that, hiding their nastiness behind booze as though it wasn't their fault at all.

We were using each other. Happened all the time. I used my informants, my informants used me. I was an iron pipe for McClan to beat on T.M. DeBlase with. Other than that, McClan had no more use for me than he had for toilet paper with fresh brown stains on it. After getting their revenge, McClan, and other informants would sit back with a cool drink and put their feet up. Informants and reporters used each other. Each time they did, somebody got hurt.

"McClan, find out, if you can, what they're talking about over there."

"Yeah, well . . ." There was silence, which meant he was thinking, or drinking, or had passed out. "See what I can do."

"Good enough. Check with you later."

"Yeah. Later. Fuckin' bastard."

"Me or T.M. ?"

"Both of yez."

I exhaled, closing my notebook. Jesus, I hated drunks.

"McClan?"

"What!" He slammed the word into my ear as though driving a stake into the ground.

"Tie a knot in your dick."

"What!"

"You heard me." I hung up. Dumb drunk.

Twenty-five minutes until my Florida shuttle. Time to call Regis Cooler and Malcolm Mullen. So far, they'd come through every time. My information was piling up— information on businesses T.M. DeBlase had set up in seven countries, businesses that weren't businesses at all. Fronts. Trojan horses.

Even without T.M.'s side of the story, and something told me don't hold my breath until he talked to me, the story was coming along nicely.

Anyway, T.M. DeBlase would have to wait until I finished this defector story.

Trotman. I wondered what else he had for me. Shit, I couldn't call him. If I wanted to see him, I had to place a small personal ad in a Washington newspaper, calling him "Horace" and myself "Mildred." Unbelievable. Our meeting was always a day earlier and the time an hour later than the ad said. When he saw it, he'd leave his office and call me from a public telephone. It was enough to make me wish I had my Little Orphan Annie decoder ring.

I dialed Regis Cooler's publicity firm, Amalgamated Communications Counselors. Mr. Cooler was out to lunch, said a frozen voice in an English accent. English secretaries were status symbols in some business firms.

I dialed Malcolm Mullen. He was napping and his wife, whose quivering voice placed her between a hundred and extinction, absolutely refused to wake him. Why fight it, I thought.

Twenty minutes later, I was on my third airplane of the day, heading south, eyes closed and trying to sleep through the next couple of hours, since it didn't look like I was going to have a sexual experience with a beautiful stranger anytime soon. My dream was bad. I dreamed I was being hit by ears of corn thrown by men in masks who laughed and laughed and laughed. When I woke up, my hands were clenched into fists and I was breathing hard.

8.

"City ain't nothin' but black beans and rice these days," said Tucker John Delk. He drove with the top down on his Thunderbird, letting the same Miami sun that shone on Anita Bryant and her oranges shine down on me. So far, all the sunshine had cost me was a seventy-five-dollar plane fare from New York.

"Cubans bothering you, Tucker John?" I leaned back in the front seat and closed my eyes, getting to work on my tan in a hurry.

"Officially, they ain't supposed to." Tucker John Delk was a detective lieutenant on the Miami police force, allegedly with an open mind toward ethnics.

"Unofficially?" I looked at him. A soft breeze, pleasant and harmless as a baby's kiss, was playfully rearranging what little hair Tucker John had left.

"Unofficially, old buddy, workin' with these suckers can sometimes be as much fun as a blow job from an alligator."

"Why?"

"Gunplay. Like the OK Corral around here. Cubans killin' Cubans over narcotics, politics, or a nasty word.

Fuckin' people all got hair-trigger tempers and more guns than an armory. A Cuban would just as soon shoot you as tell you his name.''

Tucker John Delk had picked me up at Miami International Airport. He drove well, in command and aware of what he could get away with behind the wheel. At thirty-six, he had ambitions that would keep him busy the rest of his life. Tucker John Delk wanted to be chief of Miami Police. After that he wanted to be governor. That's why he made a point of always having manicured fingernails. You never know whose hand you'll be shaking and what kind of power that hand wields.

His remark about Cubans and gunplay made me sit up straight and turn in my seat to face him. We were on the way to meet Estevez-Blanco. If for some reason Estevez-Blanco decided he didn't like me, I wondered if that would lead to bullets flying. Damn, Harker. You just can't do anything the easy way, can you?

We drove past palm trees with their drooping, long, jagged leaves of dark green, past girls with bronzed skin and hair streaked gold by the sun. On the other side of the street, a blond in shorts the size of a hair ribbon came toward us, tits bouncing like rubber balls on concrete. I waved and smiled at her. She ignored me.

"Harker?" Tucker John didn't take his eyes off the road.

"Yeah?"

"That's three times you've looked behind you. Anything you want to tell me?"

I gave him one of those grins that don't mean a thing.

"No. Nothing to tell."

"Suit yourself." He turned right on West Flagler, his eyes hidden behind the wire-framed, mirrored sunglasses cops all over the world are addicted to. Tucker John Delk was five foot ten, with one hundred and ninety-five pounds packed solid on big bones, the way it should be on a cop who wanted things done his way the first time around. While he didn't have that much hair on top, he'd put the rest of his face to work growing hair in a big way. Reddish-brown sideburns ran down both sides of his square

face, then along his jawbone, almost meeting at the Kirk
Douglas-like hole in his chin.

His moustache, also reddish brown, was the size of a
hot-dog roll. It hid his upper lip and clogged both nostrils.
Somehow, Tucker John managed to breathe. He was a
smart cop. With some ethics.

He had the confidence of a daytime burglar, with the
quiet faith in himself that comes from starting with nothing and getting everything you ever wanted. On the street,
Tucker John stepped aside for no man—white, black, or
Cuban. He could shake your hand and ask about the family
or kick your ass and put you in traction. All of it done
with manicured nails.

As he drove, he waited for me to tell him what I was
down here for. I didn't have to. He owed me, owed me
big. And I was collecting. He knew he had to pay and
that's what he was doing.

"Cross West Eighth," he said, "you're in Little Havana. That's what they call it. Little Havana. Blocks and
blocks of them people, drinking coffee thick enough to tar
a road with and chatterin' away in Spanish like monkeys
in the jungle."

"How are you dealing with it?"

"Like I'm supposed to. Polite but firm. Head bustin's a
no-no these days."

"Shit, just look upon them as potential votes."

"That I do, my man, that I do. Gettin' back to what I
said, if it gets heavy for you down here, let me know."
He was a proud man, a man who paid his debts whether
it meant money owed or a leg broken. Tucker John Delk
was still on the Miami Police Force because of me. Because of me, he was still alive.

" 'Preciate it, like you folk say. Not sure what's going
down myself. I know that Estevez-Blanco's on the fringes
of it. That's why I called you from New York. Thanks for
setting up the meeting with him."

Tucker John Delk dismissed my thanks with a wave of a
manicured hand. Once he'd been within an hour and a half of
being kicked off the force, framed, and sent to the slammer.
Some of the people messing up his life at that time

didn't even want him in jail. They preferred him dead. There had been a vote or two in favor of taking Tucker John out into surrounding Florida waters and dumping him in the deepest part, after first wrapping his feet in cement to make sure he didn't go walking around.

I'd stopped that from happening.

Tucker John's ass had gone on the line around the time I was researching my book on union leaders ripping off millions in pension funds. I'd checked out a party in a Miami luxury hotel, a party that had got out of hand, resulting in one dead prostitute, age sixteen. She hadn't died from eating canapés.

She'd died because one of the country's biggest union leaders was a sexual sadist away from wife and church. The union bastard had immediately started throwing his weight around. His union was planning a hundred-million-dollar hotel in Miami, with convention space that the union itself would be occupying in years to come. That was a lot of money staring Miami city fathers in the face.

That much money stacked up against a dead sixteen-year-old whore brought out the worst in a lot of people. Tucker John Delk was not one of those people. He'd known the girl. And he wanted to make the case. That brought him trouble. He didn't want to go along, making him a man alone. It also made him a man with his ass in a sling. In no time at all, the local power structure had worked a frame that made Tucker John the man who had supplied the whores for the party. The tip I'd got on the case from a call girl said that Tucker John was a cinch to end up in jail and/or dead.

In New York, where I'd been finishing the book, I made sure enough people knew the story before I flew down to Miami with a copy of the book.

An hour and a half before the hearing that was to hang Tucker John and keep Miami safe for union leaders to party in, I walked into his lawyer's office with my book. Tucker John's lawyer made some quick telephone calls, emphasizing, as I'd told him, that enough influential people outside of the state of Florida knew about this little scheme to frame a cop, and, when all was said and done, it was better to be publicly virtuous about it while they still could.

Tucker John Delk was exonerated and a lot of prominent people posed with him for newspaper photographs, praising him for being a good cop, something they "knew" all along. My story broke nationally, since I had the inside track to Tucker John, his lawyer, and most of the facts. And Tucker John, promoted to Detective Lieutenant, nodded knowingly and said the right things, the way a man should who wants to be governor.

I liked him, though I reserved the right to distrust him a little bit. Ambitious men are always to be distrusted. You never know when you're expendable in their world.

"I checked our records," said Tucker John, with just a touch of South in his voice. "Got some complaints on your man, Estevez-Blanco. Has this rag called *La Luz Fuerte*, means 'strong light.' People say he rips them off for ads. Takes the money and the ads don't appear."

"Sticky-fingered bastard, ain't he?"

"There's more. He's got a side business. Booking agent. Show business. Books acts on cruise ships sailin' 'round the Caribbean. Small shit. Jugglers, children's acts, singers that can't carry a tune in a bucket, piano players that play in the cracks. Shit stuff."

We stopped for a red light. I yawned and stretched.

"Show business, huh?"

"Yeah. Talk is he runs broads on the side. Lot of Cuban ass in this town. He might as well make him a few pesos pimpin', I suppose."

"Another fugitive from Castro's tyranny who made good in the land of the free."

"Sheeit. A lot of them clowns who run off from Castro ain't got no more morals than a dog in heat. Dope peddlers, rapists, hit men, whatever. Some of 'em stay straight, some don't. Same as anybody else. You expectin' somebody? That why you keep lookin' behind you?"

Turning my back on Tucker John would end that line of conversation, I hoped. "Just counting palm trees, Tucker John. Wanted to make sure I didn't miss any."

He shook his head slowly, eyes hidden behind those big mirrored sunglasses. If he believed that, he believed his letters were getting through to the North Pole.

"If you say so, Harker. Anyway, your man Estevez-
Blanco has an apartment on Alcazar. Theatrical agency's
there, too. Works out of his pad. Gives him a chance to
chase broads around the desk."

"What did you tell him about my wanting to see him?"

"Told him you wanted to do a story on Cuban immigrants in Florida, on the prominent ones with influence.
He was flattered."

Another Harker improvisation, called a lie by some
people. Still couldn't get that photograph of Fragan and
me out of my mind. Who the hell had taken it?

"You're frowning, Harker. Airplane food get you
down?" Tucker John had had a lot of practice looking at
people out of the corner of his eye.

"No, no. Something else. Having my picture taken
bothers me."

"Jesus, you sound like an African. They claim a camera
takes away your soul. They been known to put a spear through
a photographer's belly button to get their point across."

"Well, that can do something to your peace of mind."
Goddamn it, who the hell was after Fragan and his friends?
If not Roy Lupus and his merrymakers, then who? I
wanted to know because I didn't feel like running through
any more cornfields.

"Want me to go in with you?"

"No," I said. "Thanks for meeting me and everything."

He shrugged. Tucker John Delk. A man with manicured
nails and a heart full of ambition. He would have liked to
know what was going on, but he was too much of a man
to ask. A man paid his debts and didn't butt in until asked.
I just might have to ask, if things got as hot as they had
in Winslow.

I wondered if Tucker John's debt to me covered using
that Smith & Wesson .38 he wore on his left hip. It was
something to think about as we crossed West 9th Street
under a pleasant sun.

9.

"You lied to me, *señor*. You are here, shall we say, under false pretenses." Leaning back in his chair, Enrique Estevez-Blanco gave me this news with his bloodshot brown eyes almost shut, one slim finger tracing a line down the side of his clean-shaven, heavily cologned jaw. He stared at me as though deciding whether to tell my mother or spank me with a machete. Ice in his voice and his refusal to smile told me he didn't like being lied to. I began getting out from under in a hurry.

"Now just a minute, Mr. Estevez. Just one minute. *Me* lie to *you*? *Me*? OK, I did ask to see you, that's true. Now Lieutenant Delk, now I don't know what he told you. But—"

"I believe he told me you wanted to talk about the success of Cuban immigrants in your country. But you, *Señor* Harker, you seem to want to talk about other things. Other things." He shook his head slowly, sad at the deception in the world. His Cuban temper was being held in check, but not by much. The long nostrils flared, widening, then contracting like a horse in heat. His breathing could be heard blocks away.

"Mr. Estevez, all I said to you just now was I'd like to talk to someone you know, a Walter Fragan. He subscribes to your paper. Mr. Fragan is in some kind of difficulty and I thought perhaps you might help me locate him. That's all." We sat across from each other in an office cooled by a rattling fan. The fan made slightly less noise than two men swinging at each other with garbage-can tops.

Enrique Estevez-Blanco, who was in his mid-forties, had a long ax-blade of a face, pockmarked and reeking of a heavy cologne that smelled like vanilla and gasoline. Like all Cuban males, and some of the women I'd seen in Miami's Little Havana, he had a moustache. His was pencil thin, a tiny black line over thick pink lips resembling Mick Jagger's. He couldn't have been over five foot five, with three gold teeth in the front of his mouth to match the three thick gold rings he wore on his long fingers. His thick black hair, with sideburns down to his jawbone, was soaked in enough oil to fill a tanker. There was nothing strong about him, not physically, not mentally. He gave the impression of a man who was cruel out of weakness.

We were alone in his apartment–theatrical office, except for a fat, sleepy-looking Cuban woman out front in the vestibule behind us. She was typing so slowly she had to be doing it with her elbows. She fielded all telephone calls. Apparently, Enrique Estevez-Blanco had thought my interviewing him would take up a lot of his time, so he hadn't wanted to be disturbed. We were in a living room–office filled with eight-by-ten glossies hanging from the wall, mostly of smiling, dark-haired Cuban women.

Some of the photographs were of men, one or two were of dwarfs, and there were a couple of kids among those grateful show-biz folk whom Estevez-Blanco was apparently pushing down that stardust trail. Show biz might be the reason why he was such a lousy newspaper publisher and editor, whose journalistic specialty seemed to be collecting for ads he never intended to run.

To the left of the wooden desk was a green couch,

probably for gals who wanted to be stars overnight. I wondered if Estevez knew that the first couch-casting in
movie history was said to have been done by D.W. Grif-
fith, the first superstar director. According to the story,
D.W. used a green couch. Knowingly or unknowingly,
Enrique Estevez-Blanco had become part of America's
artistic tradition.

The rattling fan clanged along merrily, sending out no
more cool air than a forest fire. Estevez didn't seem to
mind. His tan skin perspired quietly, the sweat trickling
down his pink, pockmarked, smelly face, along his neck,
and into his hairy chest. The man definitely did not like
anybody deceiving him. His hot eyes said so and I thought
of what Tucker John Delk had told me about Cuban gunplay in the Sunshine State. That was all the reason I needed
to keep on talking and hope he would pardon my ambition. Frankly, it didn't look like he would.

"Mr. Estevez, if there's been any misunderstanding, let
me apologize. You're a newspaperman yourself. You understand, right?" I grinned, winking at the same time. All
us ink-stained wretches together.

Enrique Estevez-Blanco looked at me as though I were
trying to get him deported. His thick lips were twisted in
an expression of disgust and impatience. Slamming both
palms down on his desk, he leaned forward and linked
eyes with mine, trying to stare me down. Having tried that
trick more than once myself, I shifted my gaze to a spot
high on the bridge of his nose and began looking at that.
The spot was hairy and greasy, but it didn't stare back at
me, which made this nonsense a lot easier on my part.

Sighing, he looked at his watch, his way of covering
having looked away first. He leaned back in his chair.
Staring down at his crotch, he began stroking the hairs
coming from his nose with a long finger. For a few seconds, he filled his cheeks with air and blew it out over and
over as though he had suddenly remembered he'd been a
pair of bellows in a previous life. This was one son of a
bitch who didn't like to lose.

"Señor Harker, if that is your name . . ."

"I showed you my press card, didn't I?"

"Such documents can be faked, can they not?"

"Mine can be checked. A telephone call to Lieutenant Delk—"

"Lieutenant Delk seems to have trouble remembering from one minute to the next." Estevez savagely jabbed a pencil into an ink-stained blotter, breaking the point. A bad loser.

"A telephone call to my paper, then." Damn, I wasn't used to having to identify myself beyond a few seconds' effort. But, then again, prize-winning investigative reporters are not household names, no matter what they or their relatives like to think. The only people who recognize them immediately are journalism students pestering them for a job, and creditors pestering them to pay back loans.

"Let us say, Señor Harker, that you are who you say you are."

"Let us say."

"What do you expect from me?" He drummed his fingers on the blotter, leaning his head back and giving me that hooded-eye look again.

"Walter Fragan," I said. "I'd like to talk with him, that is if you've seen him recently."

"You said something about trouble." The drumming stopped, as though he didn't want to miss a word of my reply. Behind him, the fan clanged and rattled. Behind me, the telephone rang, and the fat Cuban lady who couldn't type said softly, *"Quién?"* dropping her voice as if she were in church.

"Trouble?" Had to pick my words carefully now. "Trouble. Oh, yeah. Some people had a disagreement with Walter Fragan and—"

He leaned forward, slithering onto the desk like a worm crawling around after a rain. "These people, you know them?"

"I might. Yeah, I might."

"If this—this Walter Fragan knows these people, why should he talk to you?"

"Because I might be able to help him settle things with these people, to convince them to leave him alone. You tell him that. When you see him."

For a few seconds he stared at me again, and I was all set to start gazing at that hairy, greasy spot at the bridge of his nose, when he reached to his right, pressing down a lever on the intercom.

"*Si?*" The fat lady's voice came delicately over the wire as though she weighed a hundred and ten instead of two hundred and ten. She must have had a great telephone voice. She sure was nobody's typist.

Keeping his eyes on me, Enrique Estevez-Blanco started rattling off Spanish like a teletype key reporting an Indian massacre in a Western movie. I couldn't understand one word of it, but bad vibes squeezed my stomach until I belched. If he wasn't talking about me, he was talking about one of my closest friends. When he finished, he snapped the intercom button off, leaned back in his chair with both hands behind his neck, and gave me his second smile of the day. I'd got the first when we'd met in his office earlier and shaken hands. At that time I was supposedly in town to massage his ego. I had a very bad feeling about this second smile.

So far, he'd been playing it coy about Walter Fragan. According to Delk, Estevez had had practice keeping quiet. It seemed that back in Cuba, Estevez had been associated with the Mafia. He'd done all right for himself in the land of the free. A tacky newspaper, a tacky theatrical agency. Both of them paying off, it seemed.

I uncrossed my legs, pulling my pants away from my crotch. It was like a sauna bath in here, a sauna with garlic. And that cologne he wore. The bastard must have put it on by the bucketful.

"Mr. Estevez, I—"

That was as far as I got.

Behind me, the front door opened in a hurry and three men burst into the apartment as though they all had to go to the john at once. It would have been better for me if they had. I turned around in time to see them run into the living room and stop behind me in a semicircle. They weren't smiling. Neither was I, but my not smiling had more to do with a strong sense of personal fear than a hatred of the press.

My mouth was as dry as hot sand and when I turned around to Estevez-Blanco, I had to cough twice to get my throat wet enough to speak. "Uh, well, I mean, uh, was it something I said?"

His smile belonged on somebody who got kicks out of pulling the wings off butterflies. I was in a bind, a bind of *his* choosing, on *his* turf. His bloodshot, watery brown eyes seemed uglier to me now, but that might have been prejudice on my part, influenced by recent events.

He slid from behind the desk, taking an ice-cream white jacket from the chair as he did so, slipping into it like a man who had done a good day's work and was heading for a home-cooked meal and a romp with the children.

"Señor Harker, if that is your name, I am leaving you now. My friends will entertain you for a short time. When I return, we will talk some more. Good-bye, Señor Harker." He walked slowly toward the front door, smoothing out his jacket and brushing imaginary hairs from both sleeves. In the back of my mind, I remembered that I couldn't hear the fat lady typing anymore. The telephone rang. And rang and rang. Fat lady wasn't there.

I pulled my eyes from Estevez-Blanco's retreating back and looked at the three men standing several feet away from me. All three were Cuban, with dark hair, tan skins, and oily moustaches and sideburns that gleamed like a wet mirror. They weren't exceptionally big, average size to a little above. But there were three of them, and one of me. What's more, they were here for the express purpose of giving me a hard time. I was scared but chewing my bottom lip and blinking a lot wasn't going to help me much.

I heard the front door open, then close. *Adiós*, Estevez-Blanco. *Adiós*, Harker, too.

The Cuban in the middle, a young man with a yellow T-shirt that said *Cuba Libre*, snorted, smiled at me, and reached into his pocket. His hand came out with a sliver of bright metal. In the empty room, the click of his switchblade was the loudest sound I'd heard in some time. "Hey, *amigo*," he said in a friendly voice. "Welcome to Miami."

I backed up, both hands on the chair I'd been sitting in,

dragging it in front of me. I hadn't far to go. My ass
bumped into the desk and I stopped as though I'd hit a
brick wall. In a sense, I had. Behind me, the fan's blades
rattled and clanged as if everything were normal and I
wasn't about to get hurt. Times like these, those poison-
pen letters I get didn't seem much of a problem.

Clearing my throat, I gripped the chair hard enough to
leave holes in the wood, as I slowly eased sideways, feeling the desk pass across my ass like one long continuous
goose. These clowns were between me and the door. I
could leap out the window, four stories up from the concrete. But if I did that, then I wouldn't be here when
Estevez-Blanco came back. If I did that, I wouldn't be
here when Jesus Christ came back.

The smiler, in yellow T-shirt and with switchblade,
moved closer in small steps, turning his wrist in tiny circles like a man who knew how to carve. Shit, I'd ridden
the New York subway, where Hispanic types often apply
group therapy with a blade. What did I do then? Remember, Harker, remember! What did you do then? Oh, yeah,
now I remember. I panicked, that's what I did. Fucking
panicked. But I survived.

And my instincts said survive again. I swung the chair
as hard as I could, bringing it off the floor and right at
Yellow T-shirt, hitting him in the left hip and spinning
him around. He danced off sideways, like an old-time
vaudevillian leaving the stage while still doing a hokey
routine.

The chair slipped from my hands, flying between Yellow T-shirt, who was still off-balance, and the Cuban
between me and the door. Fuck it. As soon as I got a
shot, I was heading for that door like it was eternal salvation.

I got a shot, a small one, but a shot. The man nearest
the door, a guy with a big gold cross hanging from his
neck and a white shirt with food stains on it, ducked as
though I had something else to throw, and that left me a
small opening to hotfoot it toward the door. Which I did,
running like a man who had eaten Mexican food for the
first time.

I almost made it. Almost.

I was in the clear and my heart jumped around in my throat urging me on to run faster. If I could get to the door . . . if . . .

My legs gave way and my knees went down fast until they bumped the floor. The shock registered in my brain as one huge disappointment, but I kept on trying. Man, did I try. I'd been tackled from behind and I was falling, falling, reaching out for the door with outstretched arms and open mouth, a door that was still a good fifteen feet away. Something hard slammed into my spine. Knees, fists, and elbows, I didn't know. But it hurt, hurt like hell. I went down all the way, mouth into the carpet, hands clawing at it as though that were enough to bring me closer to the door.

A sharp pain appeared suddenly in my right side. I'd been kicked like a soccer ball. I pushed up, trying to scramble to my hands and knees.

From the corner of my right eye, I saw that foot coming at me again. I pushed at it with my right arm. An ankle bone crashed into my forearm, but it didn't hurt much.

However, I wasn't going anywhere. They pulled at me, shoved me, and were doing a damn good job of dragging me back into the living room, where I guess all the fun was going to take place. Estevez-Blanco was not the kind of bastard to forgive and forget.

I was moving backward, much too fast to suit me. A forearm was across my windpipe, making air hard to come by. Somebody had my right arm and leg. And my left arm, try as it could, wasn't doing shit about getting that forearm away from my windpipe. My throat hurt like hell, and the room was turning red around me. Air was gold right now. I couldn't get enough. Here lies Harker, choked to death by a sweaty, smelly Cuban with a forearm as hairy as King Kong's.

Bam! The front door slammed open and through the hot red darkness that had swollen my head up to the size of a house, I heard somebody yell: *"Freeze! Goddamn it, freeze!"*

Thump! They dropped me and I lay there, breathing

loudly and wondering how long I had had this fucking headache. It seemed like I'd had it for the last year at least. Massaging my throat gently, I tried swallowing. It hurt too much to do that, so I stopped and gave all of my attention to breathing again.

Tucker John Delk said, "You OK?"

I sat up. But I didn't get up. I wasn't anybody's fool. Last time I was on my feet, somebody had thrown me down and fucked me over. No more. If I sat here, no one could throw me down.

"Harker, you OK?" Tucker John's voice was louder now. It should be. He was standing over me, patting my head as though I were a cocker spaniel who'd finally learned to pee on the newspaper. I looked up and saw the biggest fucking gun I'd ever seen in my life. The prettiest, too. The gun was that Smith & Wesson .38 he carried, and from where I sat, it was twelve inches over my right temple, but pointed in the right direction—at those assholes who'd red dogged me a few seconds ago.

"Yeah. Yeah. I'm fine. Just fine." I got to my feet in a reasonable amount of time and staggered over to the casting couch. Falling back on it, I rotated my head around. My throat hurt less, but that wasn't saying a lot. It still hurt too goddamn much.

"Jesus, how'd you get here?" I sounded like Lauren Bacall.

"Hung around. Estevez ain't a solid citizen. And you ain't the type to come a long way for nothin'. Just hung around. These dudes go runnin' into the buildin' and, a minute later, Estevez comes out in a hurry. You wasn't with him."

I nodded, hand still on my throbbing throat. "No, I wasn't. Can't argue that."

Tucker John was pointing the .38 at the three Cubans and they had, as requested, frozen. Tucker John's manicured hands had a two-handed grip on the piece and he looked for all the world the way you want a cop to look. He wasn't blinking and he was all business, not breathing noticeably and on top of the situation. The man made John Wayne look like a transvestite.

His eyes were on the three silent, rigid Cubans the entire time he talked to me. They must have known his reputation because they weren't moving. I don't count sweating a lot as moving.

"Harker, you always make the big play." It was a statement, not a question. He was asking me something in his own way. And right now, the man did have a claim on me even if he didn't want to come out and say so. He sure as hell did.

I cleared my throat, hoping to raise it a few octaves from the depths it had dropped because of that near tracheotomy laid on me by these three pricks.

"Yeah, Tucker John, I go for the big ones. And all I can say is, one way or another, you're in. Can't tell you anything right now, but when I put this thing together, you're in one way or another. And that should push you a step closer to the inaugural ball. Or a chief's hat."

He lifted a corner of his mouth in a small grin. Tucker John and I understood each other.

"Harker?"

"Yeah?"

"Close the door."

"Tucker John, I'd like to stay and dance on somebody's balls, really I would. But I got to get going. Got to get after Estevez-Blanco. Jesus, that cocksucker really set me up." I rubbed my throat. I'd be cutting my meat into tiny pieces for a while. Easier to swallow that way.

"Harker?"

"Yeah, Tucker John?"

"You know where Estevez went to in such a hurry?"

I frowned, looking at him. "No. No, I don't."

"Close the door, Harker."

I did, moving slowly and stiffly because walking was new to me at the moment.

I turned from the door in time to see Tucker John kick Yellow T-shirt in the balls, dropping the Cuban to his knees. The Cuban's eyes quickly shut tight, as though he didn't want to see the rest of his life anymore. His mouth was opened, with nothing coming out, and both hands were across his crotch, vainly pushing the pain down as though trying to keep it from spreading to the rest of his body. He wasn't doing a good job of it.

Slowly, I came back into the apartment. I wondered if the Cuban had done something dumb while my back was turned, but I couldn't recall hearing anything. Not a word, not a sound.

Tucker John had his back to me. His voice was easy to hear, though. ''Want them to get the point. You're a man in a hurry. You deserve answers in a hurry.'' Considering what these clowns had been doing to me, I was more than willing to overlook Tucker John's being playful.

He began speaking in Spanish, the sentences slow and the words distinct. When he finished, one of the Cubans gave him a quick answer while the other nodded his head in quick agreement.

Delk relaxed, holstering his .38. At his feet, Yellow T-shirt moaned and crawled around in his own vomit. Turning his back to them, Tucker John strolled over to me as though he'd done nothing more than give directions to a passing tourist.

''They both say Estevez lit out in a hurry for a ship docked at Pier Six. Caribbean cruise ship called *Oro Azul*, the ''Blue Gold.'' Tourist boat. Families, singles. Cheap six-day tours. Hits Puerto Rico, Santo Domingo, Haiti, places like that. Estevez books entertainers for the ship.''

I nodded. ''Thanks, Tucker John. Tell you something, ol' buddy.''

''What?''

I looked at Yellow T-shirt. He was still on the floor, knees up to his chest, his black hair matted by his own gray vomit. Neither of his two friends had made a move to help him. I rubbed my sore ribs.

I turned to Tucker John. ''Ol' buddy, you bring a new dimension to the art of asking questions.''

His grin was wide under his orange moustache. ''You ought to try it sometime. Leaves you free for gardening and shit like that. Come on, I'll run you over to the pier.''

10.

I leaned in the doorway of the grand ballroom, watching the ape stop dancing to scratch its crotch. After a quick scratch, the ape continued tap-dancing to the piano player's gentle music. The ape's huge hairy feet had purple toenails the size of cigars. The long nails gently scratched the dance floor without scarring it. I watched the ape soft-shoe to Bach being played by a tall man with his back to me. Actually, Bach wasn't being played for the ape's benefit. The ape was clowning around, trying to get the attention of a blond woman with knotty dancer's calves standing with her legs crossed at the ankles and reading a copy of *Variety*.

She wore a pale blue T-shirt saying *Ship's Staff*, scuffed tap shoes, and sequined red shorts. Anybody who can ignore an ape tap-dancing to Bach has got to be blind or deeply engrossed in something else. Finally, the ape gave up trying to win the lady's heart with his art. He lumbered over to her, grabbed her ass with a black fuzzy paw the size of a shovel, and made a move for her boobs with the other paw. The woman, who could have been twenty-five or thirty-five, smacked the paw that was on her ass and offered the ape her cigarette. Not once did she stop reading *Variety*.

Removing his head, the ape took a drag on the cigarette and began talking to the tap dancer. Without the ape-head, the man in the ape suit was blond, his hair bleached by the sun or a bottle, and had a once-handsome face that was lined from too much booze, sun, and fun. He must have said something funny to her, because she looked up from *Variety* and smiled, playfully pushing him away from her. Probably wanted to show her his banana, I suppose.

Tap-dancing apes. Cruise-ship entertainment was usually third-rate, with most acts either being on the way down or just starting out in show business.

As for the room itself, it was all green: ceiling, drapes, rugs, fake plastic palms, and tablecloths. I guessed that the green was to give passengers a taste of the tropics before they arrived at ports of call. To me, it was simply the biggest green room I'd ever seen.

I looked over at the piano player. He also had a distraction to ignore, just like the lady and her tap-dancing ape. The piano player's distraction was a small Cuban in an ice-cream white suit who leaned over the keyboard and spoke in a low voice, waving his arms like a traffic cop. You could tell that the Cuban was intense and trying hard to get his point across, because his eyes bulged and his hands chopped the air like a butcher working on a roast.

Out of the corner of my eye, I saw the man in the ape suit walk across the floor toward the door with his arm around the tap dancer's waist, their heads together. Maybe she would get a chance to see his banana after all. To my right, a waiter came in, bent down, and looked under a tablecloth, then stood up and walked out again. That left just me, the piano player, and the Cuban.

The Cuban looked up first. And when he saw me, his eyes went wide, as though he'd just sat on a sharp object. His thick-lipped mouth dropped open, but no sound came out.

"Well, well. Enrique Estevez-Blanco. Haven't seen you

since, oh, it must be at least half an hour. Come on, tell me you're glad to see me.''

Estevez closed his mouth, then started to blink as if he had dust in his eyes. He licked his lips, shrugged his shoulders, and looked away. Then his head snapped back to me as though I'd just threatened to blow his brains out if he didn't. The little man was extremely upset.

"Well, aren't you gong to introduce me to your friend?'' I said to the back of the tall man, who had stopped playing. "I enjoyed his playing very much. Bach. *Toccata and Fugue in C Minor.* I have it on a record.''

The tall man turned around slowly. His receding hair was dark brown now and he was unshaved, on his way to a full beard and moustache. Except for the dyed hair, he hadn't changed since we were photographed together two weeks ago.

I took a deep breath and coughed to clear my sore throat. "Walter Fragan? I'm Harker. Reporter, *New York World-Examiner*.'' My hand was out and stayed out waiting for him to go near it. He didn't touch it.

Fragan's gray eyes were bits of metal in his long, unshaved face. The face had become a little softer with the passing years, but that was just the flesh. Behind the flesh, the KGB training was being pulled out of his memory bank and thrown at us. He had the kind of stare that made people betray each other just to be allowed to survive.

Living in America might change defectors on television mystery shows, but all it had done to Walter Fragan was add a little weight to his tall frame. America was a place to stay, that's all. At this point in his life Walter Fragan gave off the impression of a man who was beyond all ideology, all morals, and, therefore, the most dangerous man of all. If first impressions were valid, this was the kind of man who was perfect for what he'd once done. He looked as if he didn't have a regret in his life about anything.

Estevez broke the spell. Stepping from behind Fragan, he took a small leap toward me, stopped, lifted his hands, then dropped them helplessly to his side and looked at Fragan. "*Señor*, I—''

He was finding it hard to explain why I was here, es-

pecially since he'd probably told Fragan I was having the
skin peeled from my balls back in Little Havana. That
reminded me. I had every right to be pissed off at this
greasy little bastard for what he'd done to me. Thinking
about it made me start breathing loudly.

"Estevez, hey, yeah, you, you little bastard. Nice try.
Don't look at me like you can't speak English. Your goons,
those three lovers you left behind to babysit for me? Well,
guess what? They didn't do a good job. Know something?
I think you should send them to bed without any supper."

"Mr. Harker." Fragan's voice was like a lead pipe
against the temple. The man had the tones of an emperor
deliberating whether you should hang or have your head
cut off.

"Yeah?" I tried hard not to show how nervous he made
me.

"You have come a long way. For what?"

"First, I'm not sure I want to talk with *him*"—I jabbed
a finger at Estevez—"around me."

"He stays." Fragan hadn't taken his eyes from me. And
his two words weren't a request. They were somewhere
between a command and a thunderbolt hurled earthward
by God the Father.

"All right, he stays. But if I decide to kick his tiny ass,
what are you going to do about *that*?"

"I asked you a question, Mr. Harker. Why have you
come this long way?" Walter Fragan, alias Colonel Viktor
Mikhail Valentine of the KGB, was falling into his pre-
Winslow ways. And they were not very nice.

"Two weeks ago, somebody took a photograph of you
and me on the campus of Winslow University. Now before
you deny who you are, and so far you haven't confirmed
it either, I might as well tell you that you've been identified in that photograph as Colonel Viktor Mikhail Valentine of the KGB. You've been positively identified also as
Walter Fragan, your new name, your defector name."

"By whom have I been identified?" He seemed calm,
sitting on the piano bench as though it were a park bench
and he had nothing better to do than pass the time with a
stranger.

"That's the problem. I think the people who identified you in both cases are also the people who may be trying to kill you."

Estevez frowned at me. I could have been his son reciting dirty words in a school play and embarrassing him to no end. Fragan listened without a muscle moving on his face.

"Kill me?" He made the idea seem ridiculous. Listening to him being so cool might have convinced me I was making it all up. But I thought of the two dead men Trotman had told me about. And I thought about being chased around a cornfield this morning. Christ, was that only *this morning*? Seemed like it was six months ago.

His coming-at-me-from-on-high act was starting to wear. For a few minutes, I'd been going along with it, letting this fucker treat me as if I were in Moscow and he was still wearing jackboots and a uniform. To hell with it.

"Yeah, *yeah*. Kill you. Dead for the rest of your life. That kind of kill." I took a step closer to him, leaning down so that my face was closer to his. Fuck him. I had my own reputation for interrogation. Hardass Harker. The man who asks questions and leaves nothing but scorched earth behind him. This dude had no power over me until I allowed it. As of now, I wasn't going to allow it.

"You've made your point, Mr. Harker. From your reputation, with which I am familiar, I assume you are involved with highly placed sources."

"Let's skip jerking each other off, Fragan. Two of your friends are dead. It reads accident, but that's not how some people feel it really happened. It looks like the CIA or somebody in the CIA is trying to get rid of all of you. All five. If not that, then it looks like the CIA is giving away names and addresses to your KGB friends and the KGB is doing it themselves. I want your side of the story. I want to know why it's happening and what part you think the CIA is playing in all of this. I think my story can help keep you alive, especially if I lay this whole game out in public before it really gets started."

He listened quietly, crossing his legs and folding both hands on his knee. Then he said, "How did you find me?

Did you follow—?'' He didn't bother saying Estevez-
Blanco's name. He simply jerked his head backward once
in the Cuban's direction.

"No. I went to Indiana this morning and found a copy
of Estevez's newspaper in your house. You couldn't stop
the mail. Estevez here sicced some people on me, but a
friend of mine—"

"Friend?"

"Yes. Police lieutenant. He's waiting on the dock for
me to come off.'' I didn't want Tucker John Delk around
on an interview. But, on the other hand, I didn't want him
to leave the dock until he saw me coming down the gangplank. I'd come on board alone, running all over the ship
until, suddenly, I'd heard Bach being played. I remembered a piano back in a Winslow suburb and I'd followed
my ears.

"Waiting on the dock for you to come off,'' repeated
Walter Fragan, making my security precautions sound as
silly as a child's rubber knife.

"That's right. Estevez has a habit of leaving his guests
in the hands of his buddies. If I don't come off this boat
within an hour, Lieutenant Delk is going to work on Estevez, his friends, his cat, and his dog. Lieutenant Delk
is a good cop, which means he's gonna make sure Estevez
here ends up hurting. He made me that promise. By the
way, Estevez, one of your friends is now a soprano. My
friend used him as an object lesson.''

Estevez took a deep breath and held it because that's all
he could think of doing at the moment. His ax-blade of a
face was as sad as a hound's but I didn't care. I didn't care
if his stomach acid was eating away his insides by the foot.

Fragan nodded, piecing several things together. "So,
Mr. Harker, you and I are in a photograph, are we?''

"Yes. During that demonstration at the dedication of
the DeBlase Building on the Winslow campus. We were
sitting side by side then, but we never met.''

"Yes, I know.'' He didn't seem upset about our not
meeting then, any more than he was thrilled at our meeting now. A cool customer, the Colonel.

"Somebody took that photograph. I guess it was the

people who were setting you up. CIA, looks like, though they deny it. But what else are they supposed to do?'' I shifted my weight from leg to leg. My nervousness was easing off now, but I still had the feeling that Walter Fragan was leading me around by my nose. Now why was that? Just because he was looking at me as though I were brain damaged and beyond help? I put his attitude down to snobbery.

''That photograph. Do you have a copy?''

''No.'' I enjoyed telling him that. I looked around for applause and got none. A man at the far end of the ballroom dragged a large potted palm toward the door, as if it were a drunk who'd had too much to drink and didn't want to leave the party.

Walter Fragan sighed, uncrossing his legs and leaning back against the piano. His elbows gently touched the keys, sending soft notes into the air. Even that was precise and musical, as though he'd planned it that way.

''So you think you can help me, Mr. Harker?''

''I'd like to try. Naturally, there's a story in it for me. A big one.''

''Naturally.'' He rubbed his hand across his mouth, scratching his beard with the back of his hand. He had something on his mind.

''Fragan, there's one thing I'd like to tell you. Somebody tried to kill me this morning in Indiana.''

He looked at me as though I'd just told him I masturbated a lot. His look said, ''Don't bother me with your sordid little life.''

I didn't like that. Telling him this, I thought, would make us brothers under the gun. It would show him I was in the same boat because of him.

''I take it, Mr. Harker, that this attempt on your life is somehow connected with your trying to contact me and expose the CIA; am I correct?''

''You might say that, yes.'' He was beginning to sound like Erich von Stroheim, whom I didn't like either.

''Well you are wrong, Mr. Harker. I shall tell you why you are wrong.'' His voice became harder, if that's possible.

"First, the CIA is not trying to kill me. Thomas Merle DeBlase is trying to kill me, and quite possibly because of you. You seem surprised? My, my. The famed investigative reporter caught unawares. Well, it's true. That photograph you mentioned is the missing piece. It all fits. Thomas Merle DeBlase is a careful man. His security is as close to infallible as a private citizen can attain. Whenever he makes a public appearance, his security guards constantly photograph the crowd, so that should something unforeseen occur, DeBlase's men will have a record of those involved and can secure retribution."

I started breathing again. This man with dyed hair, this Russian turned American, was shaking me to my ankles and I couldn't think of a word to answer him with. I wondered if I could even hold a pen to take notes.

Fragan continued talking as though he and I were alone in the huge green room. Estevez was forgotten by both of us.

"You were in Winslow for a story on DeBlase, I assume."

I coughed, clearing my throat. The soreness didn't bother me anymore. "Yeah, I was there on a DeBlase story. What—"

"Let me finish, please. DeBlase's men, following their normal security precautions, undoubtedly started taking pictures during the disturbance. By a quirk of fate, the two of us were photographed together, though neither of us had ever met. When that photograph was developed, DeBlase found it necessary to kill me. Quite possibly kill you as well."

I nodded. I wasn't agreeing with him. I just wanted him to keep on talking.

"So you see, Mr. Harker, you are the reason I have had to disrupt my life. Thomas Merle DeBlase saw the photograph of us and assumed we had something to discuss."

"Now wait a minute, just a minute. Why would that upset DeBlase enough to make him kill—what is it?—two people. Yeah, two."

Fragan nodded as though approving of whoever had given me a number *two*.

"You seem to be well informed, Mr. Harker. At least up to this point. Well now, let's see if we can fill you in on what you do not know. In reference to your question about the photograph, the answer has to do with three trips Mr. DeBlase made to Cuba over ten years ago. Unknown trips. I should say 'unknown to the general public.' The purpose of these trips was to meet the Cuban premier and together plot the assassination of your President Victor Evan Havilland. They—"

"You've got to be kidding!"

"I am not kidding, Mr. Harker. I do not kid about anything, not now, not ever. Your handsome, young, somewhat impetuous President Havilland was assassinated over ten years ago, twenty-four hours before he was to be inaugurated. And Thomas Merle DeBlase, along with Premier Benes, plotted the killing. Others were involved, of course, but—"

My voice was a squeak. "Do you know what you're saying?"

"I do. I was there in Havana when DeBlase met Benes. I was stationed there and I had enough spies of my own to know why one of the richest men in the world, an American who publically railed against Premier Benes, was secretly meeting Benes in Cuba. I didn't know the details, but I knew why they were meeting."

"Let me get this straight: You *knew* about the assassination? I mean knew about it and did nothing? I mean—"

"You surprise me, Mr. Harker. Your writings led me to believe you were an intelligent man. Will you kindly give me one reason why it was necessary for me to become involved in a matter of this sort? If the leader of Russia or Communist China were to be assassinated and advance knowledge was made available to your countrymen, how many of them would warn the intended target? I'll tell you how many: none."

I shook my head, hoping to clear out my ears. I had to make sure I was awake, that I wasn't just lying in bed living out a fantasy. President-elect Victor Evan Havilland, forty-three, handsome, witty, brilliant, with every gift the gods could bestow on man born of woman. "Victory Vic,'' the man who had never lost an election in his life, not even in grade school. Assassinated ten years ago in New Orleans the day before he was to be sworn in as President of the United States.

The killing had been a blow from which America had never recovered. It had shaken me up so badly, I'd gone off by myself into the country and wept for three straight days. There were rumors about an assassination conspiracy and these rumors were still around. So far, nothing much in the way of hard evidence had been produced to make these rumors stand up. Books and articles had been written and lectures given on the subject of the Havilland assassination. But the official version was still the one in the history books. President-elect Victor Evan Havilland had been assassinated by a lone rifleman, Perry Joseph, a twenty-six-year-old misfit. Unfortunately, Perry Joseph, who had denied the shooting, was killed before he could be questioned. He'd died in an attempted jailbreak two days after he had supposedly killed Victor Havilland.

"Fragan, let me get this straight. You're telling me that DeBlase planned the Havilland assassination ten years ago? Do you know what you're saying?''

"I do. I saw him in Havana, your Mr. DeBlase. I saw him meet Premier Benes. You undoubtedly know I was attached to the Russian mission in Havana, so I was in a position to know what was going on at the highest level. I am telling you that the Havilland assassination, which your government was quite anxious to cover up, was the work of powerful men. Your Mr. DeBlase, Premier Benes, and certain segments of the American intelligence community. Together, they have murdered a President and made the American people believe that a neurotic weakling acted alone, doing the killing himself.''

I had a feeling that Walter Fragan, alias Colonel Valentine, was not a man to lie about anything. He was running for his life. He could lose it any second, so why lie? If this story of his was true—

I couldn't even think about it.

"Mr. Harker, we don't have much time. Our being photographed together was an infinitely bad piece of misfortune for me. Mr. DeBlase hadn't seen me for over ten years, before he saw that photograph. Unfortunately for me, he donated a building to Winslow. Unfortunately for me, you came to cover this totally unimportant event."

"Jesus, to hell with the event. I was there digging into his relationship with the CIA. Look—are you sure about what you're telling me? About the Havilland assassination? Do you have any idea of how big this story is?"

He sneered. An actual sneer, just the way Paul Henried used to do it in those old Warner Brothers movies.

"Your story interests me only in that it may be of use to me. Since you have tracked me here and since a police lieutenant awaits you on the dock, I can neither go through with my plans to work my passage to the Caribbean, then disappear, nor can I dispose of you, without attracting attention to myself."

"Ain't that a shame?" He was something to watch. Precise as a Swiss watch and as cold as a ski run. But he was telling me that the biggest story of my life was right here in this room with him. The Victor Havilland assassination. Christ, could Fragan be telling the truth?

"Want to ask you something, Fragan. If DeBlase wants you, if he wants to keep you quiet about seeing him in Cuba, why kill others? Why the rest of your team?"

"Appearances, Mr. Harker. He kills others to make it look like someone had a mass objective. KGB revenge or some such rot. Not that my former friends would not like to run into me again. But killing my team from Havana makes it look like the Russians are active here. It does not in any way point to Mr. DeBlase. The others are merely a cover-up. I am the primary objective."

Questions, questions. I had more than my share. Right now, I just stood there looking at Fragan's dyed hair. I opened my mouth in a hurry.

"Fragan, let's say that what you just told me about the Havilland assassination is true. So why has it been a big secret for so long, like over ten years? Everybody and his brother's been poking around it during that time. Everybody. But so far—nothing; and I've read a lot on the killing."

"Not enough, Mr. Harker. Oh, yes, I know your reputation. Prize-winning investigative reporter, the man pointing a finger at society's blemishes. You've done quite well for yourself. Are you telling *me* that merely because *you've* been unable to uncover any assassination conspiracy that none exists?''

Son of a bitch. The man had one hell of a talent for making you feel a foot and a half high.

I caught myself shifting my weight from foot to foot and stopped. "OK, Fragan, OK. So I *don't* know everything. But I know the assassination of Havilland left a scar on this country that no so-called official investigation has so far erased. Hell, I'm all for a conspiracy theory. Breaking that kind of story would make me king of the water cooler around the paper. But why has it remained one of the all-time secrets? More than one person was involved. Had to be. Chances are good that somebody would have shot his mouth off before now.''

Tsk, tsk, went Walter, the Colonel. The sophisticated Russian espionage *maven* now forced to live among us yahoos. A snob and a snot he was, too. But he knew a lot more than I did about some things, a fact my ego found hard to swallow. The man was so sure of himself that you wanted to kick him somewhere soft.

"Mr. Harker, do you know history . . . specifically anything about the death of Napoleon Bonaparte?''

By golly, Mabel, I had him there. "I know what you're going to say. You're going to tell me about those Swedish scientists who examined some hairs from his head back in, I think it was '61, 1961.''

"Ah, you know the story.'' His words were a pat on the head for my standing on my hind legs.

"I know the story. They found out he'd been poisoned. Arsenic. There was enough of it in those hairs to knock down a horse. The scientists used atomic reactors.''

"Exactly. That means Napoleon did not die of stomach cancer, or malaria, syphilis, and exhaustion, as some history books would have it. He was poisoned. Murdered, Mr. Harker, a fact which does not appear in one history book in the world. More than one hundred and forty years after his death, it comes to light that he had much help in dying."

He stopped talking and waited for it to sink in. It did. The man had me hooked. I only half saw Estevez, who stood a little to Fragan's right, both hands jammed in the pockets of that awfully neat white suit. I gave a small thought as to whether or not Estevez had a gun and decided, rather hoped, that he didn't. Lord, let it be a mango he's got in his pocket.

"Fine," I said. "Tell me something else. You aren't exactly being beaten over the head to tell me any of this, yet you are. Why?"

"Self-preservation. Or, to put it another way, the kind of attention you can bring to this matter might be of help to my survival. You more or less said this yourself. Prior to Mr. DeBlase's attempts to silence me, I lived a quiet life. It suited me extremely well, though it was boring. Now it seems that I'm unable to leave the country as planned, so I must change my tactics." I could almost see him in a war room in Moscow, full uniform, boots, cap, pushing tiny toy ships across a huge table map with a long stick. Changing his tactics.

"Yeah, yeah. Well . . . uh . . ." I shook my head, temporarily inarticulate. I filled my cheeks with air and looked down at the floor because I couldn't think of anything else to do at the moment. Assuming Fragan wasn't lying, it made sense for DeBlase not to want this story out. A one-in-a-million shot—DeBlase, Fragan, and me in one spot on one particular day. But stranger things have happened and will happen before the earth stops turning. In one way, it was natural and normal for all of us to have been in Winslow then. Our lives had brought us there.

But it was the kind of cosmic knee-slapper that kept you awake nights asking God whose side He was on. Yeah, I was hooked on this one. I was going to stay with it as long as I could breathe.

"Mr. Harker?" Walter Fragan woke me up.

"Yeah, I'm listening."

"I assume you have doubts."

"You might say that. But what with Watergate, Vietnam, Cambodia, and stuff like that, this country's willing to believe anything, providing it doesn't come from its own government.''

He nodded, giving me a bigger grin, this one with the kind of self-serving satisfaction you find on the face of a man who's just cut off both your legs and is delighted you somehow managed to crawl around the floor for a little while. "There is corruption in *all* power, Mr. Harker, and in *all* governments. What made it easy to keep the Havilland assassination secret this long was the unwillingness of your government to tell the full truth. It could prove embarrassing. It *will* prove embarrassing. Secondly, Mr. DeBlase is quite powerful and he has eliminated certain loose ends.''

I thought of my romp through the cornfield this morning. Loose End Harker. Three men in jeans. Men with Southern drawls. Texas drawls? What's the difference? Men with drawls. Men with guns. Men who might well be employed by a certain Texas billionaire who gave away multi-million-dollar buildings to colleges in Indiana.

"Look, Fragan. I mean, this is one hell of a tale you're spinning. If I believe you, I could end up a fool. That is, if you're wrong. If I don't believe, I could end up a fool if you're right.'' *That* bothered me the most. Losing out on a good story.

Fragan said, "I'm sure you have been the fool more than once, Mr. Harker.''

Smiling at that, I thought of Loni, my ex-wife. "*Oh*, yeah. *Oh*, yeah. But this business of yours is a lot different.''

"Indeed. Well, they do say that truth will win out. They didn't specify when. Truth alone abides forever.''

"Buddha,'' I said.

"Correct.'' His eyebrows went up in small appreciation. Fuck him. I read hours a day when I wasn't out in the world. I read anything and everything, looking for ideas on anything and everything.

Something else was bothering me. Estevez. I pointed to the little bastard and said to Fragan, "He's heard this before. You wouldn't let him hang around if he hadn't. I want to know what he is to you.''

"My agent. Theatrical agent." Fragan grinned at his own wit. "He booked me on this ship. You don't believe me. Well, let's say that Mr. Estevez knew certain people, while in Havana. Those people, let us say, were of use to the Americans. Those people, let us say, played a part in the Havilland assassination."

"And just who would Estevez know?" I asked. Besides head-busters.

"You could ask him, Mr. Harker. He might tell you. I'll say this. Estevez's friends are involved with at least fifteen attempts by your government to kill the leader of Cuba. Since Premier Pedro Benes is still very much alive, those attempts obviously have not been successful. But those unsuccessful attempts to kill the Cuban premier, Mr. Harker, are why your President-elect Victor Evan Havilland was shot to death prior to assuming office."

For a few seconds, I didn't trust myself to speak. Fucking incredible. My eyes combed Fragan's face looking for God knows what. But Fragan looked as secure as the Pope blessing a crippled orphan.

"A hit squad, Mr. Harker. Your government had what is called a hit squad, men who murder other men. The squad killed on your country's behalf. The Caribbean, South America, Africa, Asia, Europe. Geographically efficient. Unfortunately, they were unable to kill Benes. I say unfortunately, because the Premier resented these clumsy efforts to remove him from office. In retaliation, he, with the help of Mr. DeBlase and others, killed your President-elect."

"Oh?" What else could I say? "Stunned" was a word I could have said.

"You don't think it's possible, Mr. Harker?" The bastard actually sneered at me again.

"Yeah, yeah, it's possible. Anything's possible. I'd like to ask Estevez—"

I stopped. Far across the huge green room three men stood in a doorway watching us. They weren't waiters. They started walking toward us slowly, in no particular hurry. One of them, a short man with mirrored sunglasses, limped a little, a hand going to his crotch as though his nuts were still giving him trouble. They hadn't even bothered to change their jeans, but then again, they'd been in a hurry to get down to Florida. The Cornfield Three, now appearing in Florida for your pleasure, at the Pea Pod Room of the *S.S. Oro Azul*. Shit! What a time to interrupt.

"Fragan. Listen, just listen. Don't turn around. The three guys I told you about, the ones who tried to kill me this morning? They're here, right now. Coming toward us. They—"

Estevez turned around in a hurry. So did Fragan. It was a big ballroom and a walk across it was time-consuming, like a stroll across Brazil. It was that big. Behind us at the other end, the waiters kept spreading green tablecloths like six Johnny Appleseeds sprinkling chlorophyll.

"Fragan, I'd really like to stay and talk to you but—"

"DeBlase's men," said Fragan in a thoughtful voice. He didn't stay around to say anything more. He was on his feet and running, not very smoothly, not with any particular grace, but he was running. So was Estevez. So was I.

Our feet clattered across the wooden dance floor like a trio of awkward performers. We ran for our lives, and I wondered if this was what journalism was all about.

11.

"Mr. Harker?"

"Yeah?"

"Do you have any idea where we are?"

I looked up at Walter Fragan from where I sat on the cabin floor. The old bastard leaned against the door, a tired, aging man. His unshaved face was slightly purple from fatigue. His mouth was open wide enough to catch flies and the hand over his heart made him look like a dying man saluting the flag. I wondered if he could run two more steps if he had to.

"We're somewhere below the ballroom," I said. "Why ask me? You ran along two corridors and down a staircase, with me, don't you know? I'm told you work here."

He did some deep breathing and eyeball-rolling before answering. "I was hired as a piano player, not as a long-distance runner. We were only following you."

"Don't blame it on me, Fragan. You and Estevez here, you followed. Hell, you're both lucky I started turning doorknobs when I did."

Fragan looked close to a coronary. Estevez was on his

feet, which wasn't saying much. He was doubled over, head hanging down, both hands on his knees. I'd seen that position before, on track men who'd run a hard race and were now ready to throw up.

"Mr. Harker, are we to thank you for leading us into this—this blind alley?" Fragan made a sweeping gesture at the cabin we'd just run into and closed the door behind us. It was fairly large, with racks of green jackets used by the ship's waiters and musicians. There were male entertainers' costumes on hangers and lying around on card tables. Tights, sequined jackets, a few props, and even an ape's costume. The ape suit probably belonged to that tap dancer I'd seen in the ballroom a half hour ago.

"Fragan, if you don't like being in here, why don't you step outside?" I jerked my thumb at the door. "I saw a chance to hide out, so I took it. The way you two clowns run, DeBlase's men would have been on you in a minute. We got lucky, that's all. They had to run across a huge ballroom floor, but after that, they had the edge. They're younger, maybe meaner. At least younger than you two. And I know they're meaner than me. So we rest."

"For how long, we rest?" asked Estevez, standing up straight. He stroked his pockmarked face with a perspiring hand, looking like a man buried alive and not happy with the idea.

"Beats the shit out of me. We can try sneaking out and—"

I shut up quickly, frowning and rolling over to my knees. I listened.

Fragan looked down at me and said, "What's wrong?"

"Shhhh!" I put a finger to my lips, signalling for quiet. I got to my feet slowly. The way my body ached, slowly would have to do. I leaned an ear against the door and listened hard. On the other side their footsteps were faint but coming along fast, the way bad news always does.

"What—?" Fragan again. The man just didn't know when to behave himself.

I didn't feel like being sweet. "Shut the fuck up! DeBlase's men. I think they're heading this way!"

They were. The footsteps were louder now, definitely

in a hurry to get somewhere. Or get somebody. Estevez stood rigid in his smelly white suit, his bloodshot eyes bulging as the footsteps ran past the door. My fists were clenched and Fragan stared down at the floor, moving his bottom lip back and forth between his teeth. In seconds, the footsteps faded and disappeared. Inside the room, the three of us exhaled almost at once.

"Oh, *yeah*," I murmured, shaking my head slowly. "Close."

"Close only counts in horseshoes," Fragan said snidely. "One of your American homilies."

"I'll take it, I ain't proud. You still think we should have tried to outrace those three?"

Fragan ignored my question. "They won't stop looking for us."

"Hmm, no. But they'll have a hard time finding us on board something as big as this! This ship is not exactly small."

"There is still the chance we run into them," said Estevez, in a voice thinner than a G-string.

"No way I can promise you won't," I said. "We've got a little time. Not much, but a little." I wanted to get Fragan talking again. I had some more questions. Sitting back down on the floor, I took out a notebook and a ball-point pen.

"What are you doing?" Fragan's voice climbed the scales to high C. Anyone overhearing his inflection would have thought I was going in for self-abuse in public.

"I'm a reporter, Fragan. And right now, I'm taking notes. None of us are going anywhere for a few minutes, not until we're sure the coast is clear outside. Why Havilland? Why him? Why not another target? Why not the incumbent President or some of the CIA people? Wasn't it the CIA's idea to kill Benes?"

Fragan sat in a wooden folding chair. "Benes found out that the attempts on his life were being pushed hard by Havilland. The CIA never operates without the approval of the highest American authorities. There was a very, very secret committee advising the American President on national-security matters. Still is. Havilland was on it, even though he was a young senator. But he wanted the Cuban leader dead. He pressed very hard for that to come about. The fact that Benes was bringing nuclear warheads only ninety miles off the American coast frightened many people. Havilland had no trouble convincing people around him to go along with his idea for killing Benes. The CIA, the President of the United States, they all were, as you Americans say, hot for the idea. With Victor Havilland coming into office as President, Benes knew his life would never be safe. Once the CIA had the President's OK— Havilland or his predecessor—they would never stop trying to kill Benes. So, he defended himself.''

I looked up from my notes. "Did Havilland hate Benes *that* much?''

"Mr. Harker, Victor Havilland represented the American people, and, like the American people, he had a blind hatred of the Cuban premier not always supported by facts. Benes may have been a bogeyman to you, but to Cubans he was a George Washington and Abraham Lincoln.''

"Not to mention Lenin and Trotsky.''

"If you insist. But Benes had as much right to defend his country, his life, as your American President did. One patriot versus another. Havilland was your country's brightest and best, I think the saying goes. Cutting him down in his prime, at the top of his career, was the same as cutting off your country's legs at the knees, was it not?''

I nodded, remembering that unforgettable hurt of over ten years ago. "So Benes gets an American, Perry Joseph.''

"Perry Joseph?'' Fragan sneered again, pronouncing the name as if it were Mortimer Snerd. "Perry Joseph couldn't wipe his own ass. DeBlase and Benes wouldn't have trusted a killing as important as this to a weakling like Perry Joseph, a neurotic, a man who wasn't sure if he was sexually interested in women, little boys, or farm animals. Perry Joseph? Mr. Harker, sometimes you amaze me, you really do.''

I stopped taking notes. My eyes went to Walter Fragan as though he were doing wonderful magic tricks. Estevez grinned at me.

"I amaze you, huh?"

"You don't give a job like that to a Perry Joseph. You don't give a job like that to even *one* man, no matter how good he may be."

"You're saying Perry Joseph didn't kill Victor Havilland?"

"Yes, that is what I'm saying. I know your Congress has investigated the assassination and I know a report has been issued saying one man, one bullet, and such nonsense. But ask yourself, Mr. Harker. If you were Benes, would you place your country's survival, your *own* survival, in the hands of a man like Perry Joseph? Would you?"

"Hey, look, Fragan, I've read tons of stuff on the assassination and I know a lot of it's bullshit. But there hasn't been any proof of a conspiracy, as much as I'd like to believe one exists."

"Mr. Harker, you say you read a great deal. Specifically what?" He twiddled his thumbs and looked down at me with his head leaning to the right like a fuzzy-faced, wise old owl. The Colonel was an aristocrat and believed the rest of the world existed to be spat on.

"History. A great deal of it, specifically ancient and medieval. Some contemporary, but most contemporary history is shit. It's too soon for objectivity, so all you get are press releases and applause for national virtues existing only in somebody's mind. Newspapers, magazines. I read them looking for ideas, facts, anything to kick off a story. Philosophy, because it's a hell of a gymnasium for the mind. Voltaire, Montaigne. Eastern philosophers like Vivekananda of India, probably the best thinker of the last hundred years. Plato's getting more and more dated, and—"

He held up a hand like a traffic cop at a school crossing. "Spare me. It's fairly impressive. Anyway, you must know that historical accounts of the deaths of kings are not always accurate."

Estevez looked at the two of us as if we were speaking a language he couldn't understand. We were.

"I know that," I said. "Many kings were actually poi-

soned, but history reports it as death by natural causes.
There was no forensic medicine in those days, so you could
literally get away with murder.''

"That's not all, Mr. Harker," said Fragan. He made a
steeple of his fingers, tucking it under his chin. "At all
times in history, certain men along with certain agencies
have managed to hide facts, at least for a while. Sometimes even longer. Most history contains all the truth of a
political promise. I include Russian as well as American in
that. However, people such as yourself engage in careful
research, intense inquiry, and persistent pestering. You do
get results, though it does not always make you popular.
Be that as it may, such is the case with the assassination
of President-elect Havilland. Your country covered up,
your intelligence community—CIA, FBI—distorted and hid
facts. And that is why this particular assassination has remained a much-discussed mystery. The killing was carried
out by more than one man. Was it not, Estevez?''

That last sentence was dropped on me so casually I
almost missed it. Almost. When I shifted my eyes to the
Cuban, I was looking at a nervous man. It was as if even
the thought of those long-ago events were too dangerous
for him to toss around in his mind.

"I—I—'' He folded his hands, wringing them as though
pulling the skin off the bones. This was a man who had a
lot on his mind. I couldn't wait to hear some of it.

Fragan's voice was surprisingly friendly. "It's all right,
Enrique. Mr. Harker could be a help to us with his story.
He won't print your actual name; will you, Mr. Harker?''
That wasn't a question. It was an order, a leftover from
the good Colonel's days of interrogating the enemies of
the state and giving them more than a hotfoot for wrong
answers.

"No problem, Estevez," I said. "A reporter covers his
sources or he's dead himself. Nobody's going to talk to a
bigmouthed newspaperman. So let's see, how's Juan
Gomez suit you? That always seemed to me to be the
Cuban equivalent of John Smith.''

Estevez must have licked his lips twenty times in less
than a minute, leaning left, then right, and shoving his

hands in his pockets, then taking them out. A very nervous man, our Cuban.

"I din't do nothin'," he said, shrugging his shoulders and showing his hands palms up.

"Didn't say you had. Just tell me something about yourself. Did you work for the CIA at any time?"

"*Sí*. I mean yes, yes I did."

"In Cuba or the U.S.?"

"Both. In Cuba, I carry money to people. CIA pay them, I take the money."

"Who?"

Silence. I looked up from my notes to see him staring at Fragan, a pleading look in his brown eyes. Fragan nodded once, a half-smile on his unshaved face. He could have been a proud father encouraging his retarded son to keep struggling with the alphabet.

Estevez shifted his eyes back to me. I waited, letting him get back into it in his own good time. It had better be damn quick. Visitors could be on the way.

"The Mafia, *señor*. I pay the Mafia to do things."

"What did you pay them for?"

"To kill Benes."

I didn't want to break the spell. So I didn't look up. I sat on the floor, my ballpoint pen scribbling faster than I'd ever written in my life. Then—

"Obviously they didn't. Why did the CIA think they would?"

"Because, *señor*, the Mafia lost much money when Benes kicked them out of Cuba and closed down their casinos. Also, they lost much money when they could not bring narcotics into Cuba and so easily bring the narcotics into America. Also, some of the Mafia had been stealing money from the casinos, and they hid this money and they wanted to go back to Cuba and get it. So they work for the CIA."

"Who was your CIA contact? I'm guessing now, but I think you and Fragan, here, you two got together under the direction of this man. Am I right?"

A smile on Fragan's face told me I was. "My, my, my, Mr. Harker. Your brain begins to warm up. Yes, Señor

Estevez and I were assigned to several CIA agents, but the man in charge of bringing us both across was code-named Voltaire. That was the only name we knew him by. Voltaire. It may have had something to do with his cultural interests, perhaps. I never really found out."

"*Sí,*" said Estevez. "Mr. Voltaire. He say make contact with the Colonel here and send back information. I was the go-between. For the Colonel and the other people."

Good old Estevez. The man in the middle, and I'm betting he made a lot of money out of it. Voltaire. Could that have been one of Trotman's code names?

Something told me to ask about Voltaire, which I was ready to do, when Estevez coughed and said, "*Señor,* I think we leave now. We cannot stay here too long. I think we go."

Scrambling to my feet, I shook my head. "No! Jesus, we're just getting started. I—"

Estevez's hand went into the pocket of his jacket and came out with a nickle-plated .22 that could have been a cigarette lighter. It wasn't.

"Colonel?" Estevez turned to Fragan, who looked amused by it all. Standing up slowly, Fragan said, "I tend to agree with my *amigo*. We have tarried here to excess. I shall contact you again, Mr. Harker. Rest assured I shall not leave the country prior to doing so, assuming I can leave at all. The Caribbean would have been an excellent place to hide, what with this ship docking at six ports of call. However—"

He shrugged his shoulders, a calm loser. For the moment.

I stood with a notebook in one hand and a ballpoint pen in the other, watching them walk past me. Fragan opened the door slightly, looked out, then opened it wider. Estevez kept the gun aimed in my general direction, looking over his shoulder at me, then out into the ship's corridor. I didn't like their leaving without more chitchat, but there wasn't much I could do about it. The notes I had so far were dynamite, but notes aren't a story. And investigating a story like this was going to take a hell of a lot more work than I'd put in so far.

Voltaire. Mafia. Yes, indeed, I did have things to do besides stand here and try not to get pissed off. For one thing, I was on to a story that was so explosive that I didn't even want to think about it. For another thing, I couldn't keep standing around here forever because I soon might have company. The waiters or DeBlase's men could show up any minute.

Time for Harker to get his ass in gear. And I knew how I was going to do it. I had a damn good way of getting off this ship, past the Cornfield Three, past any of their friends who might be on the dock with one of the photographs taken of me and Walter Fragan in Winslow. Yes, sir, they didn't call me Harker the Smiling Schemer for nothing.

12.

Walking through the ship in that ape suit was like walking in hot mud up to your neck. Slow, tough going. I felt as if I were in a steam bath that itched. The suit weighed a ton and the head kept slipping forward, which meant I was totally blind until I adjusted it. So I had both hands on the head most of the time, keeping the ape's eye sockets level with my own eyes. I was dragging my feet. Not because I wanted to but because the ape feet were almost two feet long, one foot wide, and heavy as concrete blocks. Don't forget those cigar-long toenails.

Reaching the staircase, I clutched at the railing with my paws and suddenly went blind. Shit! The fucking ape's head again. It had slipped forward, and I couldn't see a thing. To hell with it. I climbed the stairs anyway, pulling myself up, going to the top on my knees. An ape on his way to the top. And without Fay Wray. To calm myself and assure anyone who might turn up that I was in show biz, I began to hum a few bars of "One Night of Love." I was at the top. Lord be praised. I was exhausted. Wear-

ing that suit was taking pounds off my body and years off
my life. But the scheme was working. So far.

I stood up, adjusted the ape's head so I could see again,
and, still humming, I walked along another corridor.

In the passageway, a couple of waiters brushed by me
without saying a word. A bald, pudgy man with a clip-
board stopped me and said, "Tony, you know you're doing two shows tonight, right? Not one, two." He held up
two fingers to make sure I got the point. I nodded, holding
onto the ape head. "Good," he said, patting me on my
hairy arm. He squeezed past me and walked away whis-
tling. Wait until Tony found out about working two shows
tonight.

I was running out of air under this thing. How Tony
managed it, I didn't know. But I was sweating buckets.
Walking in it was like running a two-minute mile. Once
you got used to wearing it, it was probably a lot of fun.
But I didn't plan to get used to it.

I was about to step on the gangplank and walk down to
the dock, when I saw them. Two men leaning against a
parked car looking up at me and laughing. They weren't
driving pickup trucks, but they had that look about them,
a hard-faced alertness you only find in men who are hunters. Even when laughing, they were like vultures circling,
waiting for somebody to drop so they could eat.

I had to take my hands off the ape head. No other way
of getting down the gangplank. And I damn sure wasn't
taking the head off so that the hunters could stop laughing.
Let them laugh. Laughing at me was better than shooting
at me.

Gripping the ropes on either side of the gangplank, I
eased down it as carefully as my size 24's would let me.
The ape toenails scratched, caught, and pulled at the wood
beneath me. At the bottom, the two hunters were still
laughing and pointing at me, but that didn't stop them
from looking up at the ship from time to time. I adjusted
my head so that I could see.

Now I knew how women in short skirts felt when walking past construction workers.

Tucker John Delk was parked around the corner, behind

a warehouse. Even though I was out of sight of the hunters on the dock, I could still be spotted by someone on ship with a good pair of eyes. That's why I still had the ape head on when I shuffled up beside Tucker John. Tucker John was sitting in his car reading the sports pages when I came up to the open window.

He turned, looked at me, and softly said, "Jeeeesus Christ! Who the fuck you 'spose to be?" Tucker John wasn't scared, shocked, or impressed. Just mildly surprised.

"Harker. Who the fuck do you think?"

I wanted air in the worst way.

"Harker?"

"Tucker John, let's get the hell out of here. I can't take this head off now. Come on, man, come on, goddamn it, don't just sit there!" Being overheated made me irritable. It got a smile from Tucker John, who mumbled, "Well, I'll be dipped. Shit, Harker, it *is* you."

"Yeah, yeah, it's me. Come on out and open the door. I can't shit with these paws." I couldn't. It was like having no hands at all, an uncomfortable feeling.

Tucker John not only had to open the door, he also had to push me into the back seat because I was too fat in that ape suit to get through the door on my own.

Seconds off the dock, I took off the ape head and did a lot of deep breathing. Air felt good. It was cool against my sweating face. I leaned back and sucked in air like it was going out of style.

"Hey, man, what the hell happened back there?"

Tucker John smiled into the rear-view mirror, shaking his head in wonder. I shook my head. "I'm not sure. If I hadn't changed into this thing, I might be a dead reporter by now. Look, you know where I can get a cheap suit?"

He stopped for a red light. "What's wrong with the suit you're wearin'?"

"Funny. Ha-ha. I ain't wearing shit under this thing. Only way I could get it on. My wallet, notebooks, change, keys, everything, they're all in the feet of this thing. You ought to try stepping barefoot on keys sometime."

"No thanks." He chuckled. The light changed.

"Nothing expensive," I said. I'd gone through two suits today already. I was spending more money on clothes than Elizabeth Taylor.

"Tucker John? After the suit, a telephone. Public phone."

He nodded, eyes in the rear-view mirror like a Gypsy looking into a crystal ball. But all he would see is what I was telling him. For the moment, that wasn't much.

13.

Like all career military men, Malcolm Mullen couldn't stop giving orders. Even over the telephone, he was a man on horseback, a saber in each hand.

"Damn it, Harker. You should have ordered the wife to wake me."

"The wife wasn't in my platoon," I said.

"Exert yourself, man, exert yourself." His voice roared like Teddy Roosevelt out to build another Panama Canal.

"I'll try to remember that in the future. What's up?" I pulled a small white tag off the sleeve of my new twenty-two-dollar polyester suit. My third suit of the day. *Guiness Book of Records*, here I come.

"Tried to reach you earlier but no one at your paper seems to know where you are. What kind of way is that to do things?"

"It gets me there and back. What's on your mind?"

"Hmm, yes. To business. DeBlase. He has a big meeting coming up."

"I know, Iran. Flying to meet the Shah. Hush-hush."

"*Oh?* Oh." A few seconds of silence hung between us

as he thought about something. I got the impression that T.M. DeBlase's meeting with the Shah of Iran was a surprise to Malcolm Mullen.

It was. His voice confirmed that he'd heard my news for the first time.

"Didn't know that. By God, I didn't know that. No surprise, though. No, that's not the meeting I'm calling you about. This meeting's got panic written all over it. It's a scramble, an alert. Every top security man working for DeBlase has been ordered to show up in Las Vegas five days from now. *Everybody.*" His voice underlined the last word, as he remembered how good it had been to order people around and watch them jump.

I thumbed my notebook open to a clean page.

"Sounds like something's about to happen. Who called the meeting and why?"

"DeBlase and Harley." Malcolm Mullen said the name *Harley* like it was an expletive deleted.

"Harley? Who is Harley?"

"Runs security. The man brought in to replace me. Gaylord Ran Harley, formerly of the CIA and—"

"Hold up, slow down, Gaylord *who*?"

"*Ran*, Mr. Harker. As in what you do with your feet."

"Don't remind me. Gaylord Ran Harley. Jesus. CIA?"

"DeBlase favors the type. So does Harley himself. Harley is always ready to give an old comrade a job. Fact is, the Company goes out of its way to take care of its own, find them civilian positions when their government service is complete. Harley has filled DeBlase's security with ex-Company men."

"Ain't that the way it goes," I said. "The businessmen of America go out of their way to influence the government and the military."

Malcolm Mullen coughed, clearing his throat. "*Some* of us perform valuable services, Mr. Harker." His voice was wrapped in the flag. I wondered if he was standing at attention while rationalizing to me.

"Let's talk about one Gaylord Ran Harley and why all of the security chiefs working under him are going to be flying to Nevada in five days."

He cleared his throat again. "No one knows why, except that it's an alert. There's some kind of problem that Harley and DeBlase won't discuss with more than one or two people. Unfortunately, my contact isn't one of those one or two."

"Unfortunately." I squirmed around in the telephone booth. Public telephone booths in Miami were not built for comfort. "Mullen, how good *is* the contact you have?"

He snorted in my ear. "Good enough. Harley brought in his own men for the top positions, ten years ago or so. But some of the electronic equipment I acquired for security purposes is still being used. My men still run that equipment, Mr. Harker. *My men.*"

My men. I wondered if Malcolm Mullen would have *his men* prove their loyalty by riding horses off a cliff at full gallop. A Prussian emperor once did that years ago. I decided not to ask.

"OK, so much for your source. These security men, how many would there be?"

"Hmm, I think one or two might be from outside the country. Total would be under a dozen. Most are from the U.S. They're in charge of protecting top oil fields, factories, buildings, things like that."

"This Harley. How important is he to DeBlase?"

"Very." Malcolm Mullen filled that one word with enough bitterness to poison a reservoir. "He's DeBlase's shadow, his right-hand man. All the executive vice-presidents, accountants, whatever—none of them have as much influence with DeBlase as Harley does. None of them do." Mullen's voice held hate and envy. The power Gaylord Ran Harley now wielded could have been his.

I stopped taking notes and leaned back in the small phone booth as far as I could, which wasn't much. Gaylord Ran Harley was tight with Thomas Merle DeBlase. And their public hand-holding had begun over ten years ago, just about the time President-elect Victor Evan Havilland had been shot to death.

And hadn't Walter Fragan just told me that ten years ago he'd seen Thomas Merle DeBlase hobnobbing with the premier of Cuba? And hadn't the Colonel and friends crossed over with the CIA's help a little more than ten years ago? A lot had been going on then. With one particular CIA case officer hovering in the background: Voltaire.

"Mullen, do you remember if Harley had a CIA code name? Well, he did, they all do. Remember what his was?"

"Hmm, can't say as how I remember. It's been a long time. If I ever heard it, I've forgotten it by now. Harley's not one of my favorite people."

I shifted the telephone to another ear. There wasn't an investigative reporter who didn't have sore ears. The telephone was our lifeline. I ran up a bill each year that made Ma Bell dance in the streets. Fortunately for me, the *World-Examiner* paid it. Not willingly, but they paid it.

"Did Gaylord do anything to you specifically, other than take over your job?" My instincts said that Gaylord had.

Malcolm Mullen took a deep breath, letting it out in his own good time. The silence grew longer, followed by more deep breathing. Malcolm Mullen was obviously in the grip of bad memories.

"Let's just say he made sure that I wouldn't sue DeBlase for *any* reason, nor would I publicly make a fuss about my dismissal. He made sure I'd leave the building quietly. Let's say that."

"Mind telling me what that was? Did he threaten you? Your wife?"

"*Mr.* Harker." Malcolm Mullen was his old saber-wielding self again. "I'd rather not go into it. Harley did not threaten me or my wife, per se. He just made sure that I would regard my past association with DeBlase as classified. Top secret."

"In other words, he dug around until he found something you'd done, something you didn't want anybody else to find out about. And he told you that as long as you kept quiet, nobody would know. Right?"

Malcolm Mullen's silence said that he would like to see me tied to a wagon wheel and bullwhipped into bleeding strips.

His voice dripped acid. "Harker, sometimes you are too smart for your own good."

"I'm good-looking, too. Anyway, back to Gaylord. He's calling this meeting in Las Vegas five days from now. Is the meeting at one of Mr. DeBlase's hotels?"

DeBlase owned three Las Vegas hotels, which also explained why it was easy for him to meet the Mafia if he needed a favor done. The mob built Vegas and has had its hooks in that city ever since. I was thinking of the kind of favor Estevez said the Mafia had tried to do for the CIA in Cuba. The kind of favor that was to have ended up with Benes dead and somebody else ruling Cuba.

"Yes," said Mullen. "The Argonaut. My man doesn't know why, so it must really be top secret." He sounded disappointed at not being more in the know. He was now on the outside looking in, like the rest of us civilians, and he missed being one of the insiders playing at power.

T.S. Eliot was right when he said that all the trouble in the world was caused by people wanting to be important.

"Mullen, find out why. I'd appreciate it."

I wouldn't have been surprised if the meeting didn't have something to do with that photograph of Walter Fragan and me. So far, I'd filled up two small notebooks with what I'd heard or come across in Indiana and Florida today. Usually I keep three or four cheap notebooks shoved in my pockets, along with as many ballpoint pens. Occasionally I use a tape recorder, but I don't depend on it. I keep paper and pen at hand, because if the recorder pulls a mechanical failure on me, I'm shit out of luck. I blew a big story once because the batteries went dead and I didn't have a goddamn thing to write with. Never again.

Mullen's military voice came back at me as though he'd just accepted a mission of the highest order. "I'll see what I can do. Won't make any promises. I can tell you this much. There isn't a thing on paper about this meeting. No memos, nothing in house organs, newspapers, not one word in a secretary's notebook regarding time and date. You'd think they were planning to overthrow the government or something."

"Or something. I'll try to get back to you tomorrow, to see if you have anything for me."

"Might be going out to Vegas myself." He seemed happy now.

I wasn't. My heart jumped and I had more than a little anger in my voice. I had a lot. "*You've* been invited to the meeting? You've been holding out on me, you son of a bitch!" Never trust a Lieutenant Colonel, Retired.

"Get a grip on yourself, man." His voice reminded me of a Sahib in India telling those around him to stand fast in the face of a charging elephant.

"Jesus, Mullen, have you been holding out on me?"

"No such luck, I'm afraid. I've been invited out to Nevada to see some war games. You once wrote about them being a waste of the taxpayer's money, I believe. Naturally I have my own opinion on that."

"Naturally."

"Some friends of mine, top-level brass I might add, have invited me to come out and stay with them for a few days. Watch the games out in the Nevada desert. Ah, that desert air. Could use a little of that, me and the missus. I'll be there at the same time DeBlase will be having his meeting, but I won't be going anywhere near the hotel."

Whatever Gaylord Ran Harley had on Malcolm Mullen, it damn sure was good. Mullen didn't want anything to do with DeBlase or Harley.

"Too bad you can't go near the meeting," I said.

"That's not my job anymore," he snapped. "I'll be in Nevada for my own enjoyment, personal reasons. To watch military maneuvers. That is all."

I closed my notebook, tucking it inside my new suit. My new puce suit. Fags said puce instead of green. Tucker John, who'd taken me to the store, said the suit was the color of parrot shit.

"Are these maneuvers worth the trip?" I couldn't care less, really.

Mullen did everything but cartwheel. "Magnificent, my boy. Splendid. More than sixty thousand troops, plus support. Armor, small arms, wheel guns. Some rockets. The purpose is to learn how to best deploy troops under conditions of mechanized warfare." He sighed the way the rest of us do after orgasm.

"One more thing. Did DeBlase ever say anything about Victor Havilland?" I asked.

Mullen was silent for a few seconds. When he answered, his voice was a lot smaller. "What made you bring that up?"

"Who knows? You going to answer the question?"

He cleared his throat. Some of the military starch was gone from him now. "If I remember correctly, he, ah, he, well, he didn't like Havilland. Thought he was too liberal, much too liberal. He gave a lot of money to Havilland's opponent. He may even have preferred Havilland's vice-president to the man himself. He thought if Havilland ever became President, there would be black and white sex in the street and that America would slide into the sea or something like that. The man despised Havilland, if I remember correctly."

"Yeah? Go on." My notebook was out and I was writing again.

"Well, I do remember one thing. I thought it was sort of extreme myself."

"I'm listening."

"When we got word that Havilland had been assassinated in New Orleans, DeBlase and a few of the people around him drank a toast to celebrate. *Celebrate.*" Mullen's voice was very low now. That toast had obviously been too much for Malcolm Mullen. A man had to draw the line somewhere and, obviously, Malcolm Mullen had.

I threw a high, fast one at him. "That was around the time Harley went to work for DeBlase, wasn't it?"

"Yes. Yes, I believe so. Wait a minute—what are you getting at with all this? You off on some wild-goose chase? I thought sensible people considered all such rumors dead and buried. There's no such thing—"

"The only thing dead and buried is Victor Evan Havilland. Does the name 'Voltaire' mean anything to you?"

"No. Can't say it does. Harker, are you up to something? Acting out your fantasies again? God, you newspapermen!" His voice was high, at its most prissy. "Let me say, Harker, that any such inquiry on your part, re the Havilland assassination, would be a fool's errand." The tiny click in my ear could have been Malcolm Mullen's false teeth. Or the CIA, depending on how paranoid I was feeling.

I dropped the subject in a hurry. "Whatever you say, Lieutenant Colonel. Check with you later about that meeting. Enjoy the war."

Regis Cooler was next. I could have saved the wear and tear on my fingernail and credit card. Regis Cooler wasn't in the office. The image-maker was still out drinking his lunch. That meant he'd been chewing olives and looking through the bottom of martini glasses for at least three hours.

I hung up the receiver and stared at the traffic. It didn't inspire me. Not at first. But after staring at it for almost a minute, I snapped my fingers and pulled out one of two little black phone books I carried everywhere.

I regarded these collections of telephone numbers and addresses as a mother regards her firstborn. The pages had everything from senators' unlisted phone numbers, to massage parlors in seven cities, to the clubhouse numbers of the last three Superbowl winners. At home, I had other numbers written on everything from the bathroom wall to the label on a jar of Ovaltine. The thing that surprised me was that I somehow managed to find any number I was searching for. God protects the good, I suppose.

I dialed Boston. While I waited, I looked over at Tucker John. He was pointing off in the distance, his forefinger being watched intently by an old couple, the man and woman each holding an unfolded map. Tucker John, tourist guide to senior citizens. Up until then, he'd been leaning against his car, girl-watching and smoothing his sideburns.

I had a short wait. The man I wanted to speak to was in a university laboratory and somebody had to go and get him. Usually, he worked until eight or nine at night. Since it was a little after five, that meant he'd either be in the lab or playing poker somewhere on campus. I hoped he wasn't playing poker. If he was, he wouldn't come to the phone for Sophia Loren.

"Yeah?" Edmund Hale Peltz had an unfriendly manner

over the phone. He was a fifty-eight-year-old pathologist, best in the country. In over thirty years, he'd performed and supervised some twenty thousand autopsies for police departments and universities. The man knew more about dead bodies than God and all the worms of the world combined.

"Hey, Peltz? Harker."

"Harker, who? Who the hell is this?" His voice roared like a lion waiting too long for his red meat. The stocky man with a thick chest, short gray hair, and eyes that didn't miss a thing, always got to the point. Even if it meant sticking the point up your ass.

"What the hell do you mean. *Harker who*, you fucking Nazi!"

"Hey, Harker, it's you. Why didn't you say so?" Suddenly, he was a pussycat. His raw, throaty voice, with a touch of German hiss, was friendly. We could have been in a Berlin tavern singing beer songs.

"Why didn't I say so . . . Jesus, has anybody ever told you what a rotten telephone manner you have?"

He chuckled. "No. When I get them, they don't talk much. You vant something, you prick. What the hell is it?"

"You sound like Kissinger, you cocksucker. You know that?" I liked talking to Peltz. He had more funny stories about corpses than anybody I knew. Funny and unprintable.

"Kissinger, Kissinger. He's not a true German. He hasn't declared a war in over ten days. Vat's on your mind? Ven you coming up here?"

"Never, I hope. Come on down to New York. Maybe I'll fix you up with a live one."

"Funny. Very fucking funny. You didn't call to pimp for me, or did you?"

"No. Some questions."

"Go."

"The Victor Havilland assassination. We've talked about it and you said the official autopsy on him was one of the worst you'd ever seen."

He sighed. His beer belly probably shifted a couple of

feet. "Fucking vorst. Whoever did it was in a hurry. Sloppy. Did it in New Orleans. The official report's a piece of shit, you know that. Cover-up. Right?"

"Yeah, yeah. We've kicked it around, but what the hell, nothing's come up to really knock it down. I want to go over some of the things you and I talked about."

"Like vat?"

"Like the wounds. You said for sure that more than one man did the shooting."

"Shit, I'm not the only one to say that. Some others did, too, but who listens? Books out, shitty books, good books, but nothing's being done, you know? Hey, Harker, you up to something, you—"

"Come on, Adolf, keep your armband on. Just asking questions, that's all."

"Ask."

"OK. Wounds. Entrance wound in the back, just under the shoulder blades. Exit wound in the throat."

"Yah."

"Frontal wound, too. Part of his skull came off."

"Yah. I told you. That's the reason I'm sure more than one assassin was in on it. Vounds from the back, vounds goin' in the front. The official report doesn't go into this. One bullet, one assassin, they say. It's a cover-up, everybody knows that. Why you so curious? You never vaste your time, that's why I like you."

"Well, don't stick your tongue in my ear yet. How many men you think were in on it?"

"You quote me?" His voice was Prussian exact, like a computer. We all cover our ass. To stay alive, we have to. He didn't want to be quoted.

"No, you bastard. Even though you've shot your fat mouth off on television more than once."

"Vell, I been told to shut up. How you like dem apples?"

"I don't. By who?"

"The university, who else? They say it's foolish, ridiculous. Makes them look stupid. They *are* stupid."

"Yeah, OK. So tell me."

"At least two gunmen. Maybe three. They vould have

been smart to use three. Backup, you know? In case the other two get cold feet or their guns don't vork, or some-thin' happens. You protect yourself. That's my theory and a few other people too, yah?''

"Yah. Something else. How can I get my hands on the stuff nobody's talking about?"

"Like vat?"

"Like autopsy reports that so far nobody's been able to look at. Like slides of wounds, clothing, photographs of the body, that kind of shit."

"Jesus, ain't you see that yet?" He seemed surprised, even disappointed.

"No reason to, until now. Actually, I've seen one or two things out of curiosity. But now I want to see more. And don't ask why, at least not yet. Now, Peltz, I got it figured that a good cold-meat specialist like yourself has his ways."

He blew air into the phone. Then he said softly, as though rocking a baby to sleep, "Fuck you."

I grinned, not that he could see it. "Thanks for letting me know how bright I am. In return, I'll donate my body to science."

"Soon, I hope."

"There, there. Come on, Peltz. You know people who know people. I want a closer look at the Victor Havilland assassination report, that shit that's around Washington and not opened to slobs like me. I want a look at anything else you think I should be looking at."

"Harker?" There was a pause. It meant the price was going up, or that the dumpy white-haired German was having second thoughts about our friendship.

"Yeah?"

"My name does *not* appear. You got that? It does *not* appear." Edmund Hale Peltz wasn't angry, just deter-mined. I wondered if that would happen to me when I got older. Would they be able to lean on me and squeeze my eyes out of my head for not playing the game the right way. A hell of a thought.

"Peltz, I promise. Just give me a name or two. Then

call your people and let them know I'll be in touch. What's it gonna cost me?'' It usually does.

''Your left ball, you cunt.'' He sounded a little angry, but that was normal for him.

''Got a pencil?''

I sighed. A good days' work, Harker. ''Have I got a pencil? Does the cat have an ass?''

Tucker John Delk was still leaning against his car when I walked over to him. He was also still girl-watching and still stroking his sideburns.

''How'd you make out, Harker?''

''Two out of three.''

''Sheeit, that's the majors, Jim. Let's go.''

''Where?''

''Called the station while you were jawin' away. Had somebody run over to Estevez's *hacienda*. He's there. Looks like he found himself a way off that boat, too. God-damn boat must be runnin' out of ape suits by now.'' His grin was obscene.

I frowned, remembering how heavy that ape's head had been.

''That ain't funny, Tucker John.''

His grin stayed right were it was. ''The fuck it ain't, Harker. Fuck it ain't.''

14.

"Harker?"

"Yeah, I see 'em." Two police cars and an ambulance, all parked in front of Estevez's apartment house. A sinking feeling in my gut said that Estevez's telling days were over.

Tucker John Delk was all cop now. His eyes narrowed like Gary Cooper staring at something far out in the desert. He sat up straight behind the wheel, shoulders back, chest out. "Best drive on by. There's a restaurant, Alma's, just three blocks from here. You go in there and wait. I'll come back and see what's shakin' here. I'll telephone you at the restaurant. What's your middle name?"

"Shit, you got to be kidding?" My middle name. I didn't even want that on my tombstone.

"Harker, the fucking around is over. I'm a cop. You know what that means? That means if your friend Estevez has gone on to his reward, anybody near him has got to be dragged down to the station house and asked some hard questions. You follow me?"

I was beginning to . . . and didn't like it. However, Tucker John was right, as he too often was. He was trying to cover *my* ass, in violation of the rule I lived by, which was cover your *own* buns and fuck the rest of creation. Life is full of surprises. A thinking cop was one of them.

Damn. My mouth was watering to know what, if anything, had happened to Estevez. Tucker John continued telling me why I could not walk up to one of those squad cars and ask.

"Harker, the law's got us both by the short hairs. If somethin's gone wrong back there and you're around, well, I got to take you in. At least for questioning. Publicity ain't gonna help you in your work. You get out here and walk back three blocks. Alma's is in the middle of the third block. Wait there. Just wait. Order some rice and beans. Make sure you pay with cash. No credit cards. Leave a tip, not too big, not too small. Don't do nothin' that's gonna make nobody remember you."

He slowed down, braked at a curb, and kept the motor running. Thanking people doesn't come easy to me. "You did it again, Tucker John. Helping a visitor from the North. Whatever happened to all those fat-bellied Southern cops who drink Dr. Pepper by the gallon and tie hippies to the back of their squad cars and go speeding by the light of the silvery moon?"

He was looking straight ahead, almost as if I weren't in his life anymore, for the time being. "They're still around. Less than you city folk think, more than we need. Maybe one of these days—"

His voice trailed off. He was looking far, far away, to the governor's mansion and some changes he had in mind. The man had made a convert out of me.

"Albert," I said, opening the door and looking both ways to avoid getting an assful of fender. "Middle name's Albert." I slammed the door and leaned in the open window. "You tell anybody, you bastard, and—"

"Damn!" He broke his cop pose long enough to give me a smile with one corner of his mouth. "Albert. *Alllllll-bert.* My, my." He still had the tiny smile as he pulled away from the curb.

I looked around me. Every other shop appeared to be a coffee bar. The strong smell of Cuban coffee was everywhere and people stood around drinking it like they were getting paid for a commercial. The smell was punching me in the nose and I quick-stepped to Alma's.

Alma's was small, plain, with more strange odors than you'd find in a busy chemical lab. I suppose it was a matter of taste, but Cuban food was heavy on the garlic and the garlic was heavy on my sense of smell. No one looked at me, the visiting Anglo, and I fingered a menu, my mind on Estevez. Maybe the squad cars and ambulance weren't there for him at all. Maybe somebody else had run into bad karma. Sure.

I'd taken three forkfuls of beans and rice and semi-relaxed, when the telephone rang near the cash register. A slim woman with dark glasses, hairy arms, and a face that treated smiling as a capital offense, answered it with a brutally curt, "Alma's."

Then she covered the mouthpiece with a thin hand and said aloud, "Alberto? Señor Alberto?" Her voice was dusty.

I turned from her and went back to my black beans and rice. Then it hit me. Señor Alberto. Alberto. Shit, that was me.

"*Sí,*" I said, standing up and letting my napkin slide to the floor. "Señor Alberto. *Sí,* me. Me." Charlie Chan was more articulate than that. I hustled over to her. She handed me the phone. You could braid the hair on her arms.

"Alberto speaking." I gripped the receiver with both hands, one hand cupping my mouth. My eyes swept the restaurant in the kind of paranoia reporters feel all too often these days.

"Albert, honey," said Tucker John in a hard voice that killed what was left of my appetite. Bad news was on its way when he talked like that. "Haul ass out of there. Go somewhere, anywhere. Don't bother telling me where. I don't wanna know. Estevez ain't with us no more. Somebody put one of them blood-pressure cuffs around his neck. They pumped it up until Estevez turned purple and his eyes 'bout near came out. That sucker was strangled by some highly imaginative people. You still there, Albert?"

My throat was tighter than a miser's fist. But I forced it open with more willpower than I was feeling at the moment. The beans and rice started to come up, but I pushed them back. I breathed deeply. I was a man in trouble and not because of what I had just eaten.

"Yeah, I'm still here."

"Don't see why," Tucker John said, and he hung up.

15.

Trotman said, "This place is an armpit, Harker. Thought you people had expense accounts." He snorted in mild disgust. I could have been a black who had been given a chance for acceptance in white society and, instead, had pissed in the punchbowl during a lawn party.

I was tired. And unfriendly. "We *have* expense accounts. I'm sleeping here tonight because I want to wake up in the morning. If somebody shoots your eyes out during the night, you can't very well greet the dawn; can you now?"

Too many plane trips in one day. Too many people forcing me into footraces I wasn't in shape for. A kick in the ribs from a nasty Cuban in a yellow T-shirt. That's why I was tired and unfriendly. My nerves were raw. Someone I couldn't see was painfully scraping them with a broken bottle and doing a good job.

"Sound uptight, pilgrim." Trotman leaned back in the small room's only easy chair, crossing his thick legs at the ankles, folding his large hands across his stomach. His hands hadn't become any smaller since last night. They were still big enough to strangle a rhino.

"Yeah, I'm uptight. Shit, who wouldn't be? Just left Florida one step ahead of the posse." I sat on the edge of the bed, thumb and forefinger gently massaging the corners of my eyes. I had planned an early night. Phone calls to set up meetings with some of the people Peltz had recommended me to, then sleep until I couldn't sleep any more.

But when I'd called Mrs. Karakas in New York, sleep dropped to last on my list of things to do. "Horace" had called, she'd said. *Emergency.* The telephone number she'd given me to call was a Washington bar on E Street, which seemed safe and unbuggable. While waiting for Trotman to pay me a quick visit, I picked up the phone and set appointments for myself tomorrow. Meetings with Peltz's people.

Trotman didn't waste time getting here. My hotel was the Auden, a hole on Constitution Avenue. It was a place you'd sneak into for a sexual quickie with a woman you wouldn't want your friends to catch you with in daylight.

"Step ahead of the posse," Trotman said slowly, repeating what I'd said in order to get me started again. I noticed he was wearing red socks.

"Estevez-Blanco. You know him? Mousy, greasy Cuban with gold teeth and a face like a flattened rat."

Trotman's big head nodded once. "Bag man, sort of. Used him to pay off Cubans we were working with." His yellow eyes narrowed, burning into me. He waited to hear something he wished I hadn't learned. It struck me that even Trotman could be trusted only *so far*. How far was that? I wondered. Fuck it. I was too tired to follow my suspicious mind anywhere tonight.

Besides, you don't challenge a man's integrity to his face, especially when he's big enough to terminate you with extreme prejudice by using just his thumbs. I stared at Trotman's narrowed yellow eyes, wondering just what his crafty brain was up to. He was using a giant thumb to stroke his red nose. As far as I could figure, that's the closest he came to having a nervous gesture.

"What about Estevez?" he asked.

"Dead. And he did more that just spread money around. He also worked with the Mafia in Cuba, maybe even here. I'm not sure."

Trotman continued slowly to stroke his nose. But his thin mouth had puckered up, like a man tasting pure lemon juice. His bright slits of eyes looked through me as though I were made of cellophane.

"Dead, huh?" Trotman frowned, turning thick black eyebrows into one hairy line at the top of his red nose. He was thinking. Hard.

"Can't get no deader. Somebody took his blood pressure. One of those rubber things doctors use around your arm. Put it around his *neck* and kept pumping until Estevez stopped living. You were going to tell me something."

Trotman scratched a thick thigh, sighed, then leaned back and looked up at the ceiling. He could have been watching the paint peel. He could have, but he wasn't.

He didn't look at me while he talked. "I came over here to tell you that you've got the Company shook up. Roy Lupus saw you out in Indiana. When he told the powers-that-be, they got their drawers in an uproar, to put it mildly. They don't want this defector thing out. They're scared shitless 'bout people learnin' we can't cover our own. When you get back to New York, you're gonna find the pressure's been put on your people so hard, you ain't gonna believe it. They ain't playing now. They brought in the first team. You might even get word from the man himself."

"Oh? And who would that be?" I yawned. Not at Trotman. I was tired, flatter than hammered shit.

"White House."

"Won't be the first time. But I'm impressed. They don't usually bother."

Trotman stopped staring at the ceiling and looked at me. "Something else. Can't pin it down, but I think there's outside pressure, too. Somebody's been leaning on our people to make them work harder at keepin' you quiet. Somebody outside wants to see this defector thing stopped yesterday. And whoever it is, he's got juice, a *lot* of juice. He's got clout. What's more, he doesn't mind using it. Somebody's listening to him, that's how heavy he is.'' Trotman understood power.

I opened my tired eyes wider. Beneath me, the cheap bedspring sagged like big tits after the age of forty. ''Somebody outside the Company. Could that somebody be one Thomas Merle DeBlase?''

The second the words left my mouth, I knew that this thought had also danced across Trotman's mind. He nibbled a corner of his mouth, exhaled, and shrugged. If a man was to tackle big power, even in his mind, he didn't do it head on. He snuck up on it. Trotman's voice dropped a couple of octaves.

''Why'd you mention him?''

''Those photographs of me and Fragan. The CIA didn't take them. You may have ripped them off from the Company, but another bunch of fun seekers took them.''

''Like who?'' His large head was tilted to the right, carefully watching me the way he probably watched all people he had dealings with. I forced myself *not* to think of what had happened to *some* of those people when the dealings were over.

''Those photographs were taken when I was in Indiana two weeks ago. You and me both figured the CIA or KGB had been stalking Fragan, getting ready to move in and zap him. No way. DeBlase took those photographs. His goon squad, his security boys. A precaution in case DeBlase gets hurt. This way his boys can go to work without waiting for due process of law, if you know what I mean. Tell me something. Obviously you got these candids from your people. Under what circumstances, may I ask?''

I got as much smile as I've ever seen the big red-faced man give me. This was a quickie, speeding across his wide, thin-lipped mouth.

''Got 'em the way most good things in life happen. Almost by accident. I was out at Langley, hanging out near a photo lab, bullshitting with the guys. I wanted to pick up some more poop on defectors getting burned. So I'm

out there, just hanging out, listening. And like that—''
Trotman snapped two cucumber-sized fingers.

The sound was as loud as lightning splitting an oak tree.

"Like that," he continued. "Some guy in the lab is
laughing and he calls a bunch of us over to look at these
pictures. We all laughed. We thought it was funny you
running like hell so that flying student wouldn't land on
your nose. Everybody laughed. I guess you realize that if
something happens to you, there is gonna be dancin' in
the streets.''

"Nice to know I'm doing something right. The photographs—''

"I just ripped them off when I got a chance. There were
piles of them hanging around. When nobody was looking,
I copped a few and that's that. Nobody even mentioned
Fragan's name. Everybody was getting their jollies watching you run for cover.'' He smiled at the warm memory
of it all.

"Trotman? Who's *Voltaire*?''

He looked up from his red socks in a hurry. Both eyes
snapped to me, grew wider, and focused on my face as
though it were the strangest thing he'd ever seen. Then he
leaned his big head back on his wide shoulders, aiming
his chin at me. The atmosphere in the room changed. I'd
stepped across a line, into a territory where men play
worldwide games that end with somebody getting killed.
Or having his testicles jabbed with a cattle prod.

"Voltaire?'' His voice was a whisper.

Mine wasn't much louder.

"You heard me.''

"The name. Where'd you get it?''

"Oh, no. Oh, no.'' I sat on an inch of mattress, leaning
forward and jabbing a forefinger at a man tough enough
and mean enough to do root-canal work on me with a
chain saw. But that's how you do this kind of reporting.
You bull your way through and hope you're far away when
your bluff is called.

"Trotman, you've told me what you wanted me to know.
Now tell me what I want to know. *Who the fuck is Voltaire?*''

I stood up, yelling out the last sentence as if it were a college cheer.

Trotman didn't look at me when he answered. He stared at a chest of drawers that looked as though it had been dropped from a tall building twelve times, then brought directly to this room after the last fall.

His voice was low, somewhere deep in that huge chest. But it came out loud enough for me to hear.

"Gaylord Ran Harley. A Cuban expert. Knew a lot about that country, the Caribbean, too. He was in charge of several of our Cuban operations. A fucking individualist, a wild man. Case officer on the Walter Fragan defection. I was in the field on that one, his second in command, in charge of direct contact with Fragan and his team."

I sat back on a couple more inches of the drooping bed. "Harley. Did he run a hit squad for you people?"

"Shit, you been busy, ain't you, Harker?" He didn't seem sad or glad about that. "Let's just say Harley had a bunch of men loyal to him and they never asked him why a thing should be done. Let's say that. His people did things his way or they got themselves transferred in a hurry."

"Was there a hit squad or wasn't there a hit squad? Did the CIA have a bunch of triggermen who went around *officially* killing people in the name of the United States government? Yes or no?"

He looked at me, then at his red socks. He nodded. "Harker, why the fuck you askin' me what you already know?"

The man was giving me credit for more than I had right now. But I took the credit anyway. Estevez had told me this bit of news before somebody stopped him from auditioning dwarfs and pretty girls. As I stared at Trotman staring at his red socks, I decided something. I decided I wasn't going to ask him if he'd ever killed for Gaylord Ran Harley. Let sleeping big dogs lie.

"Harley. Would you say he and his men were rogue agents, the type to go off on their own?"

"Yeah. Yeah, you could say that. That's one of the

problems the Company's always had. Too many guys gung-
ho about what they thought was their job. Too little control
over them. Sometimes an order comes down from the top.
But it has to pass through a bunch of people. And when
it hits the field, the last guy either doesn't know what the
original order was, or his instructions are so wide open,
he can do any fuckin' thing he likes. A guy like Harley
always ended up doing a lot of what he wanted.''

"Like killing people.''

"Harker, sometimes these people *had* to go. Sometimes
it had to go down that way.'' He looked at me in a way I
didn't find reassuring, given my present nervous state.

"Sure, Trotman. Like 'Operation Phoenix' in Vietnam.
Twenty thousand people had to go. Killed, tortured. And
the Company in blood up to its elbows on that one.''

"I didn't like that one either. A lot of guys didn't.
Twenty thousand people killed. Jesus. Man, you know
some guys just don't know when to quit. They got to go
on and on and on. Yeah, Harley was a lone wolf, acting
like he was in business for himself and the rest of us were
along to applaud and throw money. Harley. Jesus.''

Trotman shook his head. I got the feeling he didn't like
Harley. But there was also the feeling that Trotman was
feeling pangs of Company loyalty. Not huge pangs, but
pangs. The Company did that to almost all of its people.
It made them so goddamn loyal to it that nothing else
mattered. Not even the United States and its people.

"Harley left the CIA around ten years ago,'' I said.

"Yeah,'' said Trotman, more like his old hard and cold
self now. "Became top security man for—for—'' He
looked up at me. "DeBlase,'' he whispered. "He went to
work for DeBlase.''

I smiled. Trotman was no mental giant. But he wasn't
excessively dumb either. Point him in the right direction
and eventually he'd stumble down the road and end up
almost where he should have ended up. "Ran Harley went
to work for DeBlase. What's more, he took some of his
team with him. Got 'em jobs, good payin' jobs in security.
He was very particular 'bout who he hired from us. Only
certain people.''

"How come you didn't go with him?"

"He didn't ask me. We didn't get along that well. Sometimes he went overboard doing certain things. I didn't see it his way all the time." Trotman went quiet, shifting his legs, running a finger around his sticky collar to scrape off the sweat. So Trotman had scruples. That meant he might kill three, but draw the line at four.

I sat back farther on the sagging mattress and almost fell into the abyss that was gong to be my sleeping area for the night. Pulling myself out of it, I said, "So Harley quit the Company and took some of his flower children with him. Certain hand-picked people. All just about the time Victor Evan Havilland was assassinated."

"So?"

"So the CIA did not like Victor Evan Havilland, right?"

"Aw, Harker, you too?" He waved a huge hand at me in dismissal, squirming uncomfortably in the chair. "Shit, everybody and his brother's gone down that road. Knock it off, will you? We didn't blow away Havilland. I mean *why*?"

"You tell me. First of all, no killings of the type the CIA does can possibly go down without an OK from the top—and I do mean the top."

He stood up and my heart dropped to my ankles. The man was big enough to do me incredible physical harm. But all he did was pace as much as the tiny room would allow. "Harker, let's say what you claim is true. The OK has to come from the top. So if Victor Havilland gave a go-ahead to certain projects, wouldn't that make him one of us?"

"It would. Until he changed his mind. He'd be one of you unless he decided that a senator okaying assassinations is one thing. A President of the United States okaying them is another."

He stopped pacing long enough to look at the scarred chest of drawers. Then he continued pacing. He had a lot more to deal with now. It wasn't just defectors getting killed. It was a lot more, a hell of a lot more.

"Trotman, would Gaylord Ran Harley kill a President who tried to harm his beloved CIA? Would he?" I kept my voice as low as I could and still be heard. My eyes were on his unsmiling face, with an occasional quick glance at his giant hands, now clenched into fists that could hammer spikes through railroad ties. Trotman stopped pacing, his back to me. He touched the wall in front of him, nodding his head once. His back was to me. In the silence, we both sweated and breathed and nothing more. It took me a few seconds to realize that Trotman, big, big Trotman, a man capable of a lot of nasty things, was *weeping*.

I cleared my throat and stood up. Seeing a man this large weep was unnerving. It didn't make him less in my eyes. I've wept before and will again. A popular American president shot to death. It had all hit Trotman at once and he knew the truth. Or he knew a *lot* of the truth.

So he wept because of it. Perhaps the weeping was a release of what he had denied to himself for so long. But he wept and I sadly watched it, knowing there was nothing I could do.

After a little while, I said softly, "Trotman?"

"Yeah?" He kept his back to me. A big hand was still pressed against the wall. His head was bowed, beaten down by life the way it does us all in the end.

"Trotman, I talked with Estevez and Fragan in Miami this afternoon. Both felt DeBlase was out to get them, to keep people from talking to me and getting something started. The defector killings are just a cover-up. It's DeBlase all the way, and it's all happening just because I got photographed with Walter Fragan and didn't even know it. I need something from you now, need it badly."

I stopped. He said nothing. He didn't move.

"Trotman, I need files. The files you people have on Havilland's killing. The commission didn't have its own investigators. It used you people and the FBI. Both of you have files and stuff on the assassination that you *never* made public. It's around, I know it. I've been told it's there. I need it. I need to look at anything you've got that's been kept secret. It's asking a lot, I know it. But I *need it*, goddamn it!"

Shit, I didn't know what he'd do now. And whatever it was, I hoped I would live to talk about it.

His back was still to me. He sniffled. A big man. A proud man.

He wasn't talking, not just yet.

"Trotman, I need you." I was pleading. The Havilland story was what my life had come down to. Flunking out of college, breaking my ass to please my old man, seeing my mother cry when everybody told her I wasn't ever going to be a fucking thing, seeing Loni and me both cry when we recognized that I was addicted to my kind of reporting and didn't have that much left over for anything or anybody else.

I wanted the truth. And I wanted to be the one to tell this truth.

"Trotman, Harley's managed to con some of your people into working with him. I don't know what the fuck he's told them, but he's getting everything from inside information to photographic assistance from Langley. Goddamn it, are you listening to me?" I was angry, almost angry enough to grab him by the arm and spin him around. Almost but not quite.

His back was still to me and it stayed that way as he left my room. He never said a word, not one word.

I exhaled. Nice try, Harker. Nice try. Zilch. That's what you got to show for trying so hard. Zip and zilch. Nothing. Zero.

16.

The phone rang nine times before she picked it up. I counted every ring.

She'd been asleep. Her soft voice was tentative, and vulnerable, the way a woman is when she's suddenly awakened.

"Um, yes? Who is it?" She made little noises in her throat, getting in touch with this world slowly and not too surely.

I cleared my throat, swallowed twice, and kept staring at the ceiling. My hotel room was dark. I lay naked on the bed in the humid night, both sweaty hands gripping the receiver.

"*Who is this?*" Her voice was stronger now. Irritation was edging over into anger, reasonable enough when somebody pulls you from sleep and just breathes into the phone. It was good to hear her voice, anger and all.

"Me," I said finally. Might as well kick it off with a clever line. I was bare-ass naked in the hot night. Lonely and scared, too. That's why I'd dialed Loni in New York.

"*Me?*" Her voice was slightly higher pitched now, effectively getting across the idea that *me* was a silly name for a grown man. "Harker? Is that you, Harker?"

I sat up on my sagging mattress. It was like sitting up in a canoe, except a canoe was softer. "Yeah, Loni, it's me. I thought you might have the machine on. Took a chance. Called anyway. Never did like that recorder. I . . . I—"

Jesus. I'd run out of things to say. Me, the master of words. Tapped out. I pawed the air with one hand, trying to make the words come so I could say something to this woman who was so much a part of me.

"Harker, are you all right? Is anything wrong?"

In everybody's life, there is one thing he wants badly and shouldn't be allowed to have. It can be fattening foods, booze, sex with animals, narcotics, driving down crowded highways at two hundred miles an hour, free falling from planes. It can be making love with whips, swallowing broken glass, gambling, riding on top of elevators, drinking turpentine. Mine was Loni.

I had two things in common with those who wanted this particular something that they shouldn't be allowed to have: mine was no good for me. And I wanted it anyway.

"Hey, baby," I said. "You know me. A cat that lands on its feet."

"Cat that lands on its feet, huh? Harker, do you know what time it is?"

"Almost three in the morning. Couldn't sleep. Things on my mind. Hey, did I disturb you? I mean are you—?" It hurt like hell to ask her that last question, which is why I stopped asking it. She understood.

"I'm alone. What's going on? Three o'clock in the morning!" She seemed surprised that such an hour actually existed.

I was feeling sorry for myself, scared, alone. But calling her was tough enough. No sense groveling unnecessarily, I always say. "You know me," I said. "Don't know where I'll be, when I'll get a chance to call. So, I just—" I sagged down on my mattress some more. It was like a hammock, minus the shady trees at either end.

"So you just dialed a number at random and it turned

out to be mine." She was less excited now. Less concerned, too.

"Yeah, I did that thing, all right. Wanted to hear a friendly voice before they come and carry me away."

I was feeling sorry for myself. That's why I wanted to hear Loni's voice. Did I really believe somebody was out to kill me? Was I tidying up my life before my meeting with eternity? Or was I being overdramatic and just using this as an excuse to get next to Loni again. Place a check mark beside one of the above.

She sighed. A woman being patient with men and their dumb ways.

"You're probably in some sort of trouble," she said. "As usual, you're obsessed with whatever it is and it'll probably turn out to be earth-shattering. Whatever it is."

I chuckled. "To say the least. Doesn't it always? You sound good."

"At three in the morning? Hold on, let me get a cigarette."

The phone went quiet. Then in the background I heard a few soft noises.

"Back," she said. A lighter snapped open and she inhaled. The lighter clicked shut. "You need any money?"

I shook my head. "Thanks, no. The paper still pays off on expense accounts."

"Just offering."

"Appreciated. How long have we been divorced?"

"Six months. Little over. Why?"

Leaning back on the sagging mattress, I stared up at the ceiling.

"Just wondering," I said, "if the divorce is going to work."

She exhaled and kept quiet. Then, "Harker, we've gone over this before, I mean, really—"

"Yeah, yeah. You're right. Conflict of interests between both parties, your honor. Anything I can do for you?"

"Umm, not at the moment. Sing me a lullabye, maybe. I probably won't be able to get back to sleep." She blew some more smoke in my ear. I shivered, remembering what she could do to a man's ear when she really tried.

"How's your new apartment?" I asked.

She laughed once, a short, delightful sound. "Expensive. Don't ever go into business for yourself."

That hurt. I don't think she meant it to, but it did. I dropped my chin down to my chest.

"Harker? Harker? You still there?"

"Still here."

"Anything wrong?"

"The heat. I ought to stop banging on the radiator. It's like a pizza oven in here."

"I'll send some anchovies."

We both chuckled politely. Not too loud, not too long. We weren't yet relaxed enough with each other to laugh. We used to be. This was turning into one of those phone calls everybody makes at one time or another. The kind of calls where you both end up saying little or nothing.

Loni was a call girl. That's what she'd been when we had met and fallen in love. That's what she'd gone back to when we got divorced.

During the marriage, she'd left "the life," as she called it. She told me she had. I didn't believe her. I turned out to be wrong. That was one reason we'd ended up apart, me not trusting her. Habit, you might say. In my business, I didn't trust anyone. Not politicians, not generals, not secretaries of state. After a while, it became easy not to trust. Eventually, it ended up costing me the one thing in life I really wanted—Loni.

Then there had been the matter of living. Just living. I had my life and it took me all over the country and half the world for weeks at a time. It consumed me, my energy, my body and soul, and eventually my marriage. Loni was alone. And I didn't trust her. I should have. She was faithful to me, but I found that out when it didn't matter to the marriage anymore. Because once the marriage was over, Loni decided that "the life"—her life—was preferable to waiting for me to come home and argue with her.

"The life"—*her life*—at least meant she was living. As a call girl, the expensive kind, she had more than a source of income, stock tips, and trips to the Caribbean with dress manufacturers. She had freedom and power, not the kind

of power the National Council of Churches would approve
of, but power nonetheless. That had come out during
one of our arguments. "If *you* need power," she had said
to me, "then why can't you understand my need for the
same thing? *Why*?"

She was no ordinary whore. She was beautiful, intelligent, cultured, knowledgeable about everything from di-
plomacy to wines to fabrics to the best hotels in the
Bahamas. She was the kind of woman who belonged in
the Renaissance or at Versailles during the reign of "The
Sun King." In another life she'd be a courtesan, a titled
noblewoman serving tea to powerful cardinals and princes.

Except that this was the twentieth century, and Loni
didn't have a palace. She had a seven-hundred-and-fifty-
dollar a month apartment on Sutton Place, a neighborhood
as elegant as anything Manhattan had to offer. And her
customers were elegant, too. Referrals and personal con-
tacts, men who wanted more than just to use her body.
These men wanted to be seen with a special woman, a
woman they could take to a diplomatic reception or a business conference in St. Croix and not be embarrassed by
her company. For that, they were willing to pay a lot.

I was paying, too. Not alimony. Loni had refused to
take a penny. I was paying with a heartache that wouldn't
turn me loose. Beautiful slim Loni. Twenty-eight years
old, smooth skin, green eyes with flecks of brown, dark
brown hair. Somehow she'd taken hold of me and there
wasn't a fucking thing I could do about it. Except bleed.
I still loved her. Two years of marriage, six months of
divorce, and the woman still had me. I thought she still
felt something for me. I hoped so. But she had her own
life to lead, in her own way, and if anyone didn't like it
or understand it, that was his problem. She was a call girl,
because she wanted to be one, because she liked it, because she liked the money, the power, and the freedom it
gave her.

On the surface, she wasn't the one with the problem. I
was.

"Loni?"

"Yes?"

"I'll be coming back to New York—"

"God, I forgot to ask. Where are you now?"

"Washington. You wouldn't believe the hotel I'm staying in."

"The great Harker in a dump?"

"Better believe it. There's a reason for it."

"There usually is."

I had to grin at that one. Usually I got so caught up in a story, in getting at the truth, that I didn't see anything else. I don't want to see anything else. Before Loni, I hadn't cared. Being a reporter was all I'd ever wanted out of life. With Loni, I had someone else to think about.

"Loni, I might call you when I get back. Is that—"

"Yes." She said it easily, the word coming out without tension, doubt, or reservation.

I let out a long breath of air, leaning back on my rotten bed. For the first time in what seemed to be months, I felt relaxed.

"Get some sleep, Harker."

"Yeah, you too. Take care."

"Yes."

She hung up.

I kept the receiver to my ear. I whispered, "I love you, baby."

I hung up and sank down in the mattress. I don't remember dropping off to sleep, but I suppose I did.

17.

Harriet Rita Good wore pink-tinted eyeglasses. The frames were thin silver metal, contrasting with her frizzy black hairdo. She was Jewish, at an age where she could be planning to stay twenty-nine for another three years. Her blue and white summer dress, short-sleeved, was unbuttoned at the top, showing me and the world that she didn't have much in the way of tits. But her legs, bare and shaved, thank God, were nice. She was fairly pretty, no glamour girl, just a woman who had done a lot with what she had. The result was more than passable, except for her habit of always keeping her mouth slightly open. You got the impression she was about to say something, but had forgotten what it was.

We were in the front seat of her car, parked four blocks away from the National Archives, where she worked. She was one of the people recommended to me by Edmund Peltz. At 9:30 A.M., she was also my first appointment of the day.

"You can keep that," she said in a voice that was slightly nasal. "It's a copy I made for you this morning.

I came in around eight; practically nobody was there. Easy to get around and not asked questions. I told them my car needed fixing and I'd be back in a little while.''

"Smart," I said, giving her the Harker smile.

What was mine to keep was a list she'd made of missing evidence connected with the Havilland assassination.

"Who else knows this?" I asked.

She shrugged. "Not many. One or two congressmen, a handful of pathologists who keep trying to look into the autopsy. If you're asking if it's been published, no, it hasn't. My uncle knows." Peltz was Harriet Good's uncle, a fact neither she nor Peltz wanted spread around. She was a researcher at the National Archives.

"These items"—she tapped my list with a pink-tipped nail—"were turned over to the Archives after the assassination. I wasn't working here then. But I found out about it. They disappeared, just like that. Disappeared right *after* the assassination committee completed its report."

It was an interesting list. Among the missing were Victor Havilland's brain, bloodstained shirt, coat, tie; a copy of his tour itinerary, along with personal correspondence he'd been carrying that day. Missing, too, were medical slides of entrance and exit wounds, along with conflicting autopsy reports.

She leaned toward me. Her perfume smelled of roses and lemon. Her hand touched mine as she looked down at the list I was holding on to.

"Most of these things disappeared before I came here. Some after. Thing is, they're listed, categorized. Everything is. Has to be. Whoever took them couldn't remove all of the listings." She smiled triumphantly at somebody's stupidity.

I smiled at her. Why not? Let a smile be your umbrella, someone once said.

"Harriet, tell me something. Why is it so hard to get access to this material?"

She pursed her lips, swung around in the front seat as best she could, and faced me, clapping her hands once. Time for a short speech.

"Harker, this is a town of who you know. Power is the

one big thing that keeps everybody here. Nothing else, believe me. Four women for every man. Honey, that ain't good odds, no pun intended. Crime all over the place. Look, there's always been something funny about the Havilland killing. Did you know that something like eighty people involved with that assassination have been killed?''

''How did they die?''

''Well—'' She leaned closer to me, giving me another look at her flat chest and another whiff of lemons and roses. ''Accidentally and not so accidentally. See, we aren't always that busy, so I get a chance to look around. To read. You read?''

''Sure do.''

''What do you read?''

''Name it. Everything. Sex papers to the Congressional Record.''

She leaned back, waving a hand at me. ''The Congressional Record. I wouldn't put that on the bottom of my birdcage. I read a lot, too. Read your stuff all the time. You're good, really good. It's nice to meet you after reading you all these years.'' She smiled, looking younger as most people do when they smile.

''All these years? Damn, woman, come on. I'm only thirty-three.''

She shrugged and didn't volunteer her age. I didn't press. Let her stay twenty-nine for a couple more years. I waved some other papers at her. ''These I *can't* keep.''

She turned serious in a hurry. ''God, no! I'll have my thumbs cut off if they know I've even taken them out of the building. Take notes, use a tape recorder. Anything. But these go back with me.'' She lifted her eyebrows, gave me a weak smile that said *you understand, I'm sure*, and touched my hands with hers. Hers were cool.

''All righteee, Harriet Rita Good.'' I gave her a gentle James Cagney-like punch to the jaw, the kind where you just press the fist against the face and push a little bit. She liked it.

I began taking notes in a hurry.

The papers had a lot of things that interested me and I was scribbling until 10:15. My fingers ached, and sitting in the front seat of Harriet Good's car had made my drawers creep up again. Cars and hot weather did that to me, and my balls were unhappy about it.

Among the facts I copied from this batch of papers were the following:

At least thirty witnesses had testified to the commission that they had heard shots or seen gunsmoke coming from a direction *other than from behind* Victor Evan Havilland. Perry Joseph was supposed to have shot Havilland from behind.

Several people had testified that Perry Joseph, dishonorably discharged from the United States Army, was a poor shot. It had taken exceptionally good shooting to kill Havilland in New Orleans that day. He'd been in a long motorcade a nice distance away from Perry Joseph, who had supposedly done his shooting with a rifle from a rented apartment.

There was also testimony that Havilland's route had been changed *thirty* minutes before he'd gone on his tour. The change had taken him right past Perry Joseph's window.

There was testimony saying that Perry Joseph had been in Mexico, Cuba, Russia, France, Santo Domingo, and parts of the United States—almost simultaneously. How could one man do that? Well, the testimony submitted the possibility of more than one Perry Joseph. Now that was interesting.

But the most interesting fact of all was that in twenty volumes of the commission's assassination report, based on testimony and interviews with twenty thousand witnesses, *none* of the information that I was taking down had ever appeared. *None of it.* The American people had never been told all of the information uncovered by the commission. Far from it. It seems that the commission, which did not have its own investigators, relied entirely on an investigation of the assassination by the CIA and the FBI. What had been done with this testimony? Answer: nothing. It had been ignored.

I finished writing all of this and more. Then I looked up at Harriet Good. "Thanks."

She grinned. "What for? I haven't done anything yet."

Her grin got more personal. "God, you work hard. You just kept writing and writing, you didn't even look up. No wonder you win all those prizes."

Yeah. Win prizes and lose your wife. That's how you do it. I squeezed Harriet's hand. "You're beautiful, Harriet. Can't thank you enough."

"If there's anything else I can do—" She wasn't letting go of my hand.

"Who knows? Don't want to trouble you—"

"Oh, no trouble. No trouble at all. You're kinda famous around here." Her eyes were wide with admiration and she looked as though I meant more to her than Robert Redford and Walter Cronkite combined. I probably did.

"Well, if anything comes up—" I said.

"I'll give you my home number. Call me there." She held out her hands for my ballpoint pen and notebook. Why not? She wasn't all that bad and, besides, why hurt her feelings? I gave them to her and she wrote carefully, slowly, printing the telephone number. We all live in hope.

18.

"Was it Mrs. Evans herself who asked for me, or just Patsy, Maxine, and Laverne?" Julius Ramey, executive editor; Jack Sommers, managing editor; Ruben Weiner, city editor. Which of the three was *it*?"

"All *three*," said Mrs. Karakas emphatically into the telephone.

Pressure from on high. Somebody was leaning on *them* and *them* was leaning on me.

"When my name was bandied about, did anyone seem nervous, irritable, or maybe in a jolly mood?"

"Forget the jolly mood. The other two had some kind of control. Ramey's voice was squeaky, so he was uptight the most. They all send copy boys, copy girls over to ask. Secretaries buzz me and ask. When they mention you, it's like . . . well, it's like they're waiting for leprosy to strike or a plane to land with flood relief."

I smiled, sticking my ballpoint pen in the dial holes one by one. Trotman was right. The squeeze play was on. Hot and heavy after Harker.

"Anybody asks when I'm coming in, tell them I'll be there when I get there." *If I get there.*

"They're going to love that."

"They can all take down their pants and bend over. Phone calls. Let's go."

"Yes. Oh, almost forgot. Patrick Maxian. *He* telephoned asking about when you were coming in." Mrs. Karakas was slightly impressed. Slightly.

"Patrick Maxian, did you say?"

"None other."

Patrick Maxian. Mr. Fabric. My name for the man who spent more on clothes each year than small nations spent on food and jet planes. Patrick Maxian was the richest and most brilliant of Mrs. Evans' legal corps. A highly paid watchdog over the grande dame's pile of money. He'd had the dubious honor in the past of combing my stories for libel and lawsuit possibilities. A couple of times, he had suggested that such and such a thing be cut. I'd howl like hell and Patrick Maxian's snake-oil-salesman's voice would calmly point out that it was Mrs. Evans' money which stood to be taken away in court, not mine. In court, all I'd have to do was sit with a Bible in my hand and look up at the heavens.

I didn't like his logic. But I couldn't get around it.

The man spoke as though he and God were lodge brothers with a secret handshake. In another age, he would have been a prince of the Church. I sometimes wondered if Patrick Maxian didn't keep a bright red cardinal's robe in his closet, along with a garter belt.

Patrick Maxian was white, rich, and well connected. He was slicker than greased ice, a man who believed he could talk you out of, or into, anything. He usually could. There was no reason to dislike him, so I was planning to dislike him without a reason.

"Maxian gets the same message as everybody else," I said. "I don't give a damn if he does play bridge with senators and flies to Hawaii every three days for a tan."

"Got it. Other messages."

"Ready."

"Regis Cooler. You have his number. Malcolm Mullen, and a Juan Gomez."

I stopped writing. "Juan Gomez? I don't know any— Hey, hey!"

"What's wrong?" Mrs. Karakas sounded ready to give mouth-to-mouth resuscitation.

"Nothing, nothing." I made a fist, pushing it hard against the wall in front of me. Juan Gomez. That would be Walter Fragan. Had to be, goddamn it.

"Gomez leave a number?"

"No. Said he'd call back. Now that I think of it, he didn't sound too Spanish. Is he—"

"Don't ask. Look, if he calls, tell him to leave a number where I can reach him. He'll understand."

19.

My telephone call to Regis Cooler was as shocking as falling off the edge of the earth. *"Regis, you're fucking putting me on."* Thomas Merle DeBlase wanted to see me.

I closed my eyes, then opened them as wide as they could go. Nothing had changed in those few seconds of darkness. I was still in a steaming telephone booth, credit cards and notebooks on a small brown metal shelf in front of me. If I twisted and turned, I could catch a peek at the Washington Monument, that tall piece of concrete which looked as though somebody were giving God the long gray finger.

"It's the *emiss*, Harker. Gospel and such." Regis Cooler was New York media cool. That meant he talked in tightly edited, hip-magazine prose that sounded like a combination of bitch fashion reporter, Eighth Avenue black pimp, and moronic rock star. If there was a momentary cliché floating around, Regis had it stacked in his memory bank waiting for a chance to use it. He was forty-two, trying to pass for younger.

"Regis, do we have a bad connection?"

"Harker, booby baby, everything's copacetic, my man. He of great wealth has granted you an audience, my pet. Surprising to me as well. All this time he had me believing you were barely a cut above dogshit at your best, dear friend."

"Fuck you."

"Do we have time?" He made his voice sound *oh so bored*.

"Regis, cut the shit. When did DeBlase decide to see me?" I forced myself to think clearly. DeBlase was trying to stamp me out. And now he wanted to see me. Jesus.

"Yesterday, my pet. That man, he do have strange ways. Dig it. Guess he considers a dialogue with you to be viable or some such. Wants to know where he can reach you."

Wanted to know where he could reach me, huh? I bet he did. Son of a bitch. He tries to plant me in a cornfield and now he wants me to walk up to him and lie down in front of his steamroller. Too much.

But the invitation was intriguing. Exciting as skydiving. Now I knew how a moth felt when it saw a campfire. You know you shouldn't, but you wanted to anyway. *Loni.* Yeah, I'd had that moth feeling before.

"Regis, did he say why?"

"Nay. You are being honored, dear one. Many have called and all have been frozen." He chuckled like George Sanders always did, deep in his throat, teeth locked together.

"Harker? Harker, dear one, are you there? Have you flown away?" The smugness in Regis Cooler's voice made me want to shove my foot down his throat all the way down to the knee. He was acting as though I were overwhelmed and speechless at the thought of a meeting with Thomas Merle DeBlase. I was. I just didn't like being reminded of it.

I found my voice before I got much older. "Where's this meeting to take place?"

"Washington, dear heart. D of C. He's on his way somewhere, and I suppose he must touch base with the

powers-that-be. This trip is *el secret-o*, Jaçk. Ain't none
of po'folk know where he be headin'."

One of us does, I thought.

Jesus, what a challenge. Right to my face. I could run
and hide and maybe keep on living. All I had to do was
get something in print and the bastard would have to lay
off. Or I could do what no journalist had ever done in more
than thirty-five years. Talk with Thomas Money DeBlase.
Sure, it could be a scheme to lay hands on me. But maybe
it wasn't. Or was I fooling myself again, as I am wont to
do on occasion? It was too good an opportunity to pass
up. It appealed to my curiosity as a reporter. If I set the
meeting in a public place . . .

I took a deep breath. "Tonight?"

"Yes, indeedee do. Give me your number and I'll get
back to you."

"No phone numbers. You talk to DeBlase or his people.
Find out what airfield he's using in D.C. Tell him we'll
meet *at* the airfield. *At the airfield.* Public place. You tell
him that. Tell him I won't be alone." Harker, the man on
a tightrope with nothing below him but a concrete floor
and a bunch of people yelling, "Jump, sucker!"

"Harker, you out of your tree?" Regis Cooler's voice
was high C.

"No, Regis, I ain't out of my tree. I ain't comin' out
of my tree either. Don't call me, I'll call you. I—"

"Hang on, I'll call now, see if I can set it up. *Airport?*
Man, you are *el weirdo*, you know that?"

I leaned back in the phone booth. Thomas Merle
DeBlase wanted to see me. Too much. That meant Harley
might be there. My stomach started to act up again and I
wondered if being an investigative reporter meant climb-
ing into the lion's cage and kicking it in the ass. I decided
that it did.

Regis Cooler didn't take long. "A-OK. Tonight. Nine.
Dulles. Just ask at the information desk for Voltaire. Mr.
Voltaire."

I stopped breathing. My hand holding the ballpoint pen
shook. My eyes watered out of stone fear and I felt as
though I'd taken one of those mysterious substances that

the police throw you in jail for swallowing or injecting. Except that I never touch drugs. What had me dazed was the thought of meeting a man who may well have pulled off the crime of the century. Face to face. Harker and Voltaire.

"Harker?"

"I'm here, I'm here. Tonight. Dulles. Information. Voltaire."

"God, you sound like Tonto."

"Talk to you later, Regis." I hung up before he got any hipper. It took me a good hour of walking around, without even knowing or caring where I was, before I finally accepted the idea of tonight's meeting.

20.

I could tell that Malcolm Mullen was in a hurry. Over
the phone, he kept throwing in a "yes, well . . ." every
thirty seconds. The old soldier didn't want to be late for
the war games. So he was packing now. The games, along
with the DeBlase—Harley emergency meeting of all security directors, didn't start for another four days. But
Malcolm Mullen wanted to be with his old comrades as
much as possible. So he was going out earlier. On the
phone, he gave me as much time as it would take me to
pick my nose. Instead of doing that, I took down the eight
names he read off: Harley's security chiefs.

Gaylord Ran Harley's security chiefs would all seem to
be on the shy side. I was sure there would be no poolside
pictures to impress the wife and kids back home. Just some
businessmen in Vegas for a tan, a round of golf, perhaps
a quick stop at the tables, and maybe even a quickie with
a high-priced hooker moonlighting from a chorus line.
And in the midst of this desert fun, someone was going
to ask, "Any old business?" With that, Gaylord Ran Har-

ley and friends might be kicking around a bit of "old business" that had gone down over ten years ago.

Under "new business" would be a photograph taken two weeks ago. A grainy glossy of an Indiana university librarian and a New York investigative reporter.

The idea of bringing in cops to form a circle around me had crossed my mind. But what would I tell them? Who would I have arrested? On what charge? In any case, I wanted a story, a story that would keep me alive, as well as fill my craving for truth, glory, and money.

I was on fairly solid ground so far with my DeBlase—CIA—Havilland story. Fairly solid. But I needed more. Documents, eyewitnesses, testimony from somebody who was there when the smoking gun was brought out and used. If certain people at the Company had been drunk with power for years, a different Victor Evan Havilland would have sobered them up in a hurry.

A CIA man with big hands knew something too, more than he was willing to admit to himself. He knew that some of his co-workers took their jobs a little too seriously at times. And there was always the assassination investigation itself. That was a study in unanswered questions and sloppy investigative procedure. Missing evidence, reports kept secret, and all of this topped by a government indifference that was mystifying, to say the least.

Something else: Victor Evan Havilland, as a member of a secret committee advising the CIA on certain covert operations, had in effect dug his own grave. If I could get something in print on his participation in such a committee, it would go a long way toward backing up what I'd put together so far.

Time to ease off pondering the cosmic game plan. I had things to do. One of them was to wait for Trotman to come into my life again, so I could have these eight names checked out. My scheming mind told me they had all been connected with Gaylord Ran Harley at one time or another. But I wanted to make sure. Had they worked with Harley? When?

It had to be him on this one rather than my other CIA sources. Who knew how far the Gaylord Ran Harley charm

and influence had spread? For one thing, he'd had somebody at the Company develop certain photographs for him,
as well as furnish certain names and addresses, among
things that I knew about. Who knew why they'd agreed to
help out Gaylord? Maybe he'd lied. Maybe they agreed for
money or for old times' sake or because Gaylord was sell-
ing Bibles door to door and needed to build up a route.
The point is he had friends in high places.

So I was sticking to Trotman on this one. Whatever else
the big man would do, he wouldn't go running to Gaylord.

21.

My telephone conversation with Lanford Greeve Paugh began with my mispronouncing his last name. He corrected me with Southern charm, in a bass voice impressive enough to announce the end of the world.

"Poe," he said, "Poe, as in Edgar Allan." There was a tired kindness in his voice, tending to exaggerate his slight Kentucky drawl.

I could have listened to him talk about shoelaces, that's how good he sounded. He'd been out of politics for six years. Though no longer Senator Lanford Greeve Paugh of Kentucky, he was still called senator by everyone. Somehow he inspired you to. His voice did.

Senator Paugh. I'd pronounced it *paw*, as in the end of a dog's leg.

"Mr. Harker, sir, I hope you don't mind if I entertain myself while we talk. I'd made myself a liquid libation just before you telephoned. Since the Bible has told us 'waste not, want not,' I intend to neither waste nor want regardin' this glass of sour mash I now hold in my right hand. You *will* understand, I trust."

I smiled. "I *will* understand, Senator."

"Excelsior! Peltz's faith in you has not been unwarranted. May I say that I do read you from time to time. You are an interesting young man. Washington especially seems to offer fertile ground for your sort of inquisitiveness." His bass tones filled my head. The man sure had some voice. He had more than that, too. Lanford Greeve Paugh was no suspender-plucking, Bible-quoting Southern politician. He was intelligent and he had as much integrity as politics allowed him. Which wasn't as much as the church would like. But it was more than most congressmen had.

"I hope that was a compliment, Senator." I wasn't sure.

"It was." He chuckled, a golden rumble in my left ear. With that glass of booze in his hand, he had something to feel happy about. Lanford Greeve Paugh now lived and practiced law in Lexington, Kentucky. Occasionally he taught a law course at a state university. According to Peltz, the senator with the pearly gates in his voice drew packed classrooms. I could understand that. Anyone with a sense of hearing couldn't help but be rooted to the spot when Paugh opened his mouth. That voice of his was created to win friends, influence people, and mesmerize whatever was left over.

I wanted him to tell me what had gone on when he'd served on the committee investigating the Havilland assassination.

At the other end of the phone, I heard something that sounded like someone swallowing a baseball. If I had doubts about the ex-senator's ability to think and drink, he dispelled them as we went along. Whatever the sour mash was doing to the rest of him, it was bypassing his brain.

"Mr. Harker, Peltz tells me you're pokin' around the Havilland assassination." The sly implication in his rock-of-ages voice said that I should tell him why. I didn't. But it was an effort not to.

"Something like that, Senator. Nothing definite, you understand."

"I understand." He chuckled. A man who knew the value of keeping secrets.

"Senator, did you serve on the committee from the beginning?"

"Yes, sir. Indeed I did. One of the first ones chosen. They wanted a cross-section, whatever the hell that is. North, South. Didn't waste no time lining us up. Havilland's body wasn't even cold when we were told that the whole thing had to be solved in a hurry."

"Told?"

"Told. Told to hurry up, reach a conclusion, and have a report ready by yesterday. *Yesterday.*" A quick silence let me know that the sour mash was being attacked again.

"Who ordered the speed-up?"

"Who do you think? Vice-president Byron Graham Wilcox. He succeeded Havilland on the spot and it was his ball of wax after that. He went into action faster than one of them Texas quarter horses he raised." Paugh spoke like a man more interested in yesterday than tomorrow. If you're over seventy, that's usually how you tend to see life.

"Wilcox?"

"None other. The man from Texas hisself. Boots on the Oval Office desk and horseshoes on the White House lawn. Down home comes to Pennsylvania Avenue."

Lanford Paugh was both sympathetic and cynical about the Texan who'd been forced to curb his own presidential ambitions, accept his party's vice-presidential nomination only to back into the presidency after all. Back in over Victor Havilland's dead body.

I looked up from my notebook, chewed on my pen for a few seconds, then said, "Anybody on the committee complain about being rushed?"

"Sheeit, son, did we ever. Didn't do no good. We didn't even have our own investigators. Had to use the FBI and CIA to dig up facts for us. They told us what they wanted us to know, 'bout how it was."

"You're kidding."

"Son, I'm seventy-three. No time left for kiddin'. The FBI, CIA, and the New Orleans police, they all come up with stories that didn't hold a forkful of cat's piss far as me and Sisson were concerned."

"Sisson?"

"Damn, son, you can't be that young? Riley Sisson. Georgia senator. On the committee with me."

"Yeah, yeah. Now I remember. He died, didn't he? Plane crash."

He took his time answering. When he did, his bass voice was slow-rolling thunder. "Plane crash. Senator Riley Sisson died in a plane crash."

If ever a sentence was crying out to be read between every word, that last one was.

"Senator, uh, I may be imagining this, but I think you've got something on your mind that you're not telling me."

He let me wait. It could have been the sour mash. Or it could have been something else. He sounded as sober as he had at the beginning of our conversation.

"Did Peltz tell you 'bout Riley?" The bass voice softened. "Me and him was friends, you know. Came to Congress only three years apart. Tighter than two ticks on a hound dog's ass. Got picked the same day for the assassination committee. Same day." His deep voice faded. Memories had slowed it down.

"No, Senator, Peltz didn't say anything about your friend." I had the phone tight against my ear. The feeling was there again. Something was about to happen.

"Riley was plannin' to come out with a minority report on the killing. I was even thinkin' of going in on it with him. He didn't like what he'd been told by the CIA, FBI, by nobody. The New Orleans police, they ticked him off most of all. Feisty little rooster, that Riley. Told me once that he wanted to be President. Imagine that. Dumb redneck from Georgia, wanting to be President. He'd have done it too, you know? Damn redneck would have got his ass in that chair sure as my name is Lanford Greeve Paugh."

"The minority report, Senator. It—"

"I ain't forgot you, son. Riley Sisson was my friend. At my age, your friends are mostly waitin' for you to come on across and meet them."

"I understand, Senator."

"Anyway, we felt—well, not that we was *always* lied

to. We *was*, part of the time, no doubt about it. But what mostly happened was that a lot of our questions just weren't answered. We'd ask the CIA fifteen questions 'bout the killin' and they'd answer maybe three. Same with the FBI. When it came to the New Orleans police, they seemed to be comin' at us through them other two groups of patriots, so we didn't get much out of them either.''

I shook my head. Incredible. "Senator, how could anybody get away with that kind of attitude? I mean, this wasn't just somebody getting flattened by a hit-and-run driver. This was the killing of an American President-elect in downtown New Orleans just hours before—"

"I *know* what it was, son. Believe me, I know." His bass voice rolled right over me. "But you young people don't understand somethin' and maybe that somethin's the key to this whole thing. Back ten years or so, nobody *ever*, I repeat, *ever*, questioned the FBI *or* the CIA. You understand what I'm sayin'?"

If I didn't, I was either deaf or demented. The truth is that the American press had been gutless and without balls for so long that the American people had got used to it. With Vietnam, Watergate, and Cambodia being exposed as total deception and bullshit, with the FBI, CIA, and IRS fuckery shown to be a matter of policy, more and more questions were now being asked. But that was now. *Today*.

Who had covered up and why?

"Senator, I am beginning to understand things a little better."

He grunted. "You'd be one of the few, son. Anyway, lacking the freedom of dissent that is currently in vogue, we had to go along with things. Not Riley Sisson. He didn't want his name on no Havilland assassination report. He didn't believe what we were told, and he stood alone. Damn. I loved that goddamn redneck. Stood alone. Said he wanted to issue a minority report. Wanted me to go along with him. God forgive me, I didn't."

He went quiet again. So far, the sour mash knew its place. It wasn't bothering him that I could see.

"Senator? Riley's accident . . ."

"Yeah. Remember it well. I was watchin' a college football game not far from here. Somebody come up to me, gimme a note sayin' Riley had gone down in a private plane. 'Spose to have been on a huntin' trip, him and a friend. Some prison warden from Texas. Three of 'em died. Them two, plus the pilot. Plane crashed in Texas someplace."

Unless I was mistaken, Lanford Greeve Paugh had his doubts about Riley Sisson's death being an accident.

"Senator Paugh, I have the strong feeling that—"

"That I consider Riley Sisson's death, shall we say, questionable? Let's just say I don't wanna meet my maker with another lie on my aged soul. 'Scuse me. Time to refill." It didn't take him long to do that. In less time than it takes to pop a cork, he was back throwing his doubts at me.

"Son, let's consider a few things. You writin' any of this down?"

"Every syllable."

"That's good. Lot of books out 'bout that killin'. Most ain't got no more truth in 'em that a hen's got teeth. Quick money. That's all they're about, I expect better things from you."

That made me feel damn good. I hoped I'd live to see his expectations come true.

"OK, son, let's see. First of all, lemme say that Riley Sisson hated huntin'."

"What?" I almost stopped writing. The street-corner public telephone booth I was now using was one of the few that hadn't been rendered inoperative by roving switchblade freaks.

"You hear correctly. Riley would just as soon shoot his wife as shoot an animal. The man hated huntin'. Secondly, he weren't too fond of private planes either. Thought they was put together with spit and wire. He had to be practically drunk to get on any plane. His wife will tell you that. She's living in Virginia. Alexandria."

"So there was no minority report?"

"No." He sighed. He didn't like remembering that fact. "No minority report. Riley died and the rest of us let

Wilcox, the FBI, and the CIA stampede us like cattle. We turned in a piece of shit called an assassination report; we all signed it and threw it at the American people." This was as bitter as he'd sounded during the entire conversation. I got the feeling that he now wished he'd stood up and opposed the report. Riley Sisson had. And look where it had got him.

"Did Riley give you *any* idea who he might be talking with outside the committee?"

"No. Grieves me to say this, but I guess when it looked like he was the only holdout he stopped trustin' everybody, includin' me. . . . Just occurred to me—his wife might know. Pretty little Delia. Yeah, she might know." Lanford Paugh was still drinking and thinking. And never the twain seemed to meet. His liver was probably strong enough to be slipped into an atomic reactor and emerge without a mark on it.

"Senator, is there anything you can tell me about the CIA and FBI reports on the assassination?"

"Damn little, son. Goddamn little. Somebody's still sittin' on them, that's for sure. Couple facts or rumors, call 'em what you will. One is that Perry Joseph was workin' for the FBI at one time. Maybe even the CIA."

"I've come across that."

"That was the talk, but nothin' was done 'bout it. And when Riley Sisson mentioned it to them two investigatin' bodies, he got a wall of silence for his answer. 'Nother thing we never got an answer to was whether or not there was more than one Perry Joseph."

"I don't get it. Senator, what would be the point in more than one Perry Joseph?"

"It might explain the story 'bout him being an informant for certain people. That would be one reason he was everywhere. The FBI and CIA specialize in infiltration whenever they can pull it off. What's to stop them from using the name 'Perry Joseph' for one of their men and gettin' him inside one organization or another? The Perry Joseph we investigated was no more dangerous than a paper cup. Yet all the available—I stress that word *available*—evidence pointed to this rag doll as a man capable

of killin' a President. Sheeit.'' The silence might mean he
was working on more sour mash. Or just reliving the
doubts he hadn't had the courage to stand behind ten years
ago.

I chewed on my ballpoint pen some more. The Perry
Joseph we were all familiar with had been a twenty-eight-
year-old misfit, kicked out of the Army and unable to hold
a job anywhere. His wife had left him and he had no
friends. His Army records said he was a total washout,
from marksmanship to driving a jeep. He couldn't do anything, according to the available background on him. Yet he
had killed a President. With some excellent long-distance
shooting. And then conveniently died in an attempted New
Orleans prison break.

"Excuse me, Senator, but did you come up with anything about Perry Joseph's marksmanship? I mean, Army
records say he couldn't pull a trigger worth a damn. Yet
he shot exceedingly well on the day in New Orleans.''

"Damn, boy, that was one thing Riley didn't like either.
Don't know where he got it, but he told me that Perry
Joseph was left-handed. Now that was no secret. But did
you know that the scope and sight on the rifle Joseph's
'sposed to have used was set up for a right-handed man?''

"Uh, excuse me, but I don't remember reading that in
the report. I admit that I didn't read all twenty volumes,
but—''

"Wasn't in the report.'' He dropped the news on me
without a buildup. He could have been telling me the day
of the week.

"Wasn't in—''

"Lotta things the committee turned up wasn't in the
final report.''

"Like what?''

"Like witnesses who said they saw shots comin' from
more than one direction. Thirty witnesses said that. Ain't
a word on *this* testimony in the final report. Did you know
that Havilland's motorcade route was changed at the last
minute? Just thirty minutes before he was to ride through
the city, somebody ordered a shift. One route changed to
another. The new route took him right by that apartment

house where Perry Joseph just happened to be waitin'. Hell of a coincidence, ain't it?'' His bass voice showed he did not like coincidences.

"Yes, sir. That might explain some of the missing evidence. Like papers from his jacket, his itinerary, stuff like that. He might have made notes on the changes, who suggested them. Yeah, yeah!'' I was ready to kick a hole in the telephone-booth wall. Jesus Christ. No wonder somebody was ripping off evidence.

"See where you been tippy-toeing into the National Archives, ain't you, son? Yeah, I been hearin' 'bout that missin' stuff. Brain's missin', they say. Sheeit, why not? Brain would let you know that he wasn't just shot in the back, with a hole coming out of his neck. That brain might back up them thirty or so ignored witnesses, that some shots come from the front as well. You know that a couple of doctors say Havilland got part of his skull shot off from the front, don't you?''

"Yes, sir. But nobody's made too big a thing of it.''

"No, they ain't. If they do, they got to deal with more than one bullet, the bullet that supposedly went into his back, come out his throat, and wounded somebody else sittin' in front of him. To admit that there's more wounds is to say there is more people involved. Nobody's inclined to do that little thing. Sure wish you could taste this mash. Damn good stuff.'' He sighed with pleasure.

"Take your word for it, sir. You said something about ignoring witnesses.''

"Yes, sir, Mr. Harker. The committee on which I served ignored witnesses, evidence, and anything else that did not lead to a one-man, one-bullet theory. Everythin' had to fit neatly around Perry Joseph. If it didn't, it got tossed in the wastebasket. You take that and add it to a don't-ask-questions attitude on the part of the FBI and CIA. Now take all that and add it to a government-is-sacred attitude that was damn stronger then than now. And you have got yourself one hell of a stone wall, mountain high and valley low. Too much for anybody to climb over. Too strong for anybody to knock down. With pressure from the highest in the land to close this investigation in a hurry—and I am talkin' 'bout the *highest*, son—well, the Lord Jesus Himself would be hard pressed to find the truth under them circumstances.''

He wasn't bitter. He just sounded like a man coming to the truth a bit late in life. A man like that sounds thoughtful, even wistful, as though he'd like the chance to do it over again.

''Mr. Harker?'' He called my name in a way that made me feel like I was the key to a pending billion-dollar tax cut and he was sounding me out as to whether or not he should go ahead with it. When I hung up, I was sure going to miss hearing my name pronounced like that. It grew on you.

''Yes, Senator?''

''You wouldn't by any chance have friends who could get you a copy of those heretofore secret CIA and FBI reports?'' His evangelical voice dropped to an even lower pitch. I was almost afraid to tell him I was even thinking of something as dastardly as what he'd just suggested.

''Senator, the thought's crossed my mind.''

He seemed to brighten up. ''Well, you keep in touch now, hear?''

''Yes, sir. Oh, one thing, Senator. Could you do me one small favor?''

''Name it, son.''

''Put in a call to Riley Sisson's widow for me. Please tell her I'd like to talk with her about her husband. If you give me her number and address, I'd be grateful.''

''I'll do that, Mr. Harker. But I can't promise a thing. She kinda cut herself off from everybody after Riley got killed. She and I talk once in a while, but I understand she lives alone. Don't see hardly nobody 'cept her church and ain't even set foot in Washington in years. She couldn't stand livin' in Georgia without Riley, so she moved to Alexandria permanently. They used to keep a house there when Riley was in Congress. Yeah, I'll call her, tell her that you'll be gettin' in touch with her. But don't expect much from the dear little lady. Been almost ten years since Riley died and she ain't got over it yet. I think she's bitter at what she thinks really happened to Riley.''

"What does she think really happened?"

Lanford Greeve Paugh took a very deep breath. He let the silence stay in place for a long time. I chewed my pen some more, blinked my eyes, and waited.

"She thinks her husband was deliberately killed because he was getting too close to somethin' involvin' the Havilland assassination. She once told me that Riley had a good idea who really did the killin'. Then she shut up, like she'd already said somethin' she shouldn't. I think what happened is that after Riley's death, she just stopped trustin'. Stopped trustin' everybody."

"Yes, sir," I whispered. I wondered if he even heard me. The Washington heat wasn't on my mind anymore. Riley Sisson. Senator from Georgia. A man who didn't hunt and who hated flying. A man who died in a plane accident on his way to do—what? To hunt. Died with a Texas prison warden beside him.

When I hung up, I stepped outside of the booth and stared at the traffic. My hands were shaking. Because I knew that I was as close to finding out what I wanted to know as I'd ever been in the last forty-eight hours.

I wanted the truth more than I wanted anything else. At the moment, I wanted the truth even more than I wanted Loni. That, my friend, was saying a hell of a lot.

22.

"Lanford Paugh called me about you, Mistah Harker. He urged me to see you. He's an old friend. I don't see many people these days. I'm sure you understand." Delia Sisson sat upright in an easy chair, the way they teach you at Southern charm schools. Delia Sisson was in her sixties, a small woman with rimless glasses and sensible shoes. She was barely five feet tall and certainly not over a hundred pounds. Her hair was bone-white, cut short and combed straight back. The Southern drawl still was there, but not strong. What strength she had left wasn't in her body. It was in her heart and mind. Delia Sisson had manners, dignity, and the kind of presence no one instills in their children anymore.

"Yes, ma'am. Want to thank you for that."

She nodded once, a regal gesture. A queen of the old South.

I sat directly across from her, on a couch covered by a patterned fabric of red roses the size of basketballs. Delia Sisson's house was small, like her, and antiseptically clean, the way a house is when the people living in it have nothing else to do but clean. Floors were waxed. They gleamed like George Raft's hair.

"You're here to talk about Riley."

Her tiny face barely had room for eyes, nose, and a small mouth that had almost been removed by age. Her eyes were blue. The blue was fading. I wondered if weeping had worn the blue away.

"The Havilland assassination, ma'am." I stopped breathing and didn't take my eyes from the little white-haired woman who wore a short-sleeved brown dress, a thin slash of pink lipstick, brown sensible shoes, and a plain gold wedding band.

"Yes, I would imagine that to be the case."

"Senator Paugh tells me that your husband favored a minority report." No sense wasting time. She seemed to be a no-nonsense type herself. As surreptitiously as I could, I pulled notebook and pen from my pocket. I wasn't nervous. Just anxious.

"He did. But, as you know, the committee report *was* unanimous." She was dignified and polite. But there was no doubt about what she was really saying. The unanimous Havilland assassination report was as genuine as the tooth fairy.

"Why do you think the report was unanimous, Mrs. Sisson?"

"Pressure, Mr. Harker. It was believed in certain quarters that the nation would be torn asunder were a report not issued as quickly as possible. To avert what some thought would be anarchy and possible civil war, the report was issued with what you might call extreme haste." Her hands were folded in her lap, the backs covered by blue veins and the brown spots of aging. They never fidgeted once. Once, a tiny finger reached out and stroked the gold wedding band. Her voice held its dignity. I was talking with a very special lady. Riley Sisson had chosen well.

"Your husband was aware of this, I assume, and didn't like it."

Her lips moved toward a smile, then stopped. She was remembering her husband. I guessed the smile had stopped because remembering him was painful.

"My husband was righteously angry, Mr. Harker, the way Southern men can be when they are religious. His conscience, his God, would not let him be less. He stood alone. Alone." The smile came back and stayed longer this time. The widow of a Georgia redneck, my ass. Delia Sisson would not marry a man who was only a tobacco-chewer with big dreams. He would have to be a lot more.

"Yes, ma'am. Were there other pressures?"

"There most certainly were, Mr. Harker. The CIA and FBI pushed extra hard to have the report read a certain way. They did not like my husband and my husband did not like them. The fights that went on, *my Lord*. Riley was a scrapper, Mr. Harker. He would fight Jesus if Jesus were in the wrong."

I smiled at her. Pride in that wedding ring was understandable.

"He sounds like a man worth knowing, Mrs. Sisson."

She sighed gently. The gesture was as lovely as a sunset. "He *was*, Mr. Harker. He most certainly *was*. After his death, I withdrew. I guess you could call it that. Grief was a big reason, but not the only one."

"What were the other reasons?"

"Disgust. Fear." Her eyes looked into mine and never blinked. She was in control of herself, a tiny, white-haired woman who would have graced the White House in the finest tradition of grand first ladies. If Riley Sisson had been anything like his wife, the country could have done a lot worse for a leader. It damn sure had in recent years.

Somewhere in the back of my mind, I wondered why she was opening up to me when, as far as I knew, she hadn't talked to a reporter since her husband died.

"Disgust, Mr. Harker. My husband worked extremely hard to get at the truth. He died because of it. After his death, I was disgusted at what happened. Cover-up, that's what happened. The truth was buried even deeper. And fear. Fear for my own life, Mr. Harker." She said this so calmly, I almost didn't believe her. But Delia Sisson wasn't the type of woman to merely practice her charm-school speech patterns.

She smiled at me, a sweet smile. The woman was charming.

"He was on to something, Mr. Harker. He was on his way to learning how Victor Havilland was really killed. And who had been behind the killing."

"Could you be more specific, ma'am?" My heart started jumping around again. The sun had crept across the clean room and was frying my left thigh through my puce polyester. I didn't give a shit.

"Yes, Mr. Harker, I can. My husband was known throughout the South, not merely in his home state of Georgia. He could have been one of the first Southern politicians to go beyond being merely a senator. There's no doubt in my mind. Because of that, a lot of people kept in touch with him, big people, little people. Rich, poor, black, and white. One of those people was the warden of a Texas jail, a man named Wallace Uttman. I guess fear touched the warden, too. Fear of man or fear of God, I was never quite sure. Anyhow, Warden Uttman and my husband were in touch from almost the day my husband got put on that assassination committee. He told my husband that Perry Joseph didn't kill the President-elect. He told my husband that he knew who had. Mr. Harker, he told my husband that the killing had been done by three convicts from his prison."

In the silence of her small living room, I could hear a clock ticking somewhere behind me. Out front an ice-cream wagon rolled past slowly, its bell tinkling. The sun was now searing my hip *and* thigh. I looked at her and said nothing.

"Mr. Harker, did you hear what I just said?"

"Yes, ma'am, I did." I got the words out, but after that my throat got tighter than a miser's fist.

"Three men from Warden Uttman's prison did the killing. Their names are Willard Justin, Joe Delgado, and Roger Joel."

"Excuse me, Mrs. Sisson, but how—"

"Warden Uttman got in touch with Riley. He told him that those three convicts I mentioned had been taken out of the prison on come sort of medical pretext. This had happened several times. These times had been for a briefing of sorts, practice session, dry runs. The last time they were taken out was the day before the assassination. After the killing, the men were returned to prison. Within a week after that, all three men were killed in a prison riot.''

''Who was behind this, ma'am?''

''Thomas Merle DeBlase.'' She lifted her chin. A widow passing judgment. ''Thomas Merle DeBlase also killed my husband and Warden Uttman. I can't prove it, but I know it.'' She lowered her chin. There wasn't a tear in sight. I wondered why. Unless she had cried herself out long ago.

''Did the warden ever tell your husband why DeBlase wanted Havilland dead?''

''The usual reason. Rich men always kill anything that interferes with their being rich. Victor Havilland was going to turn this country upside down. Among other things, that meant dealing fairly with blacks. This disgusted DeBlase and a lot of other men in the South. DeBlase owns Texas. He can do what he wants to with that state and everybody in it. Getting the warden to hand over three convicts was no trouble at all. Southern bigotry killed Havilland.''

She got up, crossed the room, and sat down on the couch next to me. Up close, she looked like a woman who didn't have a frightened bone in her body. The white hair pulled my eyes toward it. I wondered if it had turned white when she heard that her husband had been killed in a plane crash. Or had it turned white when she'd learned he'd been murdered?

''Mr. Harker, I have some papers you might want to look at. Letters from Warden Uttman to my husband. Some of Riley's private notes. Riley never kept them around the house. He didn't trust a soul, so he kept them in a safe-deposit box under another name. You will find the letters especially interesting, I'm sure. I'll get them for you shortly. My husband is said to have died in a hunting accident. Crash of a small private plane. Mr. Harker, Riley was meeting Warden Uttman for more information on the assassination. Riley hated hunting, despised it. And a private plane scared him more than anything."

"Yes, ma'am, I know. Senator Paugh told me."

"He was correct, Mr. Harker. My husband would never have made such a trip. But no one listened to me. Absolutely no one. Then I realized that perhaps I was better off with no one listening. Because, you see, no one ever intended to do a thing about my husband's death. It was a convenient death for many, many people. With Riley gone, there would be no minority report. No official disagreements. I was frightened for my own life, frightened that the people who had killed Victor Havilland and my husband would also kill me. I'm not frightened anymore."

"Yes, ma'am." I wondered why.

"I'm dying, Mr. Harker. Dying of bone cancer. I was informed of this last week. Terminal, irreversible."

Standing up, she looked down at me, smiled gently, and said, "I'll get you those letters, Mr. Harker. Would you like something cool to drink?"

23.

Uttman's letters to Riley Sisson pushed my story close to completion. Uttman named names. Dates. Places. Who had approached him about these particular convicts. When. Where they had met. Who had worked on the necessary forms that had got the convicts taken out of prison on several occasions and taken to a Houston hospital as "guinea pigs" in a "scientific experiment." Some experiment. Thomas Merle DeBlase's name was mentioned. So was one "Voltaire."

Warden Uttman's handwritten letters—there were five—seemed to reflect a growing fear. His conscience had bothered him, too. Whatever DeBlase was pressuring him with—fear, money, you name it—wasn't nearly as effective as what the heavenly hosts had used. Uttman had been cracking under the strain. Going along with DeBlase may have seemed like a good idea to Uttman at one time. But that idea had led him into hell. Only the first envelope had been addressed to a post-office box. The letter inside each envelope, however, bore Riley Sisson's name.

The last letter, dated two weeks before the fatal plane

crash that had killed the two men, had more apprehension in it than all the others. In this one, Uttman had put down on paper his fear that he was being followed, his phone tapped, some of his mail opened. He, too, felt that he could not trust anybody, that "they" were everywhere. This last letter suggested a final meeting to discuss the prison riot that had killed the three convicts. After this meeting, if Sisson couldn't convince anybody there had been a conspiracy, Warden Uttman was going to leave the country. Warden Uttman had been a frightened man. With good reason, as it turned out.

"More iced tea, Mr. Harker?" Delia Sisson touched my wrist with a small hand made cold by holding a pitcher of the best iced tea I'd ever had.

"Yes, please. These letters, you said they'd been in a safe-deposit box?"

"Yes, they were. I only took them out last week. The news I'd received from my doctors made me reexamine many things. One gets one's house in order, you understand." She seemed almost glad to be leaving this world. As she talked, she filled my glass to within an inch of the brim. Then she set the pitcher down on a green straw place mat.

Sitting down beside me, she touched her white hair, then smoothed her skirt. It wasn't wrinkled, but she was a lady who had always been neat. She folded her small hands in her lap, again touching the wedding band once, just once, with a tiny finger. It seemed a practiced gesture. An obligation, a remembrance. Like fresh flowers on a grave.

Now I knew why she'd agreed to see me, why she was so calm. Her house *was* in order. She was ready for something important, the one thing we work toward all our lives. Raymond Chandler called it "the big sleep." Death. When you're ready for death, your life's in order. Just like this house she and I were in. Her seeing me was just more tidying up.

"Mrs. Sisson, these letters. May I—"

"Yes, Mr. Harker. They are yours to keep. The notes, too. Paugh claims that you are quite the gadfly, the kind of man T.S. Eliot says goes about disturbing the universe.''

It was my turn to smile and bow. I did both from a sitting position. Disturbing the universe. I liked that. Letters and notes belonging to a man dead some ten years. I was cynical enough about the judicial process to doubt if anything was strong enough to bring Thomas Merle DeBlase and friends to trial. But, shit, that wasn't my job anyway. My job was to investigate, then write a news story. Leave justice to over-priced lawyers and judges who worked an hour a day, whenever they showed up in court.

"Have you had a chance to look at my husband's notes, Mr. Harker?"

"Quickly, ma'am. Very quickly. I notice that your husband had been pursuing a link between those convicts and a certain Cuban. I see the name 'Cuchillo' mentioned here several times."

" 'Cuchillo' is a nickname, code name you might say. It means 'knife.' It belonged to a Cuban who had tried to get money from Riley for giving him information on the assassination. Riley wasn't sure if Cuchillo was telling the truth. There's no other name on Cuchillo, and Riley never got around to telling me the man's real name. Some world, isn't it? I mean when men can't even tell you their right names. Cuchillo had told Riley that Perry Joseph was just a front, somebody used to get information."

"For whom?"

"CIA, FBI. Whoever paid him. That's why the cover-up. If Perry Joseph killed Havilland and Perry Joseph worked for the FBI, CIA, or both, then both would have to be investigated. The cover-up in the main was made to protect those agencies from being scrutinized too closely."

"Mrs. Sisson, tell me more about Cuchillo, Señor Knife."

"Señor Knife, as it were, was a mercenary gentleman. He wanted Riley to pay him a lot of money, which Riley refused to do. They kept in contact, mostly with Cuchillo phoning Riley. Riley told me that Cuchillo had seen Perry Joseph in Havana, talked with him, and Perry had said he was working for the American government. Undercover man or some such. Perry liked to brag, said Cuchillo. Told everyone he was getting paid regularly for his secret work and knew a lot of important people.''

"So Cuchillo could have connected Perry Joseph with the CIA or FBI or both.''

"Perhaps, Mr. Harker. He dangled bits of information in front of Riley's nose to get him to come up with money. Cuchillo was also connected with Warden Uttman's three convicts. That's one of the carrots he tantalized Riley with.''

"Oh?''

"Oh my, yes. It seems that while out of jail, supposedly in a hospital toiling for the cause of science, these three men I mentioned to you were doing more than honing their tactics for assassination. They were also consorting with women, Mr. Harker. Prostitutes. I suppose a man in prison does accumulate certain needs. Anyhow, Señor Cuchillo told this to Riley, who of course told me. Cuchillo claims to have furnished the women used by these convicts.''

I swallowed more iced tea, letting my tongue toy with a small piece of ice. A Cuban who pimped for Thomas Merle DeBlase and Gaylord Ran Harley's assassins.

"Mrs. Sisson, does the name Enrique Estevez-Blanco mean anything to you? Can you remember your husband mentioning that to you?''

She frowned, her small features retreating into a circle in the center of her tiny face. Tilting her head to the right, she thought carefully, then shook it side to side. The gestures were as small as those made by a kitten. "No, Mr. Harker. I do not recall such a man. Why? Is he part of all this?''

"He was. No matter.'' Something else I'd have to check out. Cuchillo. That could very well be the late Mr. Estevez-Blanco, a man who was in Havana during this time. A man who knew a lot of people.

"Did your husband say anything more on the possibility of there being more than one Perry Joseph?''

"Oh my, yes, Mr. Harker. This Cuchillo person was not the only one to tell Riley this. Other witnesses testified as much under oath to the commission. Nothing came of it, of course. The assassination report wanted one man, one bullet. *Demanded it.*"

She emphasized her point by tapping her palm with the back of a tiny hand. The lady was staring at death. She had no time to lie. If it had been me sitting there knowing that my demise was imminent, I'd have been jumping up and down on that rose-patterned couch like some idiot on *Let's Make a Deal*.

"My husband, Mr. Harker, was not the only man to entertain the possibility of more than one Perry Joseph." Her voice was stronger. Or seemed stronger to me. "Perry Joseph was a misfit, spineless as an eel, and I know men, Mr. Harker. I know a true man when I see one. I married one. Perry Joseph lived by pretense and weakness. He pretended to be a radical sympathizer. This allowed him freedom of movement in certain circles. The FBI and CIA both used this, paying Perry Joseph for the dubious privilege. If you dig deep enough, you'll come across this in some official report. I'm sure you know the CIA and the FBI both have their own assassination reports, both unreleased."

"Yes, ma'am. I'm working on that now."

She smiled again. I winked at her and the smile spread. "I wish you well on that, Mr. Harker. This country needs saving from the people who are running it. They tend to forget that the country doesn't belong to them. It belongs to us. They are our servants, not our overseers." She nodded once for emphasis.

"Yes, ma'am. You know, it's quite a coincidence."

"What is, Mr. Harker?"

"Three convicts die in a prison riot in Texas. Perry Joseph attempts to escape and dies in a New Orleans prison. Him and one other prisoner. Five men die violently in two prisons. All within a week after Victor Havilland's assassination."

She was filling my glass with more iced tea. Her head was bowed and she held the pitcher in her two tiny, blue-veined hands. Her Southern voice was most gentle. "Yes, Mr. Harker. That *is* some coincidence."

She set the pitcher back on the place mat, folded her hands in her lap, and looked at me. There was no expression on her face.

I reached for my credit cards. Time to get on the horn. Again. "Mrs. Sisson, I'd like to make a long-distance call. I'll charge it to my own number."

"Go right ahead." She was in her tiny kitchen, smearing homemade ham spread and relish on whole wheat, with lettuce, mayonnaise, and two slices of tomato. I had work to do and I needed all the energy I could get. Besides, the tiny woman was an excellent cook. Lucky man, Riley Sisson.

I called Ray Stance in Houston. He worked for a paper there, and sometimes served as stringer for us, covering local stories that the wires were either too busy or too stupid to touch. Ray and I were on the telephone thirty minutes.

When I hung up, Ray had his orders. Get me tearsheets from back issues of the five biggest Texas newspapers. The tearsheets I wanted were stories on the prison riot that had killed three particular convicts under Warden Uttman's jurisdiction. To put off suspicion, I told Ray to pull stories on every prison riot Texas had had two years before and two years after the riot we were interested in. If anybody asked, hopefully it would look like Ray Stance was checking back issues for information on four years of Texas prison violence. Nothing more.

I wanted this information in a hurry. So I ordered Ray Stance to stop what he was doing and get me what I needed. He was to send the tearsheets to Washington by hand. They were to be placed in a public locker at Dulles Airport. The key was to be placed in an envelope with my name on it and left at the main information desk. My name was necessary because I'd need to identify myself. I was going to pick it up in person, hopefully unmolested. To hell with waiting around for the mail to reach me. Something told me that my mail might not be a private matter anymore.

These back newspapers were my only chance of getting photographs and background on convicts killed in the riot at Uttman's prison. Because during those thirty minutes of long-distance listening, as Ray Stance made telephone calls for me, I learned a few things. I learned that a lot of records had conveniently been destroyed at Uttman's prison during this particular riot. There were no records left on most of the convicts who had taken part in what had happened on that day. Oh sure, there were now *new* records on the survivors. New records. And only on the survivors. That left out Roger Joel, Joe Delgado, and Willard Justin.

A telephone call by Ray to the Houston hospital mentioned in Uttman's letters to Riley Sisson revealed no records on any "humanitarian experiments" conducted there during that time. No one could find any.

Nor was the state bureau of medical records any help. They didn't have any such information either. The state bureau of prison records followed in step. There were no records available on *any* of the convicts killed in that riot. I wondered if somebody had managed to sneak into heaven and do a job on the Book of Judgment, too.

I listened long distance to Ray Stance knock his head against the wall some more. Warden Uttman's letter had mentioned a so-called medical team at the hospital. The doctor, researcher, and two nurses supposedly in charge of the "research program" were no longer at the Houston hospital.

The doctor had come home one night and interrupted a burglar at his trade. The doctor had been killed. The burglar was never caught.

The researcher had died of an overdose of sleeping pills. He'd been depressed for several weeks prior to ending it all.

One nurse had drowned in her bathtub. No signs of violence.

The second nurse had simply disappeared. Since she was unmarried and over twenty-one, the Houston police had not tried too hard to find her. With no evidence of criminal misdeed, why should they? *No* one seemed to be able to find her. Not family, not friends. I made a guess, keeping my guess to myself. My guess was that she was mildewing in a shallow grave someplace.

Even though Ray Stance was doing all the asking, I didn't want his ass hanging out where it could be seen. So I'd made a suggestion. He'd taken it. All of his telephone calls concerning missing records, and phantom experiments had been made under an assumed name. A real name, however. Someone from the Texas lieutenant governor's office. Official and unknown. Let the curious play around with that.

This bit of research was going to cost the *World-Examiner*. But what's an expense account for, I always say. Ray Stance was to bill the paper directly, mentioning my name of course. Five hundred dollars for himself. Transportation, plus a hundred dollars for the person flying my tearsheets to Washington. Ray was to pick somebody from his paper, preferably a young, wide-eyed reporter still caught up in the mystery and wonder of it all and dumb enough to do what he was told without asking why. My favorite kind of young reporter.

Ray Stance was to nail his mouth shut, too, under pain of pissing me off. When it came to friends and enemies, I had a long memory. Ray got the picture.

Somebody had gone to a lot of trouble to get rid of three convicts. However, that somebody might not have been fast enough to stop all news stories on the riot from breaking. That's what I was counting on. I was counting on photographs and stories having broken in the press, with DeBlase and Harley thinking that after the coverage everything would quietly disappear.

I stood up, notes and papers in my hand. One hell of a day. Couldn't recall one like this in a long time. It was exciting, this digging out what other people had kept hidden so long for whatever the reason. But, in another way, I wasn't surprised. As a reporter, I expected the worst from people. That's what I usually got.

But Delia Sisson was different. A complete surprise. A diamond in this dungheap of a world. A lot of reporters owed their newfound fame as saviors of the Republic to people like her who cared about the country in a way that had gone out of style.

"I've enjoyed your being here, Mr. Harker." She stood up, extending her hand. "You are a hard worker. So was Riley. He would have wanted someone like you to have his papers."

Jesus. I felt like a rat. I'd been planning to steal them any way I could. But the woman had given them to me. *Given them to me.* As usual my scruples were consistent. Consistently few. Some kind of lady, Mrs. Riley Sisson.

I stepped toward her, guilt and a love for this old woman hitting me with equal force. I looked down at her. If one of us was going to cry, it would probably be me. "Thank you, Mrs. Sisson. And not just for the notes and the sand-wiches."

"You are welcome, Mr. Harker. Godspeed in whatever you do. May He keep you always in His hand."

Too often it's His finger, I thought. "Yes, ma'am." I said.

I drove away from the tiny house in Alexandria, Virginia, with Mrs. Sisson standing in the doorway waving to me as though I were her son or a dear friend. I wouldn't have minded either.

24.

"Talk louder," I said. "Can't hear you. What the hell's that racket in the background?"

"You mean the music?" asked Walter Fragan.

"Racket. If that's music, I'm a wombat." Still in Florida, according to the area code given me by my secretary, Fragan was trying to speak above Latin barroom music noisy enough to make your ears bleed and stun high-flying birds.

"Hold on, hold on!" he yelled. "I'll shut the door."

I was at the back of a movie theater located in one of Washington's all-black sections. Since the town is seventy-six percent black, an all-black section's not that hard to find. Hopefully, *I'd* be hard to find if DeBlase and Harley were still out hunting. Which I was sure they were. With no logical reason for me to be in a neighborhood like this, I was hoping my pursuers would think likewise and not look for me here.

"Can you come back to Florida?" asked Walter Fragan. He wasn't snotty anymore. The sneer was gone from his voice. The man was serious and worried.

I grinned in the darkness and twisted the knife a little. "Do I hear panic? And how do you know I'm *not* in Florida?"

"Anxiety, Mr. Harker. You hear anxiety. And you are *not* in Florida, so do not waste my time. Oh, your secretary was most discreet. Do not blame her. Let's say that rumors abound. And rumor says you are out of this state and up north somewhere."

"Oh, yeah?" My turn to get nervous. "What else do rumors say?"

He sighed. Boredom or impatience. It was impossible to tell. One thing was certain. He was in a no-nonsense mood.

"If you cannot come back to Florida, then we must make arrangements to meet somewhere. Soon."

"Must?" Fuck him. When I had wanted to talk he'd run off, leaving me to sweat it out in an ape suit. Now *he* wanted to talk and I was supposed to do handstands over this fact.

"Must, Colonel? Why *must* we?"

"Mr. Harker, you were quite anxious to find me at one point. What has happened to change your mind?"

He was in a hurry, like a man in a very small room being chased by a very hungry leopard. I was willing to bet Estevez's getting killed had convinced Fragan that DeBlase and Harley meant business. It wasn't a game anymore.

"Let's say I've come across more information," I said, "possibly better than anything I could hope to get from you." My eyes wandered to the movie screen. Clint Eastwood was killing Italian extras in a spaghetti Western.

"I see. Well, I was hoping we could get together." The man was almost apologetic. Almost. Something had happened to soften him. Fear. Fear had happened to him.

"If we do, it won't be in Florida. I barely got out before the questioning started. If I go back, I can be held for a couple of reasons, all related to the late Señor Estevez."

"Yes, I know. I know." He seemed sad about Estevez. I wondered why.

"Fragan tell me something. Estevez wasn't really your

type of guy. He was a slob, let's face it. You, well, you've got some sort of polish. What did you two have going to keep you together over the years?''

He sounded tired, like an old man who had just finished running a long, hard race. His voice was flat, strained. Death does that to you, if you're around when it happens.

"Business partners. He and I were business partners. I owned a piece of his newspaper and theatrical agency. There weren't too many areas of investment open to me, ones that I could be a part of and not have to answer some questions. So I invested with someone I knew, who knew me. Someone I wouldn't have to explain anything to. Capitalism, I think you Americans call it.''

It was sad. A highly trained KGB officer, multi-lingual, with a talent for espionage rarely found in one's own countrymen, now reduced to owning points in a cheap newspaper and theatrical agency fronted by a Cuban flesh-peddler. Life plays tricks on us all in the end. I wondered how I'd end up.

"That explains it.'' I was thinking of an intelligent man like Fragan reading a rag like *La Luz Fuerte*. It was this rag that had led Harley's hounds and me to the Colonel.

"Mr. Harker, we must see each other.'' Fragan was pressing. His voice wasn't so self-assured anymore.

"Fragan, you are not getting me back on those sandy beaches. For one thing, our Texas friend has his goons out looking for us both. If the police held me for just twenty-four hours, he's the type to find a way to put something in my mashed potatoes. Thanks, but no thanks.''

Two black kids walked by me, laughing and slapping palms. On screen, Clint Eastwood was still shooting Italian extras.

"I know what you mean, Mr. Harker. Estevez's death was a shock to me. We had known each other for a very long time. Have you seen a newspaper today?''

"No. I don't think Estevez's death is going to make news outside of Florida. Florida cops will probably think it's just more Cuban violence. Benes, pro, anti, what's the goddamn difference? You and I know better. But nobody else does. And nobody else cares.''

"I'm not talking about that, Mr. Harker. I'm talking about the shooting in Las Vegas. Cannizzaro. Richard Cannizzaro. Happened late last night. Somebody blew his head off with a shotgun."

"What's that got to do with you? I've heard of Richie C. He used to handle a lot of the Mafia's Vegas business. He was the show-biz type. Liked movie stars and show girls. So somebody wasted him, so what?" Richie C. was around sixty-five or would have been if he'd lived.

"Mr. Cannizzaro had business dealings with Mr. Harley. Remember Estevez mentioning his own dealings with certain people in Havana? Gambling? Do you remember?"

I was ready to bite my tongue. Jesus, did I remember.

"Yeah, I remember Estevez saying something about certain people in Havana. And their business interests. And their wanting to do something about those interests." Like killing Cuba's premier.

"Cannizzaro was one of the people Estevez passed money to. Even political assassination costs money, Mr. Harker. Cannizzaro was in charge of the efforts those American businessmen made to remedy the Cuban situation."

"You got proof of what you just told me? It's going to take more than just Estevez's word."

"I've got proof. Rather, I know someone who does. This someone is also worried about survival. The deaths of Estevez and Cannizzaro have made this somebody very nervous. I was in Havana when Cannizzaro was kicked out. Cannizzaro was involved with gambling casinos and narcotics smuggling."

"That's public knowledge. This somebody who's worried, who is he or she?"

"First, Mr, Harker, let me say that it is indeed public knowledge about Mafia activities in Havana. But it is not public knowledge that it was Gaylord Harley who arranged for money to reach Cannizzaro, money for weapons, explosives, boats. As for the person involved—"

"Hold on, hold on, friend. One minute. You *know*

somebody who can connect Harley with attempts on
Benes' life?''

"You heard me say that, yes. The money was deposited
in banks in Mexico City and Panama. Cannizzaro and certain others made the withdrawals, under assumed names,
of course.'' Behind Fragan, the Latin music was faint but
still unkind to the ears. A singer was working over lyrics
that sounded like the eye chart.

"What's your boy got to back this up?" I asked.

"Bankbooks, cables, letters of deposit. This 'boy,' as
you put it, saved these papers against such a time as now.
He'd gone back to Cuba for a few years to make sure he
was safe. In Cuba, he got into some trouble with the police and had to leave in a hurry. He came to this country
and was living quietly in Miami, until recently. Too many
sudden deaths have made him nervous. I've told him a
news story by you might keep him alive.''

"Him, hell. Him, you, *and* me. Your friend, who is
he?''

"Just call him Julio Miranda.'' The smugness had returned. Could the sneer be far behind?

"One more thing, Mr. Harker. My friend says he can
tell you something about the mechanics of the assassination. His part had to do with escorting some women to a
practice site, where men were sighting rifles, looking at
street maps. Men who hadn't seen women in a while,
men—''

"Jesus Christ!'' Delia Sisson had said something about
prostitutes being furnished for three convicts. Convicts
from a prison run by Uttman. Estevez and Miranda. Pimps
for Harley. *Somebody else knew about the prostitutes furnished for three cons.*

"Fragan, how soon can you and Julio get started
north?'' I had my lips so close to the phone I almost swallowed the receiver. My heart was about to snap its strings
and go off someplace.

"Why north?''

"Because I'm not coming south and you need me. OK,
we need each other. Just keep driving north. Keep in touch

with me through my paper in New York. There's no other way for us to communicate, and you can't stay there."

"Can't get out of the state that easily," he said. "Airports, piers. Somebody's watching them. Not sure if it's our Texas friend or the American government. At the moment, both are equally untrustworthy. Sill, I guess there's no other way but to take your advice. Rent a car."

He sounded ready to sit in the shade. Soft living had squeezed more juice out of him than he knew. Even though the Colonel might be able to come up with a tricky move or two once in a while, he was no longer the bright-eyed young lad who'd once been the toast of Moscow and Havana.

Jesus, this assassination thing was getting bigger and bigger. If I stopped to think about it too much, I'd be too paralyzed to move. So I stopped thinking about it. And just kept on running.

Outside on the street, my head spinning around like a man who'd been beaned by major league pitching, I found a newspaper.

VEGAS MAFIA CHIEFTAIN SLAIN—COPS FEAR GANG WAR

Victor Evan Havilland had been dead for over ten years, but the conspiracy that had killed him wasn't dead at all. It was going strong. My knees ached and my ankles hurt from being folded up like an accordion in that piss-smelling booth. Still, I was in better shape than Cannizzaro.

Richie C. The man in the fifty-dollar silk ties, one-hundred-and-fifty-dollar alligator shoes, and diamond pinky rings. The man who never played blackjack for less than a hundred dollars a hand. He'd made all the papers. He would have loved that. Publicity always turned him on.

25.

"What the fuck do you mean, you can't?" I was angry. That made me slam both hands down on the table and lean across it toward Trotman. Anyone looking closely would have thought I was about to do Trotman harm. I could have done more harm to the sidewalk by biting it.

"*Can't*. That's what I mean. *Can't* get it." He swallowed the rest of his beer, setting the glass down gently on the table. Trotman had just told me he couldn't get his hands on the unreleased CIA report on the Victor Evan Havilland assassination. I wasn't happy to hear this.

"Why can't you?"

"Because of what's happening right now." He rolled the glass between his big hands. "I don't know if it's this DeBlase business or not."

I leaned back in the booth. This was Trotman's secret bar, a joint called Angelo's near M Street, North West. It was dark, with a crowd of blue-collar workers, mostly white. There were booths in the back facing the door.

"You think Harley's got his friends tightening up security?" I pushed my ginger ale to one side.

"Maybe. Fucking Harley. Always did run things to suit himself. The Company could have made trouble for him, but I guess he knew too much. Knew too many people, too. So they let him resign quietly and everybody covered up like crazy. Not about *the killing*, you understand."

He looked at me. He still couldn't bring himself to talk about his beloved CIA and the Havilland assassination in the same breath. *The killing.* Yeah, it was *the killing*, all right. *The killing* of the century, bar none.

I looked at my ginger ale. It was light brown, with three ice cubes, and it didn't have a worry in the world. "Sounds like Harley left some things behind to be covered up," I said.

Trotman shrugged. "He wasn't the only one. Guys are always resigning because it's better for us that they do. They got carried away, things happened, people got killed, so—" He shrugged again.

"So the Company let them off the hook because it couldn't bring them to trial and still stay a highly secret organization. Let me ask you something." I fumbled in my pocket for one of my notebooks.

"These names—" I flipped through the pages. "Names of DeBlase's security directors, the ones reporting to Harley. Take a look at them. See if you recognize anybody. If you do, tell me what you can about them."

He took the notebook and frowned at it in the semi-darkness. He nodded his head two or three times, started to smile but didn't. Without looking up, he said, "Harley's boys. Most of them worked with him at one time. Shit, I worked with a couple here myself. The others were fans of Harley's, agents who thought he was the greatest thing since condoms. All except this one, this one right here."

A huge forefinger tapped the name third from the top. "Rossman. Gerard Rossman. He never was one of us."

"Oh?"

"He was with the New Orleans police force."

Trotman said that calmly. It hadn't hit him yet. I chewed my lips, cleared my throat, and reached for the ginger ale. It had no taste because there was something else on my mind. The Havilland assassination had taken place in New

Orleans. So had the "attempted" jailbreak by Perry Joseph. It looked as though Harley had hired his Company teammates to work for him and DeBlase. *And he had also hired someone who used to work in the New Orleans police department.* Payoff time, said my suspicious mind.

Trotman frowned. He looked down at my notebook, a forefinger tapping the page. "Say, know something? Rossman. He was on the New Orleans force at the time of—Jesus H. Christ! That bastard was with them when Havilland got it! Yeah!" He nodded his head again and again, frowning until his forehead looked like someone had painted lines across it every day for a week. Trotman's brain wasn't that fast, but the man was not dumb.

He stared at the names again and let himself half-smile. "Stein. Fucking asshole, this guy. Always ready to work on you. Interrogation expert. Sadistic bastard. Likes to deal out pain. Bad news. Fairly, Pearson, Jakes. Good old Jakes. Thinks he's a big-cunt man. Fucking crazy people, all of them. Where'd you get these names?"

Smiling, I reached over gently, prying the notebook from his shovel-sized hands. "Now, now! None of that, young man. No names. Not yours, not theirs. No names."

Trotman lifted a corner of his mouth. "You're all heart, Harker."

"That's me. All-Heart Harker. 'Bout that report—"

"Shit, man, they're watching that thing like it's pure gold. You can look at it if you know somebody. I did get a quick peek—don't get excited. Didn't get much. I had to put it back before the clerk came back from taking a piss. Saw one thing—"

"Shit! Why the hell didn't you tell me this instead of jerking me off!"

"Saw Perry Joseph's name. He worked for us and the Feebs."

Feebs. That's what other law-enforcement services call the FBI.

"Jesus Christ, Trotman, take your time, why don't you!"

He ignored my impatience and annoyance. Better for me that he did.

"Feebs gave him a number. One-oh-one. Paid him two a month for working for them. We've got him down as one of ours; I don't know if it was at the same time. Probably not. We paid him 'bout the same."

"That's definite?"

"Yeah." Trotman said the word softly, as if he didn't even want me to hear it. His conscience was sure giving him a hard time.

No wonder the CIA and FBI were hot to keep Perry Joseph's employment record out of the final assassination report. Keep it out and avoid an investigation.

"Trotman, is there any way you can get your hands on that report?"

"Harker, you don't fuckin' quit, do you?"

"Hell, no. I want to be somebody when I grow up."

"I'll try. That's all. No promises. I'll try. Got to go. This is as safe a place as possible. But it never hurts to be sure. I'm leaving the back way. Wait ten minutes, then go out the front."

I nodded. A few days ago, I'd have laughed at this Captain Midnight bullshit. But the past forty-eight hours had made a believer out of me.

He slid out of the booth, stood up, and looked over the bar with those hard yellow eyes. Apparently satisfied that all was right with the world, he walked toward the back slowly, like a man with nothing more on his mind than beating the rush-hour traffic home. I watched him disappear through the door.

I'd decided to make a few notes on our conversation. My ballpoint pen was in my right hand and I was thumbing through a notebook looking for a clean page.

One of them slid into the booth where Trotman had been sitting. The other sat beside me, which stopped me from going anywhere.

Both of them scared the shit out of me and I guess I looked it.

Kalter said, "Boo!" His small ratlike face did its best to smile.

Lamont, sitting next to me, said nothing. He leaned his head back against the booth and stared at the ceiling. I let

the silence float around for a while. I needed time to stop
being scared.

Deep breathing helped a little bit. But not much.

"What's the matter, Harker? You look like you ain't
feeling so good." Kalter folded his hands on the table and
grinned like a child-molester moving in for the kill.

I felt sick. Had they followed me or Trotman? Shit.
Goddamn it. How had they found out? Christ!

"Hey, Lamont," said Kalter. "Harker's gone quiet.
Maybe it's you, maybe he don't like sittin' next to black
people. Hey, is that it, Harker? Lamont's OK, he's one of
us."

Lamont said nothing. He kept his eyes on the ceiling,
as though God were doing private magic tricks for him
alone. Being OK and one of us didn't seem to thrill him
that much.

"OK, Kalter," I said. "So you're here, so what."

He grinned, enjoying himself. "So we order a beer.
Waiter, two beers and—Hey, Harker, what's that horse piss
you're drinking?" He pulled the glass toward him, sipped,
and made a face.

"Jesus," he said. "Ginger ale. God, how the hell can
you drink that shit? Two beers, one ginger ale."

The fat waiter threw a towel over his own shoulder and
backed off.

They knew about Trotman. Shit, this was bad news. I
had to warn the big man as soon as possible. I owed him
that. How the hell had they found out? I wanted to know.
Trotman had made a mistake, no two ways about it.

The waiter came back. We waited until he'd set the
drinks down and left.

Kalter stopped smiling. Roy Lupus wasn't around to
keep him in check anymore. He didn't have to be polite
now.

"Harker, let me tell you something. You bastard reporters think your shit don't stink. You go 'round sticking
your fuckin' nose where it don't belong and you write
garbage, fuckin' garbage. You tell lies, you hurt the country. Russia's too good for you, you know that? You oughta
go someplace where it's nice and quiet, where you don't

have a chance to open your big mouth and sit at your typewriter and play big man. Someplace quiet. Like a hole six feet deep.''

Reaching over farther, he dropped something into my ginger ale, then smiled and leaned back in the booth. Picking up his beer, he sipped it, said "Ahhhhh," then sat it back on the table.

I looked at my ginger ale. He'd dropped a piece of chalk in it.

"Know what that's for, Harker? Guess you don't. When the cops find a dead body, they outline it in chalk. You carry that 'round with you, put it in your pocket. This way when you turn up with your eyes shut, nobody has to go lookin' for chalk. We just reach in your pocket, pull it out, and start drawin'. Saves us time.''

I didn't like Kalter. The man had a sadistic streak in him straight out of the SS. I pulled the ginger ale and chalk toward me, staring at the glass as though it were vintage wine. Then I reached over and started pouring. On Kalter's lap.

He leaped up as though the liquid were red-hot. "Hey! Hey, you crazy bastard!''

People in the bar turned around and looked at him.

He stood there brushing it from his suit. He was red-faced, angry, embarrassed.

"Harker, you prick!''

Lamont's deep voice rumbled over us both. "Cool it, man. You ain't in a public kind of business." He was ordering Kalter around like Kalter was his pet dog. "Go in the bathroom and get your act together. Don't come out till you're straight.''

Kalter caught the tone in Lamont's voice and stopped brushing. His suit looked as if it were pissed on. The look suited Kalter. His eyes jumped from Lamont to me. He stared at me like he'd decided to kill me one day real soon. It was not a look designed to make you feel loved.

When Kalter had left, Lamont sighed. "Dude's weak. Can't cut it. Why'd you do a thing like that?''

"You don't sound angry about it.''

He grinned, saying nothing. That said it all. He wasn't angry. That was a relief. I wanted to go on living.

"He pissed me off," I said. "Always threats, always big mouth, bad mouth. That business about me ending up dead. Shit, fuck him where he breathes."

"He don't like you, man."

"I don't like him."

"Yeah. We 'sposed to make sure you stay away from our people, that you leave town."

"No way you can do that." Who was I kidding? Lamont could throw me across the Potomac like a silver dollar.

"We can make it rough, dude. You know it, I know it." Practical and direct.

"It's going to look bad in the papers, Lamont. Real bad."

"Ain't my worry, man. The people 'fraid of you. They think you can hurt them, hurt them bad. Long as you out of town, for a little while, they prepared to take the consequences."

"There will be consequences. I'll come down hard and nobody's going to be happy."

He grinned. I could have climbed over him if I had ropes, picks, and a team of men.

"Harker, I only work here. Besides, if somebody gets his ass in a sling where I work, maybe it's to my advantage. I might just get promoted."

"I wish you well, Lamont. Are you kidding about that, about seeing that I get out of town?"

"Ain't jivin'. You go. Now. That's supposed to give them time to clear up things."

"Like check out my sources, cut off heads, stop people from talking to me."

"You ain't as dumb as you look."

"Thanks."

Kalter came back. He was calmer. But he didn't love me any more or hate me any less. He stared at Lamont, then at the ceiling, then at his fingernails. The man was seething and fighting hard to control himself.

He said, "Harker, let's go!"

"Fuck you. I'm not going anywhere. And you try to do it the hard way and we'll all three end up at police headquarters. Maybe I can't outfight you two, but I can outscream the both of you." I was scared. But I was ready to holler.

Lamont said, "Cool it, man." He spoke to Kalter. "We are supposed to see that he gets out of town. That's it."

"Listen—" Kalter pointed a forefinger at Lamont, as if to say, "Remember your place."

Lamont just looked at him. Kalter took his forefinger back.

Lamont turned to me. "That's the way it is, Jack. You got to go."

And that's when I got the idea of the day. I smiled, took a deep breath, and said, "Fine. I go."

Kalter frowned. Lamont leaned his head to the right.

"I'll go," I repeated. *What a brilliant idea, Harker. Fucking brilliant.*

"But," I added, "when I'm ready. Tonight. My word on that. No fuss, no screaming, no cops. I go."

"Harker—" Kalter leaned toward me, then lowered his voice. "Now, cocksucker! Now!" He was hissing like a snake. His face was red again.

"Tonight. You meet me or follow me, whatever. Take me to the airport. To Dulles." Where I was to meet DeBlase and Harley. Out in the open. I had my escort. Two of the Company's finest. Harker, you wonderful schemer, you.

"Cool," said Lamont. "We ain't 'sposed to make trouble. We don't need the poe-leece or somebody yelling his ass off while we drag him out the door. Tonight. What time?"

"Seven-thirty. Meet me at the Auden Hotel. We go to Dulles. But, dig, I'm coming back to this fair city. And you people are still going to be unhappy."

"No problem," said Lamont. "Tonight we take you to the airport." Kalter stood up in a hurry, as though I'd dumped something on him again. Turning his back on us, he stood breathing loudly. He didn't like what Lamont and I'd just agreed to, but I had the feeling he was going along with it because he knew it was smart. I could start yelling and blow their game as well as mine.

"Wait for you outside," said Kalter, his back to us. He stomped out like a rejected suitor.

"Man's got problems," said Lamont, jerking a big brown thumb at Kalter.

"Man's an asshole. How'd you find me?"

"Your people are careless, man. You ought to tell them that, you know?"

Trotman. Where did you fuck up? *Where?*

"I'll remember. Tonight. Don't play me cheap, Lamont. Anybody comes near me, he'll have to shoot me to keep me from screaming like I was being raped."

He stood up, grinning. "Don't go 'round sayin' that, dude, 'bout people shootin' you. Some people ain't got no character, you know? They just might—" He shrugged, spreading his hands palms up.

I got the message.

For a long time after he left, I sat there and felt sorry for myself. Why not? No one else was feeling sorry for me.

26.

Trotman's voice was calm over the telephone. Almost too calm. He didn't seem worried.

"What else did they say?"

"That's about it," I said. "Kalter did most of the talking and all of the yelling. Your people want me out of town, I guess so they can plug up all holes. Your name wasn't mentioned. But they showed up minutes after you left, so I got to figure you're it. They know, don't ask me how. What the hell did you do to tip them off, go down on somebody during a staff meeting?"

Trotman seemed preoccupied. "Guess I got careless. Once is all it takes."

"Like killing yourself," I said. "Once is all it takes."

It was almost five-thirty. I was in a coffee shop near my hotel and Trotman was at a gas station.

"Harker, all I can do 'bout that report is just walk up to whoever's watching the file, zap him, grab it, and run. File's under a combination lock. Last time, I had to forge two passes just to get inside the room. Let it all hang out.

That's what it's going to take. Just stick my hand in the fire, I guess.''

"You've done enough, more than enough. They've made you, man, understand that. They know. Jesus, is there some kind of story you can give them?''

"No. I probably got careless, like I said. Lot on my mind. This—this Havilland thing, you know? Hard to believe we'd—that we'd go all out to sweep it under the rug like that. Bothers me. I been hearin' rumors for a long time, but I put those down to wishful thinking. We got a lot of enemies. This thing's got me down. So you're leavin' town.''

"Yep. Tonight. Shuttle to the Big Apple.''

"Goddamn, Sam.'' He chuckled. "They really got you leavin'?'' Doubt was in his voice. That was to his credit.

"You know better. I'm splitting, but it's just a scam. They think they won a battle. That's not the same as winning the war.''

"Tactics, huh?''

"You could call it that. You can still reach me through the paper in New York, if anything comes up.''

"That won't be easy. Crackin' down on everything like crazy 'round here. Security's tighter than a cat's asshole. Phone calls being monitored. Guys looking out of the corner of their eyes. Purge time, man. People uptight. You started something.''

"Balls. The Company did. Started it a long time ago with their secret wheeling and dealing, with their phony fears of enemies, with their do-as-I-please attitude. Hell, none of it's *our* government anymore. The government, CIA, FBI—all them fuckers are totally undependable. Whatever they do, they do for themselves, not for us. Don't blame me, Trotman.''

"Too late in the day for that kind of shit, Harker. I'm going back to work.''

"Hey, Trotman, watch yourself, OK?'' For a few seconds, I felt pity for the big man who'd believed in an ideal only to see it perverted into a private, vicious game by men like Gaylord Ran Harley.

"Yeah. Watch myself." He sounded like a man ready to jump from a tall building.

He hung up first.

"Watch yourself, big man," I whispered.

I spent the next hour and a half in two different movie houses, watching neither film. I sat in darkness and worried a lot. At seven o'clock I left, took a taxi to the Auden Hotel, and went inside to pay my bill. When I turned around, Lamont and Kalter were standing by the front door. I smiled and waved. They didn't. I walked toward them.

27.

"Where you meetin' your people?" asked Lamont.

I pointed to the airport information desk twenty feet away.

"Nine o'clock. Fifteen minutes from now. After that, I take a nine-thirty shuttle back to America."

Lamont snorted at that one. But it was a friendly snort. His eyes said so. Kalter had left us alone. He'd gone off, to piss or make a telephone call. It didn't matter to me.

"Those things you took from the locker," said Lamont. "Those envelopes. They have anything to do with these people you meetin'?"

I'd picked up the key to the locker from the pudgy clerk at information. Two sealed brown manila envelopes containing the tearsheets from Ray Stance were waiting for me in the locker, as per my instructions to him. I was going to wait until I was alone before checking them out.

"Maybe," I said in answer to Lamont's question. The big black man had sharp eyes.

"You ain't makin' no fuss," he said. His small smile said that I wasn't fooling him.

"You mean I didn't shove my fist in the air and scream my ass off about my rights?"

"Somethin' like that."

"Maybe I'm shy."

"Yeah. And sharks don't eat meat."

"Aw, come on, Lamont. Can't you appreciate my making your job easier?"

He leaned toward me. We sat side by side on orange cushions, on a backless bench designed to discourage people with nothing to do but hang out in air terminals. A few people walked across the huge empty room, their footsteps clicking on the hard floor. A mechanical-sounding voice droned on about incoming and outgoing flights.

"Harker, long time ago when I was a little kid, there was this other cat. Smiled all the time. 'Specially when he was gonna kick your ass. Used to walk up to you grinnin'. Put his hand on your shoulder friendly-like, like this—" Lamont laid a hand the size of a door on my shoulder.

"Then before you knew it, *wham*! Dude dropped you. He liked to do that. Smile, then kick ass. Got so every time we saw him smile, we knew there was trouble. One day he come up to me smilin' like that. I smiled back. He reached his hand out to touch my shoulder. I went upside his head with a wine bottle. Coldcocked that nigger. When he opened his eyes, I looked down at him and said, 'I see you smilin' at me again, I ain't gonna like it.' Him and me understood each other after that. He never smiled at me no more."

"You're trying to tell me something, Lamont." I chewed my lip. Lamont always seemed to get bigger when I was afraid of him.

He grinned. "Not you exactly. Just want to tell you that when things are goin' good, that's the time you be wonderin' about what's really goin' on."

"OK if I smile?"

He liked that. He grinned again and nodded. "Yeah, man. Help yourself. Like Machiavelli says: 'Men will always be false to you unless they are compelled by necessity to be true.' I guess it just ain't necessary for you to tell us the truth.''

Lamont was big enough to *make* it necessary for me to tell the truth about everything I'd done since leaving the womb. But I had the feeling that he didn't have this kind of attitude toward me. His sense of restraint might change if he found me harming a close relative. But I wasn't planning to, so I should survive the next ten minutes.

Thomas Merle DeBlase. Gaylord Ran Harley. I couldn't believe they would actually show up. And if they did, what would we talk about? Dead people, probably.

Kalter was walking toward us.

"Here comes Chuckles," I said.

"Man's got problems," said Lamont. "He's scared, that's why he shows off. If he were cool, he wouldn't be uptight. Man shouldn't show his feelings.''

"That man shouldn't show his face.''

Kalter stood in front of us, small bright eyes on his watch. He had eyes the size of raisins.

"Few more minutes, Harker. Then you're a travelin' man.'' Kalter looked at me as though measuring me for a coffin.

"Like I said, Kalter. I talk to some people, then I leave.''

"Yeah, sure.'' He unwrapped a stick of gum, sticking it into his mouth past tiny yellow teeth. He didn't offer any gum to Lamont or me.

I looked past him. Six men were walking toward the information booth. Only one seemed familiar. White hair fringing a pink skull, round face belonging to a kindly old granddad. Medium height, wearing an off-the-rack brown suit, white shirt, and dark blue tie. He seemed at peace with the world, and if a small boy had come up to him, he would probably have given the kid a quarter, along with a pat on the head.

Thomas Merle DeBlase. Mr. Money himself. A man politically to the right of Genghis Khan. Harmless looking. But so is a coral snake.

I stood up, my heart flopping like a fish out of water. The clock over the information desk said one minute to nine. These people didn't play around even in small things. Which of the six was Gaylord Ran Harley? Harley. The man who had tried to kill me, the man who had succeeded in killing Victor Evan Havilland. What the fuck was I doing here? Jesus, when God was giving out brains I must have been at the back of the line.

My throat felt like it was filled with plaster. I was scared, excited, and I wanted to turn and run. Clearing my throat, I started walking toward the six men.

Behind me, Kalter said, "We ain't leavin' till you come back, Harker. Better remember that."

"Countin' on it, baby." He didn't hear me. Just as well. My voice was high, like Mickey Mouse after being kicked in the balls.

I kept walking, wondering if the ground would open up under me before I got there. It didn't.

If Gaylord Ran Harley hadn't gone into his present line of work, he would have been a whiz on the silver screen. He could have been Rory Calhoun's twin brother. Same dark good looks, the kind that Hollywood cried out for in the forties. Same perfect features, gray hair at the temples, same direct stare that was supposed to weaken men and women, though for different reasons. Harley was also over six feet tall and dressed like a banker—conservative, well-tailored suit that must have cost four hundred dollars on sale. He gave you the impression that you were taking up his time. He spent seconds staring at me from top to bottom. I felt as though I had shit on my nose.

Thomas Merle DeBlase stood behind him, a man on either side of him. DeBlase looked everywhere but at me. He looked at the floor, at the ceiling, at his nails, at the buttons on his suit jacket. I could have been crumpled newspaper used to train his dog.

Six of them and one of me. I had enough fear for all seven of us.

Harley said, "I'll come right to the point. You're in the way. Back off."

I felt dizzy. I was sweating, even though the terminal was air-conditioned. But I had to say something.

"Back off from what?" Great, Harker. Fucking memorable.

"Harker, you're still alive because I wanted to know what you'd found out. So far, you know very little. And your paper knows nothing. I wanted you to hear it from me. You're in over your head. Back off and live."

His voice could have come from a computer. It had no feeling, no hesitation, no doubt. He stared at me as though I were a sick child.

"You know a lot about me, Harley. You ought to know I don't take orders." My throat was looser now. But not loose enough.

"There's a first time." Behind him, one of the men snickered. They reminded me of the guys who were always named Vito and who came over from Brooklyn to break your legs when you wouldn't pay up.

"How do you know I'm not wired?"

"I know. And you're not." The man was direct, and it made me nervous. I should say *more* nervous.

"So you know. Look, Harley, you don't tell me anything, I—"

"Harker, back off. Stay alive. Do yourself a favor. You'll never prove anything. The country doesn't care, it doesn't want to know. Come on out to Vegas as my guest. Stay at one of our hotels. You want anything—a woman, three women, expenses, you got it. You've had your exercise, so rest a bit."

"I've got all eternity to rest. Goethe said that."

Harley looked at DeBlase. DeBlase was looking at the floor. We could have been seven travelers waiting to catch a plane for the Bahamas.

Harley turned back to me. "You want an exclusive interview with Mr. DeBlase. You've got it. Business, politics, changing social conditions. He'll talk about it. An interview like that will make you a big man."

"I want to talk about the Havilland assassination."

Harley moved his head from side to side, then shifted his weight. He stared at the ceiling, then ran a finger down the side of his nose. When he smiled, I could see the power he had over men. The man could have been anything he wanted to be, and other men would have followed him. He had a power of leadership given to only a few.

"Harker, you believe in reincarnation?"

I shrugged. "Hadn't thought about it."

"Think about it. You might be able to write a hell of a story on it. First-hand experience."

Behind him, three men snickered. They were large men, men with hunter's eyes and hard, bony faces. They didn't look like gardeners.

"Well," I said, "if I come back, I hope it's as a girl's bicycle seat."

Harley said, "If you change your mind, Harker, we'll be in Las Vegas four days from now."

Prick. He knew a hell of a lot about me and that bothered me. It started something gnawing at my brain and all I could come up with was that the bastard had inside information about *me*. *Me*!

"Have fun in Iran," I said.

He froze, looking at me with eyes as hard as green marbles.

Then he smiled, snapping his fingers once.

A man behind him handed him a folded newspaper, which he passed to me. Then, looking over at Lamont and Kalter, Gaylord Harley leaned his head to the right, studying them for several seconds. He turned back to me.

"Nice talking to you, Harker." The interview was over.

I gripped the folded newspaper.

"Nice talking to you, too." I waved the newspaper at DeBlase. "Hello, Mr. DeBlase."

His face never changed expression. He flicked his eyes to me, then looked away. It had all taken less than a fraction of a second. No smile, not even a glint of recognition. I could have been a grain of sand or a fly on the wall. I got the feeling that I'd have to work awfully hard to get a reaction out of that man. Well, that's what happens when you've got a few billion dollars and a warped mind. You're not easily impressed.

Gaylord Ran Harley spun around, and two men behind him stepped to the side. He walked between them until he was out front. The rest followed him, like Explorer Scouts

on an outing. Gaylord Ran Harley. Yeah, I could see him
leading his own branch of the CIA, and getting away with
it. The only one who could stop him was Errol Flynn, and
he was dead.

I unfolded the newspaper. It had been opened to page
thirty. On the bottom, a small paragraph had been circled
in red. It was today's paper, a New York City tabloid. The
paragraph said the body of a man presumed drowned had
been washed ashore at Rockaway Beach. There was no
identification, but there was a description of the man. I
may have been reaching, but I didn't think so. The man
was Drummond McClan.

I felt cold. My hands shook and I ground my teeth together to keep my jaw from shaking. Well, I couldn't say
I wasn't warned. I'd been warned in spades.

Kalter touched my elbow. "Harker? Harker?"

I turned to him slowly. Jesus, those people played rough.
"Yeah?"

"Lupus wants to see you. Now." The touch became a
pull.

I became angry.

"Kalter, if you don't let go of my elbow, I'm going to kick
your nuts all the way up to your nose." Fear can do that to
you. Make you unreasonably angry at almost nothing.

"Cool it, just fucking cool it, Harker. Lupus says you
wanted to see a certain document. Called while you were
talking to your friends. Well, he claims if you see it, you'll
believe we didn't have nothin' to do with nothin', understand?"

I frowned. Was I hearing right?

Lamont was still sitting on the orange cushions twenty
feet away, unable to hear but able to see.

"You saying that I can look at your report on the Havilland assassination? I thought you guys wanted me out of
town so I *couldn't* see it."

"Things change. Somebody decided it might be best if
we played along with you, give you a break. Then maybe
you'd give us a break." Kalter did everything but chew on
a straw and dig his toe in the dirt. There were dark spots

on his jacket and pants. The man just couldn't keep himself clean.

"Kalter, you tell Lupus if this is some sort of trick, it won't work. I'm still writing what I feel like writing, report or no report."

"He knows that. You do what you want to do. He just feels if you got a look at it, you won't be so hard on us, that's all."

"That's all, huh?" I wondered about that.

"All right, Harker?"

"All right. But let go of my elbow, I can walk."

28.

The gun was small, hidden under the folded newspaper given me by Harley. Both newspaper and gun were now being held by someone other than me. In the darkness, I'd been given a quick look at the gun, just enough to let me know it was there. A .32, I'd say. It looked like a toy, a blue metal toy with a tiny hole at the end of a three-inch barrel. Six shots, probably. All aimed at my gut.

Kalter licked his small pink lips like a night watchman peeking into a shower room packed with naked college girls.

"It's real, Harker. Believe me when I tell you. Makes holes. Get in the car."

"Lupus doesn't want to see me, right?"

"In the car, asshole. Behind the wheel. If I have to, I can leave you lying right here in the parking lot with pennies on your eyes."

"Wouldn't want that," I said. The son of a bitch had me believing he'd do it. That made me jumpy. I wanted to kick his tiny ass in the worst way. But he had the piece and it was zeroed in on my navel.

Out in the darkened parking lot, I'd started asking questions. Too many questions, it turned out. That's when Kalter had pulled a gun, covering it with my newspaper. In the parking lot, we were off in a corner away from anyone, unless you counted mosquitoes and moths. There were no cars parked near us. CIA training in all things.

Lamont frowned, looking at Kalter, then me, then Kalter. Apparently this number was a surprise to him, too.

Lamont, in front of Kalter and off to his right, started to say something. "Hey—"

Kalter turned on him viciously, his face strawberry-red. White flecks of spit were tiny cobwebs in the corners of Kalter's small mouth. This little bastard was angry and psycho, a dangerous combination in a man holding a gun.

"*You* shut the fuck up, understand? *You* don't say nothin'! I say jump, nightfighter, you fuckin' *jump*! This ain't the darktown strutters' ball. You got no say in *shit*! Harker gets in the car, he drives off by himself, that's it. Don't aggravate me, jungle bunny. Just don't. You're nothin' but a guest at the party, understand?"

Kalter fought to keep his voice low and ended up hissing like a snake. His face was now a darker red, eyes wide and bulging like those of a man craving a drug he couldn't get his hands on at the moment. When he stopped hissing at Lamont, his jaws continued to work, like a man chewing a tough steak. Kalter was a hair away from going over the edge.

Lamont kept his cool. But there were signs, baby, signs that something was going on behind that big black unsmiling face. His chest expanded to a size big enough to snap any tape measure in the land. His shoulders eased up and back. But the Lamont who read Machiavelli, and who told stories about men who smiled just before putting the hurt on you, relaxed. He grinned, wider than I'd seen him do yet. That was an indication of something. He turned his palms up, shrugging like a well-behaved government worker.

"You callin' it, dude."

"Sure I am, spade. Now we *both* know it."

Kalter turned back to me.

I was confused, which still left more than enough room to be nervous. Given the chance, I'd have leaped over cars and parking-lot fences like a champion high hurdler wearing a flaming jockstrap.

Kalter was crazy. And me being paranoid anyway, it wasn't taking much to make me more fearful.

Kalter smoothed his jacket with his bare hand, brushing the dark spots on it, then rubbing his fingertips together. Whatever the spots were, they'd come off on the little man's hand.

He jerked the newspaper at me.

"Inside."

"Why?"

" 'Cause I say so. 'Cause I got the gun. Call it 'national security.' "

"National security? Your ass, national security. Tell Lupus he's not going to get away with this strong-arm bullshit. I—"

"Yeah, yeah. Write a letter to the editor. Come on, Harker, my finger's nervous."

Kalter backed off, licking his lips some more. He jerked his head at Lamont, signaling him to back off, too.

I became aware of the heat, of whining mosquitoes, of a couple of people walking into the parking-lot entrance far, far away. What good would yelling do me? No good at all. Fear turned my tongue into something thick and dry. My mouth felt full of old socks.

Kalter kept backing away slowly.

I touched the car door handle.

From the corner of my eye, I saw something move and small bits of shiny metal go flying at Kalter's face. He crouched, crossing his arms to protect his eyes. He yelled, *"Goddamn it!"*

Lamont. The big black man moved fast, a blur in the night. A count of three and it was over, and all I could do was stand there with my mouth open, my hand on the car door handle and my stomach churning.

Lamont had thrown coins into Kalter's face. Kalter covered up. Lamont closed the distance between them, kneed Kalter in the stomach, then grabbed the little man's head

with his two big black hands. Pulling the head down hard
and fast, Lamont brought his knee up as quickly as he
could. Kalter didn't scream. He didn't have a chance to.

Kalter's face hit kneebone and there was a snapping
sound, like a branch being broken off a tree. Kalter
dropped to the concrete like a pile of rags and lay there,
his right hand still under the newspaper.

Efficient? Like a computer that's just been oiled. I was
impressed, grateful as hell, and less nervous. Less nervous didn't mean total peace of mind. It meant *less* nervous.

Lamont snapped his head toward me. He wasn't even
breathing hard, but he had the expression on his face of a
man who was all business.

"Move away from the car!"

"What?"

"Man, aw, shit!" Lamont grabbed my hand, and jerked
me away from the car as easily as if I weighed three
ounces. My armpit ached as a result of that little pull and
I stood there in the night massaging it.

"What's going on?" A good question on my part.

"Shh!" Lamont had the hood up. I looked down at
Kalter. He lay on the concrete, as quiet as a throw rug.
His head was at a funny angle and I held my breath. Squat-
ting, I felt his neck. Jesus. Nothing. Fucking nothing.
Crazy Kalter was dead. Terminated with some of the most
extreme prejudice I'd ever seen.

I turned to Lamont and was about to comment on this,
when my eyes went to his hand. He was holding something
out to me.

"Go on," he said. "Look at it."

I did.

It was dynamite, three sticks of it taped to a timer.

I took a deep breath.

"How'd you know?" I whispered.

"Man was anxious to have you drive off by yourself.
Check him out. He got some spots on him. Go on."

I bent down over Kalter again, making a face as if I
were poking around in a stopped-up toilet. Those dark

spots on his sleeve and jacket. Oil. Dark, wet. I touched them, then smelled my fingers. Son of a bitch. Oil.

I stood up.

Lamont said, "He didn't have them spots when we came out tonight. Suit had just come from the cleaners. Guess he did this here number when he left us inside by ourselves. You know why?"

Lamont didn't seem upset about having killed a co-worker. To tell the truth, it was bothering me less and less as the night wore on. The prick had tried to kill me. *Me!* Jesus, I wished Kalter was alive so I could kill him myself.

"Yeah, *I* know," I whispered. "This thing I'm working on. People I'm checking out. Yeah, I know why."

"Havilland," said Lamont, peeling the black tape off the timer.

"Yeah. How'd you know?"

"*How'd I know*. Sheeit. What the fuck you think you was asked to leave town for? That's all the people been talkin' about. You askin' questions and they uptight. *Sheeit, how'd I know?* You think I'm stupid?"

"Lamont, the next person who calls you stupid is going to have to deal with me. I owe you. I guess Kalter figured you and him could keep on backing off while I went *boom*. 'Too bad about old Harker,' the folk would say. 'He was always all over the place and now he's all over the place.' My nuts in Virginia, my cock in Maryland, and my ass out in Chesapeake Bay. Shit."

Lamont stepped past me and looked down at Kalter. "Too bad he ain't alive. Then we could put him in that car instead of you and it would be his ass flyin' to and fro. Never did like that sucker."

"That why you trashed him just now?"

"Maybe. Figured if he'd waste you, he'd waste me one of these days. Besides, a man's got to cover his own ass and I ain't in this game to do whitey's shit work just 'cause whitey's got a hard-on against somebody for no good reason."

"Good thinking, Lamont." I looked down at Kalter, and got an idea.

"Lamont?"

"Yeah?"

"You're a man of many talents, I can see that. Can you hook that dynamite up again?"

"Why? I ain't drivin' that thing if that's what you got in mind."

"No, man. Listen. Hook it up, then put Kalter here behind the wheel."

"Come on, the dude's dead. Stone cold. He ain't gonna be no deader."

"Oh, yes, he is, if you're as good as I think you are."

"Where you comin' from, man?"

"From survival city. Hook that shit up again, put Kalter behind the wheel. Better put him there *now*, before people start walking by, while it's empty 'round here. Then hook up the dynamite. Then my friend, you jump the wires. And don't tell me no black can't jump wires."

"Then what?" He didn't sound impressed. "I jump the wires and my ass is in front of God two seconds later. Fuck that shit."

"OK, jump the wires is a bad way of putting it. But you fix the wires some way, I can't tell you how. Just lean Kalter's body forward some kind of way and put those wires around his fingers. Rigor mortis is going to set in, his bones are going to get stiff. You do it right and the bastard will get stiff, the wires touch each other, and *bam*! Kalter dies in a mysterious explosion."

I was feeling inspired. I liked the idea.

Lamont wrestled with it. But not for long.

"Fuck rigor mortis. Takes hours for that to set in. Thing's got a timer. Set that and it should go off. What the hell, it's better than tellin' people why I wasted this cat instead of lettin' him waste you."

"That's one way of looking at it. Get busy. Let me ask you something—you think Lupus ordered this?"

Lamont had Kalter in his arms. In the darkness, it looked like a black friend lifting his drunken white friend into a car.

"No. They could have taken you out at any time. Why do it here?"

He placed Kalter on the front seat, then began work on the timer, setting the dynamite back under the hood.

Lamont was right. Why did the CIA wait until now to do me in? This attempt to kill me hadn't happened until *after* I'd met DeBlase and Harley, *after* I'd turned down any deal and courageously stood up to threats on my life. In retrospect it seemed courageous to me. *After.* Somewhere during that historic quickie talk with Gaylord Ran Harley, a signal had been passed to Kalter. A signal that I wasn't backing off.

Maybe Harley had blown a kiss to Kalter. Maybe passing me the newspaper was it. Whatever it had been, I'd almost ended up with a motor shoved through my pancreas and both legs torn loose and tossed to the four winds. Bless you, Lamont.

I kept quiet. The last thing Lamont needed was a loud mouth looking over his shoulder.

Mosquitoes whined past my ear. I slapped my neck, crushing one. Lamont turned around quickly at the noise, gave me a look of disgust, then stuck his head back under the hood.

OK, from now on let the mosquitoes chew away on my bod. But, God, please give Lamont the skill of a surgeon and the speed of a greyhound.

Lamont stood up, pushing the hood down as carefully as if it were made of antique porcelain.

"Finished," he whispered.

I turned and started running. So did Lamont. I gripped my notes and envelopes of tearsheets as though they were a baton. We made it to the end of one row, then cut left between cars, running like two guys with a good reason to run fast.

BOOM!

The roar went off, then echoed and reechoed. An eerie yellow light brightened a large part of the parking lot. Glass and chunks of metal bounced off car hoods and concrete like a hard, hard rain.

We stopped running and turned. Two or three people were trotting toward the blaze. But not too fast.

The fireball was bright orange and yellow, lighting up the area around it. It crackled, a cheerful sound.

"That sucker is fricasseed," mumbled Lamont.

We both stared at the fireball.

"What do you care?" I said. "When that fucking thing exploded, you were inside the terminal, giving me a hard time because I wouldn't get on the plane to New York. You had to get tough by yourself, because Kalter had said he was going to call in. Fact is, I plan on writing Lupus a nasty letter saying these things. After all you goddamn people have done, a letter from me could not possibly be misconstrued as an alibi for you, now could it?"

Lamont was back to his cool grin, the stingy kind. But he held a big hand out, palm up.

I slapped it. He kept the grin nodding once. Then he turned back to the fire. It snapped like a hundred whips. But it was dying down in a hurry. Even in death, Kalter wasn't much.

29.

"You look awful."

"Feel awful," I said.

"Been standing out here long?" She didn't seem surprised to find me waiting for her.

I looked at my watch. My eyes burned as though someone had thrown pepper into them. Lack of sleep.

"Since around two this morning. Let's see, that makes, oh, three hours. Yeah, close to three hours. Doorman said you were out."

I yawned, looking up at the sky. Dawn streaked Manhatttan skies yellow, orange, red, and blue. God wasn't being stingy with early-morning color.

Fatigue had blurred my vision. Harker, a man viewing the world through egg whites. I stiffened, trying to stop myself shivering from tension and the early-morning chill. I considered smiling, but abandoned the idea as too much effort. My first failure of the new day.

"How bad is it?" asked Loni. Her eyebrows lifted slightly, understandable since I didn't look like a man who was carefree and unencumbered.

"Bad enough. Somebody's trying to kill me." I rubbed my stiff neck, yawning some more.

Her eyebrows went up another inch with concern. Her eyes widened and her head leaned back in slight shock. "It's that heavy?" Her voice was soft with worry, as though we were both in a library.

"That heavy." I looked over my shoulder, then over hers. Habitual paranoia, a knee-jerk response. Around us, the streets were empty. Totally empty. A cab had just dropped Loni off, then pulled away. That left three of us standing on a Sutton Place sidewalk—Loni, me, and the doorman of her building, a big red-faced man who tried hard not to stare at us, but not hard enough to suit me.

I stared at Loni. One deep breath on my part was enough. I took it, then exhaled.

"You look good."

Her grin was the kind that said, "Thanks, but don't make a big deal over it."

Once, I'd told her that God had worked on her face at the same time he'd worked on Elizabeth Taylor's. And Liz had got the left overs. OK, so it was only my opinion.

Both women had oval-shaped faces, always a turn-on for me, with thick natural lashes, and the kind of sensual mouth a man would beg to suck on with his dying breath. Loni's eyes were sea green. Her hair was dark brown, and when the light hit a certain way, you could see some red in it. At five foot five she had perfect legs, as lovely as anything Michelangelo ever carved with a chisel.

Her breasts weren't big, but that wasn't a problem. Hadn't Loni and I both agreed that anything over a mouthful was a waste? We had. Loni had a mouthful. At twenty-eight, she looked younger. Some found her cold, others found her cool. She was always in control of herself, which is why she appeared frozen to many people.

Tonight—rather, this morning—she wore a pale yellow summer dress, with short sleeves and knee-length skirt. Her brown shoulder bag, which probably cost half of my weekly salary, wasn't overstuffed. Loni wouldn't want to destroy the designer's line. Her legs, which always set my mouth to watering, were bare, and she wore yellow wooden clogs. The effect was powerful, done simply and with confidence. She was delicious to look at and think about. I began to feel less tired.

We stood on the sidewalk staring at each other, saying nothing. Two people still involved with each other and not knowing what to do about it.

Loni rarely asked dumb questions, something else that set her apart from almost all women. But when your ex-husband shows up in front of your apartment building at five in the morning, unshaved, in a wrinkled puce polyester suit, papers and brown envelopes under his armpit, claiming somebody's out to waste him, a woman should say something.

"You want to come upstairs?"

I nodded once, relaxing a little. Might as well keep my dumb questions to myself, too. Like what were you doing all this time and who the hell was he?

I followed her into the building, forcing a weak, tired grin at the doorman because he'd been glaring at me like I was six feet of garbage piled under a hot sun. Snotty bastard.

In Loni's apartment, I collapsed on a long, low gray couch, closing my eyes.

"No coffee," she said. "Tea or juice, right?"

"You remembered."

"Yes." She didn't elaborate. If she remembered anything else, she wasn't going to mention it.

I heard her in the kitchen. God, did I ache. I was sore from hairline to toenail. Pictures flashed across my mind. Cars exploding in parking lots; guys chasing me through cornfields; Walter Fragan playing the piano and sneering; handsome Gaylord Ran Harley handing me a folded newspaper, then turning around and walking away; Delia Sisson sitting across from me and telling me she was going to die soon.

"Tea."

I opened my eyes.

It was on a coffee table in front of the couch. I sat up, mumbled thanks, and squeezed a lemon wedge into the hot liquid. Loni's apartment was on the twentieth floor, with huge windows facing the gray East River. While she had not finished decorating it, she'd started well, tastefully, expensively. Good Impressionist prints, copies of French classical furniture, a piano. She played well.

The apartment was huge, with a sunken living room, two bedrooms, dining room, and walk-in kitchen. A person could jog in here or herd cattle. I'd seen it when it was empty. Then we'd sat on the bare floor and talked about our divorce.

She sat across from me on an easy chair, legs drawn up under her, dress pulled down modestly. Loni never brought customers to her apartment. This place was her sanctuary, a refuge.

"Are they waiting for you at your place?" she asked. She was worried about me and I wanted that. She frowned, leaning her head forward.

"Maybe. I felt safer in the open, even more than hotels, so—" I shrugged. Fatigue ate away at me, making my bones hurt.

"Anything you can talk about?"

That had been the problem in the past. I had been too wrapped up in my work ever to talk about it with her. Obsession and ambition take up all your energy and time.

"Working on a story everybody thinks should be dead and buried. Somebody killed somebody and I don't think they should get away with it, that's all." I sipped the tea, enjoying the hot, lemony taste.

"Can they stop you?" She leaned forward, her hands folded.

"They've tried. If I get my story printed, that's it. It'll be out and everybody will know. Trouble is, I need more information, stuff on paper, stuff from eyewitnesses."

She leaned back in the chair, slim fingers pulling hair away from her eyes. "Those papers—" She pointed at my notes on the coffee table.

"Yeah, that's part of it." I thought about those tearsheets Ray Stance had sent me. Two of the three convicts mentioned in Warden Uttman's letters—Roger Joel and Willard Justin—both had looked a hell of a lot like Perry Joseph, the alleged assassin of Victor Evan Havilland. The two cons could have passed for Perry Joseph's twin brothers. Anyone seeing them from a distance would have thought he'd seen Perry Joseph. Interesting.

"What do you want me to do?" said Loni.

"I figure my place is going to be watched. Hotels, too. I need somewhere to work. Two days, maybe three. I should have everything together then."

I was undecided about going to Las Vegas and trying to learn about that meeting called by Harley and DeBlase. I wanted to know about it, believe me. On one hand, going out there seemed like backing naked into a buzz saw. On the other hand, going out there might be the last thing they'd expect me to do. Still, I was undecided about it. If I got good information from Fragan and Miranda, if I got a copy of the unreleased assassination report from Trotman or somebody else, then I didn't need to know what was going on in Vegas. *If.*

"You never made me a part of your work before," she said. She lifted a corner of her mouth in a small smile. The smile could mean, "You need me now, you prick." Or it could mean, "I'm glad you finally asked me." I wasn't sure.

"Loni, it's been tough the past couple of days. I didn't know how tough until I stopped running long enough to think about it. People have been hurt bad in this thing."

"Your fault?"

"No. Well, maybe. Hell, I don't know. I know that I'm tired and scared. Sometimes I think they'll get me before I finish this story. I've never run up against this kind of people before. They've got money, power. They're meaner than mean. Sometimes I'm sure they're going to win, that they're going to waste my ass before I get to the printer. I guess I'm saying I wanted to see you before—before—"

Before I get killed, I thought. But I couldn't bring myself to say it. Like I couldn't bring myself to say a lot of things when we were married. And look where that had got me.

"Yes," she whispered. "I understand."

I stood up. Damn, it was an effort. I ached so much. She stood up, too. We embraced. She felt good, smelled good. If I had a choice of a last act on earth, I think this would have been it.

We stood that way a long time, the dawn coming in through the window, the two of us holding each other, with nowhere to go, except bed and, later, our separate ways.

We began by going to bed. And weeping silently throughout our lovemaking.

When I woke up at twelve-thirty, Loni was gone. A note said she'd be back that evening, but she might have to go out again.

Nothing had changed. My ex-wife and I were both hard workers, always on the go, with little time for moments like we'd had this morning. Your ex-wife and love of your life is a working girl, Harker. Face the facts. You've had your therapeutic fuck, now off you go. Sure.

I read the note a couple of times.

The pain took its time going away.

30.

"We cut down trees to print this shit? Come on!" Jack Sommers turned his jowly head sideways, throwing both hands up in the air. The stocky man with receding greasy black hair and thick lips had just commented on what he'd heard of my Victor Evan Havilland story. Since the bastard had interrupted me three times, he hadn't heard that much. At fifty-five, his disposition was as surly as a ghetto drunk's.

He pointed a finger at me, his eyes hidden behind green-tinted glasses. "You take your own sweet time getting here, and when you do, what the hell do we get? Something every nut in creation has been pushin' for the past ten years. Jesus!"

The hands went up in the air again. He breathed loudly, like a bull in heat. Anger was never subtle with him. It was out in the open, the way it is with men of power who don't give a damn about anything or anybody.

We all sat around a long conference table, like the cast of an Agatha Christie mystery waiting for the inspector to come in and say, "The guilty party is one of us in this room." The room had wall-to-wall tan carpeting, brown wood panel walls, and three portraits of distinguished gentlemen—ancestors of Mrs. Evans.

"Jack," said Mrs. Evans, her voice all soft ice, "please let him finish." She grinned at me. I grinned back. Good old Eddie. Controlled and polite with her inferiors, the way a woman with a hundred million dollars should be. This morning she was wearing her usual basic black, pearls around her throat, and a thin gold wristwatch. At sixty-plus, she was well preserved, fashionably slim with gray hair cut short and well cared for.

"Yeah, Harker, finish." Jack Sommers didn't spit at me when he said that. He didn't have to. The thought was there. Jack Sommers didn't like me because he couldn't control me. He was also jealous, the way older editors are of young reporters. Sometimes an editor will ruin a young reporter out of bitterness, driving the kid out of the business. Sommers wouldn't do that. He had an eye for talent and used it well. But that didn't mean he had to like you.

Ruben Weiner, tall, sixty, white hair, pipe smoking, with bad teeth and an ulcer, let his eyes go from me to Jack and back again. Ruben had cut some of my stories in the past, but so far hadn't said anything. He may have been waiting for Mrs. Evans to tell him what his opinion was going to be. For some reason, I trusted Jack Sommers more. Jack was ambitious, therefore he'd let me get away with more. But first he'd try to break me down.

"Harker, you must understand something." Julius Ramey. Mr. Conciliatory. Silver hair, tanned, lined face, and capped teeth. At sixty, still handsome and lean and not to be trusted.

"What must I understand?" I sat sideways in my chair, a hostile position if you count such things as important.

Julius Ramey folded his hands, cleared his throat, and smiled. He looked good. "We've had phone calls from the White House, from the CIA, even from someone representing former President Wilcox."

"Wilcox didn't call himself?" A joke. Wilcox had been dead two years.

"Harker, this is serious." Ramey's smile weakened. His voice weakened, too.

"I know it's serious. That's why I got out of bed this morning."

Mrs. Evans smiled and said, "How long have you been in town?"

"Couple of days."

I let them think that one over. They didn't think about it very long.

Jack Sommers frowned until his thick black eyebrows met over his wide nose. His voice was high with rage.

"You were in town a *couple of days* and never contacted us, never—"

"Jack, Jack, I'm sure Harker had his reasons for that. Didn't you, Harker?" Mrs. Evans' voice was level, polite. But she wanted an answer.

"Yeah, I had a reason. First, I'd like to finish my story. I seem to remember little get-togethers like these in the past, with me on one side and everybody else on the other. And when the smoke cleared, guess who was right?" I wasn't angry yet. But it wouldn't take long at the rate we were going.

"I remember, Harker," said Mrs. Evans. "Go on, finish your story."

"First, let me say I'm sorry about the bill for the cornfield and those cars I totaled or didn't return. You'll understand as I go on. Next, I did come back to town and lay back. I'll explain that, too. Last, as fantastic as this tale is, I've got proof and I can get more. Proof enough to write a story. But understand something: The pressure's on because I've got something. They wouldn't be kicking us in the leg if I couldn't hurt them. I know my job and I do it goddamn well. Hear me out, just hear me out, OK?"

Nobody said anything. I took that as a signal to continue. Even Patrick Maxian, wearing one of his high-priced suits as usual, was attentive.

I began.

"Victor Evan Havilland was murdered. Not by one man. By three. Three men selected by Thomas DeBlase and a rogue CIA agent named Gaylord Ran Harley."

I stopped. I was being stared at.

I went on. When I finished it was eleven-fifteen. No one had interrupted me.

Patrick Maxian was the first to speak.

"Well, I—all I can say is *well*! Uh, you realize that DeBlase will undoubtedly sue us or pressure us for a retraction. I mean that's automatic." He didn't look happy about it. Fuck him. Worrying was his job.

"How far are you?" Jack Sommers was subdued, almost respectful. Almost.

"That's what I've been doing the past two days. Putting it together and staying off the streets, trying to keep on living. Halfway through a rough. I'm missing something, one last piece. I hate this kind of bullshit, sitting around here and talking about something before I've finished it." I was mildly pissed off, but too emotionally drained to start throwing chairs around the room.

"What's that final piece?" asked Patrick Maxian.

I hesitated. This isn't how I did a story, talking about it before it was finished. But what the hell, this wasn't any story. Not by far.

I opened my mouth, but I wasn't going to mention the secret CIA assassination report.

"Something linking the CIA to payoff money for the Mafia. Stuff on paper. Bank records and letters of deposit. Got problems with that. But I need the material. It can link the CIA, the Mafia, maybe even one or two of those convicts I mentioned. Remember I said it was beginning to look like maybe two of the convicts might have gone around posing as Perry Joseph?"

Maxian nodded.

"So when I get these financial records, I may have it all."

Ruben Weiner tapped his pipe against an ashtray, keeping his eyes down. "What about this Vegas meeting you mentioned? Shouldn't you try to check that out, maybe go out there?"

"Why? So I can get shot up and dumped out on the desert? My source for the records was supposed to be in town yesterday, but he's having problems." Fucking Walter Fragan. A minor car accident in North Carolina. No damage to him or Miranda, but the car had to be worked on. Rather than leave it and have it traced, he and Miranda were staying over until it was repaired. They were due in town later today or tomorrow. But I hadn't told anybody that. Not these people, not Loni.

"We've tried your apartment," said Jack Sommers. "You're not staying there." He sounded offended that I hadn't been in when he telephoned.

"Like the man said: When you're not here, you're there." I grinned at Jack, knowing he wouldn't like that. He didn't.

"Harker," said Mrs. Evans, "if this story is what you claim, it's going to turn this country upside down. Not that I mind. But we must be right on this. We cannot have so much as a small error. If we do, we can be sued or laughed at. Both are not pleasant." She wasn't smiling. She was a rich woman who was also a smart, careful woman.

"I know." I was tired. Tired of explaining, tired of trying to stay alive.

"Where are you staying?" Patrick Maxian. He took out a ballpoint pen and a small notebook.

"Forget it," I said.

"Aw, come on." Jack Sommers slapped the table in anger, both hands palms down and making a lot of noise.

I stood up, trying not to come unglued. "Until this story's finished, I'm holed up. Call Mrs. Karakas. She won't know, because I'm not telling her. But I'll check in with her and I'll get back to you if it's necessary."

"Harker!" Julius Ramey stood up, too, not smiling, ready to exert himself in front of Mrs. Evans. She didn't seem to notice. She was looking at me carefully, a hand fingering her pearls.

"Harker," snapped Ramey, "we have a right to know where you are! We're getting telephone calls and—"

"Sit down, Julius. We don't have a right to know that." Mrs. Evans kept toying with her string of pearls, watching me as though I were about to steal the silverware. "Harker, can you finish the story soon? Patrick and I want to check it very, very carefully before publication." She wasn't asking, she was telling. The mood in the room was subdued excitement. I still had to prove what I'd just told them.

"I'll try. No promises. Like I said, it depends on this last bit of information."

"Good. Will you be all right?"

"Sure. If I don't take out an ad where I am. This has got to be the last meeting before I bring the story in. I know you all outrank me here and I'm supposed to be humbly aware of that. But somebody did try to kill me. Maybe nobody in this room is as upset about that as I am. But I'm not making any more public appearances until I bring that story in." I thought of Gaylord Harley knowing as much about me as he did. I didn't like that.

"With backup notes and evidence," said Patrick Maxian, ever the lawyer.

"Sure. Can I go now?"

Everyone looked at Mrs. Evans, who smiled sweetly and said, "If you need anything, Harker, please ask. We don't want to interfere with you and have you take that story to another paper out of pique, now would we?" She was being excessively pleasant, but not for my benefit. She was telling her hirelings to back off and leave me alone. But she was doing it without busting their chops publicly. Stylish lady.

I grinned. So did she. Eddie and I understood each other.

"Harker?" Patrick Maxian.

"Yeah."

"If something happens to you and that evidence you've got all piled up somewhere, I suppose we don't have a story."

"Guess so."

He smiled, which seemed an odd thing to do.

"You take care of yourself, you hear?" The well-dressed man smiled some more.

31.

"What's up?"

"Where you callin' from?" Lamont's voice was hard with the promise of bad news.

"The paper. Phone booth in the lobby. Big meeting this morning with my publisher and the assholes running this sheet. My letter, it get there all right?"

"Yeah. Everything's cool. Down here they think somebody from Kalter's past caught up with him. I'm too new to have enemies. You ain't, but I didn't bring that up. Investigation goin' on. Don't look like I got to sweat it none. Thanks for what you did."

"For what *I* did? Shit, that turkey had a gun on me before you stepped in. Wasn't for you, I'd be dead."

At least Gaylord Ran Harley and Daddy Warbucks DeBlase hadn't reached Lamont like they'd reached Kalter.

"Your boy, Trotman," said Lamont. "Cat flipped out. Messed up two people and run off with some records. Ain't nobody sayin' what he run off with. But it's got to be heavy from all the shit that's goin' down 'round here. Security's tight on *all* records now.''

"Jesus, slow down! Trotman did *what*?" What the hell was going on? Trotman acting crazy?

"Man, I just *told* you. Trotman jumped two guys guarding a secret file cabinet. One's in the hospital. Fractured skull. Cat might die. Other one can walk some, but he sure can't run. Trotman just snuck up on them, dumped the cats, and copped those papers.''

"What papers?" I turned around in the phone booth, my back to the lobby. I was shouting. Sweating fast. Getting the kind of stomach that could put me on milk three meals a day, in the near future.

"Nobody's talkin'. Nothin' but tight lips 'round here. Everybody's runnin' round like the building's burnin'. You best watch your ass. You know they got you and Trotman tied together, so somebody might be comin' round to see you. Thought I'd warn you.''

"Yeah, yeah.''

I ran a hand through my hair, trying to make my brain work faster. Didn't do any good. Trotman busting heads and grabbing papers. One of those papers had to be the secret Havilland assassination report. Why else would the Company be uptight?

"One more thing," said Lamont. "Word is Trotman's unreliable as far as the organization is concerned. Unstable. Word is to close the file on him. You know what I'm sayin'?"

"Kill him.''

Lamont sighed. "You kept your word, you wrote that letter. It helped me a lot. I'm just tellin' you what's happening', that's it.''

"Yeah. I owe you, man. Trotman. Poor bastard. All he ever did was believe in his country. Look where the fuck it got him.''

"Ain't my worry. Ain't yours, now. Watch your own ass. That's why God gave you eyes.''

The CIA wanted Trotman killed. Which meant he had the secret assassination file on Havilland. *Had to*. Trotman was mentally unbalanced, said the Company. No longer safe, trustworthy. A thought hit me: I hoped Trotman hadn't flipped out to the point where he wanted to turn me into chopped meat.

"Lamont?"

"Yeah?"

"Thanks. Stay cool."

"All the time, dude. All the time." He hung up. The name he'd left with Mrs. Karakas was "Big Mac." Big Lamont, the Machiavelli fan.

32.

Loni closed her suitcase.

"I may be gone when you get back," I said.

Best for me to say it out loud. I'd been there two days and my nerves weren't as tight as they had been. Being with her had helped.

She smiled, sitting on the edge of the bed and lighting a cigarette. Her hands held the cigarette as if it were a white sapphire. A class woman, my ex-wife. After inhaling, she held her head back, blew smoke at the ceiling, and pulled a few strands of hair away from her forehead.

"You look better," she said.

Funny how one senses things. She'd agreed to my *time out*, but we both knew we had to return to living our own lives. For one thing, she was still living hers, even while I stayed at her apartment working on my story. That's why she'd packed. She was going out of town. She didn't tell me where and I didn't ask. We both knew why. Loni was a working girl.

"Feel better," I said, sitting on the bed with her, taking her hand. "Had my meeting today and survived. I'm still on the spot, but I should be OK. Thanks for the hideout. Thanks for everything.'' I squeezed her hand.

She playfully blew smoke in my face. ''Any port in a storm, right?''

''Wrong. Special port. Condemned man's last request.''

''Just call me Santa Claus.''

We sat holding hands on the bed, neither of us saying anything for a while. We both knew I would have to leave. I loved her, she had a kind of love for me. But that wasn't enough, it seemed. Sleeping with your ex-wife can be therapeutic, but painful. Therapy was drawing to a close. Time for the patient to be discharged.

She stood up. ''Plane leaves at seven-thirty tonight.''

''Four hours from now.''

She put out the cigarette, looking at me. ''Yes,'' she said softly.

I stood up and walked toward her. A little medication for the road.

The telephone woke me up, an ugly noise if you're sleeping well. I had been sleeping well, facedown on my typewriter. Nodding out in the line of duty. To hell with answering it. Nobody, not even my secretary, knew I was here. And if it was someone for Loni, a John or a friend, fuck them, too. I never touched her phone. The answering machine was turned off. She did that when she was out of town for several days. A recorded message saying she was away for a week was an invitation to burglars.

So the phone rang. And rang. And rang. I stood up, yawning and stretching. Almost two in the morning. I'd been writing since Loni had left for the airport.

Loni.

The telephone kept ringing.

Could it be her? Trouble. Shit, that was it. Loni was in trouble and had given this number. Plane crash. Hijack. A sex freak had punched her around. These cheerful thoughts and others beat a path to my brain.

The telephone kept ringing.

I ran across the room and reached for it.

"Harker?"

A man's voice. And I turned cold.

"Harker? Come on, come on. No need to be shy."

I froze.

"Harker, I don't have all day. If you won't talk, I guess it's up to me to carry the ball."

"Who—who is this?" I squeezed the receiver with both hands. My body ached from being rigid with fear.

"That's better. We met a couple of days ago. At the airport."

Gaylord Ran Harley.

I nodded. "I remember."

He sounded cheerful, like a man who had just paid off the mortgage.

"Good. Now listen carefully. I'll say this once. Once. No more. We've got your wife. She's—"

"My wife. What—"

"Harker, shut up!" His words were an icicle jammed in my ear. "Listen, reporter. That's all I want you to do. Listen. We've got her. If you don't do as you're told, she will come to grief. I think you know this is no idle threat."

He kept his voice calm, like an airplane pilot in a movie, telling the passengers he could land this thing on a dime. A calm voice playing with my life.

"What—what do you want me to do?" I sat down on the edge of a chair, ready to throw up.

"Get on a plane and come out to Las Vegas. You wanted to do that anyway, right? So here's your chance. Just in case you think I'm joking, let me describe what your ex-wife was wearing when she left New York tonight. White silk blouse, brown skirt, sandals. Carried one tan suitcase, small. One shoulder bag. Now, I can tell you what was in the suitcase if you want. I can even tell you what color underwear she's wearing. You come out to Las Vegas. TWA leaves Kennedy at three-thirty this morning. You leave now, you can make it. Don't come and you can live with the fact that you made a decision for both of you. You think about what the decision is."

Loni's life. I'd dirtied her with this mess. Christ.

"Harker? You still there?"

"Yeah."

"You sound tired. I can well understand that. You have been busy lately. Anyway, you come out to Las Vegas, rent a car, and start driving into town. Ask for a Chrysler, dark blue Chrysler. Start driving on Paradise Road. That's it."

"You've really got Loni?"

Silence.

Then—

"Ha-Harker?"

Loni. Frightened. Her voice as tiny as a child's.

"Loni? Loni?" I stood up, looking out of the window at the dark. Lights twinkled across the East River.

"I—I'm sorry," she said. "I came here to—to work and—"

"Never mind why she's here, Harker."

Harley. All business.

"Harley, you bastard! I'll kill you!"

He laughed.

"Harker, you amaze me. You butt in where you don't belong, and when the game gets rough, you cry. I can't afford to have you seen leaving New York with anybody near you. As far as anyone is concerned, you left on your own, like you always do. Nobody's forcing you to do a thing. Leave or don't leave. It's up to you. Your wife, your ex-wife, is in pain. If that doesn't bother you, well . . ."

All Loni had done was let me lie down and rest. That's all. And for that, they were hurting her.

"I'll be there, Harley."

"Thought you might. And, Harker—?"

"Yeah."

"Come alone. And bring those notes you discussed this morning. All of them."

"I'll be there, Harley."

"Like I said, I thought you might."

He hung up.

Angrily, I yanked the telephone from the wall and threw it at a mirror over the fireplace. The glass shattered. I looked at it. My reflection was ugly, a face of many, many parts. I stood there breathing heavily.

Loni. Stay here and kill you or go out there and get us both killed.

I looked at a clock. Five past two. Not much time.

I found another phone, the one in Loni's bedroom. Two calls before I left. Then out to Kennedy Airport.

I was going out to Las Vegas, and if I got the chance, I was going to kill Gaylord Ran Harley. That thought stopped me from being scared for a while.

In minutes, I was out of the apartment and down the sidewalk looking for a taxi.

33.

Nevada.

This morning, I drove the Chrysler along Paradise Road. As ordered. You can drive as fast as you want in this state, but Harker, the cautious speedster, kept the needle around fifty. Nice car. No bombs under the hood. I'd watched a bored-looking kid cowboy, with jeans, boots, and multi-colored fringe shirt, drive the car up to the McCarren Airport terminal and get out, underhanding me the keys in the same motion. I didn't tip the skinny bastard because I hated the shirt he was wearing.

At another time, the drive would have been pleasant. Cool, crisp desert air. Chilly, like all deserts are at night. Night? Hell, it was five-thirty in the morning and I was driving toward the dawn. My ass was still numbed from a five-hour flight. The time change, three hours behind New York, didn't bother me. My mind was still flip-flopping over this whole business. I didn't have time to worry about jet lag. The dawn was pretty. God had a good eye for color. Yellow, a brighter orange than New York dawn, a paler blue. Nice.

Paradise Road was still dark, which was good. The darkness hid the ugly trailers scattered along the roadside like giant tin cans.

Fucking Gaylord Ran Harley. Cocksucker. I could kill him twelve times over. Jerking me around like I had a wire in my nose. Leave New York, Harker, he ordered. We've got Loni, Harker. Gonna give her pain. Bring your notes, Harker. *The ones you talked about this morning.* I almost smiled. Almost. That had been Harley's one mistake so far. His fucking pride and arrogance, the power he thought he had with Thomas DeBlase's money, had got to him. So he had said something he shouldn't have.

That exploding car in Washington. Harley's airport conversation with me. *You're not wired, Harker. We know you're not. You haven't contacted your paper. We know you haven't.*

All that shit bothered me, because it meant Harley had somebody watching me. Somebody close. Yeah, it had bothered me. Until Harley had called Loni's apartment. I'd been too pissed off and worried to think about it during my talk with Gaylord. But my brain is as crafty as Harley's, in its own way. I now knew who Gaylord fucking Harley had watching me, checking me out, and reporting on my moves.

That's why I'd made two telephone calls before leaving Loni's apartment. Sure I was still scared, still jumpy. But before, I'd only had two chances of living through this: slim and none. Now I had three. Slim, none, and who-the-fuck-knows.

Gaylord. Slick little fucker, ain't you? Get me to leave New York alone, board a plane alone, arrive in Vegas alone. Witnesses will swear I wasn't threatened, that nobody had a gun in my back. So when accident time rolled around, it would look good. Nobody forced Harker to do shit. He went to his reward, as the old folk used to say, alone and unaided. Not quite, Gaylord, not quite.

The drive was quiet. So far. Just country music on the radio. Just like Indiana, where this thing had started.

Something had told me that I wasn't supposed to get to Vegas.

That something was right.

Ahead of me, blocking the road, were two cars. They seemed to have been expecting me. I chewed my lip, said a prayer that didn't last long and wasn't aimed at anyone in particular, then slowed down. All of this seemed unreal. Desert, wild-looking sky, and coming to a stop on a dumb dark road in Nevada. What a fucking way for a grown man to make a living.

I braked several feet away from the cars and waited. I took deeper breaths, because that seemed to help. It did. For a second or two.

Two figures detached themselves from the darkness and came slowly toward me in my headlights. They weren't in a hurry. They swaggered like cowboys trying to show off. Why not? They'd been on the winning team, you might say, for over ten years. That's how long the truth about Victor Evan Havilland's assassination had been a big fat secret.

My fingers drummed on the steering wheel. My rhythm was bad.

"You comin' out?"

The drawl was cheerful, playful. I was a mouse and the cats were going to have some fun.

The mouse opened the door and stepped out into some damn chilly air. In my hurry to get out of New York, I'd taken my gabardine jacket, throwing that over a short-sleeved shirt. Freezing on the desert hadn't been on my mind.

I shivered.

"Boy looks all tensed up," said Drawl #1.

"Got reason to be," said Drawl #2. They stayed in the darkness on either side of me. They chuckled softly, snickered, and did a good job of making me feel like I was in a lot of trouble.

"Where's Harley?"

"Yonder. In the car. You ain't carryin' nothin', is you?" Drawl #2. His voice was lower, somewhere around his belt buckle. He sounded more retarded than Drawl #1, who also sounded retarded in his own way. They patted me down for a gun and found none. I had none.

Rubbing my arms to keep warm, I walked on the highway with rubbery legs. Behind me, I heard the two cowboys poking around my Chrysler. My notes were on the front seat.

"Over here!" Harley's voice was sharp, a commander keeping the troops in line.

I walked to the first car. Harley sat near a window in the back seat. I looked for Loni, my head moving from front window to back.

"She's here," said Harley.

He opened the door and Loni climbed over him, stepping quickly to me. Her face was puffy, eyes red with weeping. Her left hand was bandaged.

Harley stepped out behind her. Tall, handsome, contained. Still with that attitude of a man who'd rather not waste time with you, but since he had to, he'd give you at least four seconds to make your point.

Counting the two drawlers who'd come over to my car, there seemed to be at least six men with Harley. Even without guns, they could have put out my lights. I'm a schemer, not the reincarnation of Bruce Lee.

"Bleeding's stopped," said Harley, pointing to Loni's hand. "Don't blame her. She had a role to play. She played it. She didn't know about it at the time, but she played it. And speaking of roles, yours is ending."

"Think so?" I sounded braver than I felt. I held Loni. She wept, trembling in my arms. I was trembling, too. Not weeping. Not yet. I could do that easily enough, if things didn't turn out like I'd planned.

"Know so," said Harley. He stood erect, watching me like I was some specimen on a slide. The man was impressive. Polite and well spoken, well dressed and in control of himself. And under it all, very evil, very dangerous.

"You know quite a bit about me," I said. Shadows seemed to draw closer. They weren't shadows. They were Harley's men. I fought against my fear. Pulling out every bit of guts I had left, I gently pushed Loni to one side and faced Gaylord Ran Harley. Me against the man who'd committed the crime of the century and got away with it. I could be considered overmatched. But what he had done to Loni had brought out a lot of hate in me. That hate could be put to good use. It could give me enough balls to save my life.

"Know a lot about you," repeated Harley. He smiled. His eyes weren't in it. Neither was his heart. The shadows snickered. "Yeah, Harker, you might say that."

One of the shadows stepped forward and handed Harley my notes. The tall, handsome man flipped through the pages, squinted at them in the darkness, then slapped them against his hand.

"All here?"

"No," I said.

He grinned. "Thought not. Now let me see, you probably called somebody, oh, like Mrs. Karakas, right? Maybe gave her a copy. Told her if you weren't back by such and such a time or if you didn't call her by such and such a time, that she should do something constructive with your notes and story. Right?"

A jolt of fear started at my feet, sped through my body, and punched my brain. I fought it like hell, balling my fingers into fists. I was close to dying and it was not a fun thing. Far from it. The man knew a lot about me. A hell of a lot.

I knew who he was getting his information from.

"Yeah, Harley. You're right. Mrs. Karakas has a copy of everything. If Loni and I don't leave here, she takes it to the paper. They'll run it."

"No, Harker. They won't. She will bring it to the paper and no one will print a word of it. Before I tell you why, look around you. Go on, look."

I did. I saw nothing. Just desert, dawn, and three cars parked on a deserted road. No other cars coming by. I might have wondered about that, but right now I didn't care.

Harley kept on talking, arms folded across his chest. He'd have looked great in television commercials. Or on a slab in the morgue.

"Today's the first day of some very special United States Army maneuvers. Road's blocked off, about now. Lot of press coverage, Harker. Not the kind of thing your Eastern liberal elite goes for. But some papers have readers who are quite interested in such things. You know, I've been on maneuvers where, oh, thirty, forty men were killed. Really. Happens all the time. Tanks back up over a fox-hole, parachutes don't open, grenade explodes before it should, live ammunition is used instead of blanks. Accidents, Harker. Happens all the time. Today, there's going to be two for sure. Two.''

"Loni and me," I said. Can't fool Harker, folks.

Harley smiled. The shadows snickered again. A fun time was being had by all. Except for me and my ex-wife. Loni was still shaking, cradling her sore hand against her chest. I tried grinning at her. It didn't feel like a grin to me.

"Loni and you," said Harley. "I wanted you to know what's going to happen to you, to you both. *You know why*. A reporter dies in the line of duty. Accident. On the job. With his beloved at his side. And a bullet in his ear.''

I looked over my shoulder. Behind me, the road was bare, except for my Chrysler.

I turned back to Harley.

"How's Patrick Maxian?" I said.

Harley's head snapped back as though he'd just heard a strange noise. He narrowed his eyes and stared at me for a long time before saying anything.

"What did you say?" His voice was very, very soft.

"You heard me." I didn't repeat my question.

"Patrick Maxian?" asked Harley.

"Yeah. One of several lawyers employed by the *World-Examiner* to keep it out of libel suits and shit like that.''

Loni said, "Oh, Harker, I'm sorry—''

Harley didn't look at her when he hit her. Just a quick backhand in the face, driving her up against the car. Loni yelped, like a puppy that's just been stepped on.

I blew my cool.

Leaping forward before the shadows could stop me, I swung at Harley's good-looking face, catching him at the corner of the mouth and spinning him around. He had a hard jaw and my fist started to hurt.

It was one of the best punches I ever threw. I didn't get a chance to throw another one. Arms grabbed me from behind, and a forearm came across my throat. I stopped breathing and started rasping.

"Let him go! Goddamn it, let him go! Can't be a mark on him!" Harley was shouting, touching the corner of his mouth. His fingertips were bloody. It was goddamn good watching him bleed.

The shadows let me go. I felt my sore throat. An ax might have hurt me more, but I doubt it. For a few seconds, I leaned over and rasped like a donkey.

Harley worked his jaw left and right. I watched his tongue probe for loose teeth. Now I knew how good it could feel to hurt somebody.

"OK, Harker, let's talk about Patrick Maxian."

I coughed. It was like swallowing broken glass.

"Maxian." My voice was barely above a whisper. The pain was sharp and fresh. "He's your inside man. He used my wife to set me up. You got her out here, gave her some pain, and that was enough to get her to come to the phone."

Loni was on her feet, holding her face with both hands and weeping. I wanted her to come out of this. If nothing else, I wanted her to walk away alive.

"Go on," said Harley, dabbing at his mouth with a silk orange handkerchief. The shadows had stopped snickering.

"In Washington, you said you knew I hadn't contacted the paper. A few hours ago, you said to bring along the notes I'd discussed this moring. That adds up to somebody at the top knowing about me. That adds up to Maxian. Where is he?"

I heard footsteps behind me. One of the shadows stepped forward into the light from the headlights. Patrick Maxian.

Not so contained now. His lips were pressed together and he had both hands jammed into the pockets of a very expensive suit jacket. He looked at me, then looked away quickly. Patrick Maxian was nervous.

I spat in his general direction and went back to stroking my sore neck.

"So you knew about Maxian." Harley finished wiping

blood from his mouth and folded the handkerchief neatly before putting it back in his pocket.

"*Before* I came out here, Harley. *Before.*"

The silence in the cold dawn was reassuring. I was still shivering, but I'd scored points with that last remark. I could feel it.

Stepping closer to Harley, I said in as calm a voice as I could come up with, "If you're counting on Maxian here to go back and get my notes and poke holes in them in front of my editors, you're fucking crazy. I've taken care of that." Sunlight began to creep closer to us.

"I see," said Harley softly, fingers lightly touching his jaw where I'd hit him. It was nice to see that. His voice was slightly less sure now. But he was a hard one to shake. My neck hurt like hell.

"You see—" I began pointing at him, wishing my finger were a bazooka.

The cars had rolled up without lights. When we heard them, they had stopped behind my Chrysler.

If I were the type to fall to my knees in gratitude, this would have been as good a time as any. Car doors opened and men got out. In the darkness and from that distance, they, too, looked like shadows. They were. *My* shadows. God is kind every so often.

Gaylord Ran Harley stepped forward, head leaning toward the new arrivals. His men turned, too, a couple of them reaching for their back pockets and sticking hands in their waistbands. They weren't reaching for a chew of tobacco. DeBlase's men, probably. Or Vegas cowboy types working for Harley in Nevada.

Me, I was excited, nervous, happy, relieved, ready to pee in my pants for the sheer joy of it all. A lot of people came to Nevada to gamble, to get divorced. I'd gambled with my life and won. I didn't have to divorce myself from living. Not this time, Charley.

Roy Lupus was out in front of his men, his coat collar turned up, face unshaved, hair uncombed, and no smile on his precise face. He didn't look so neat. He stared at me as though I'd just attacked his wife.

"Where's Trotman, Harker?"

I grinned, shrugging.

"Beats the shit out of me."

"Harker, is this some kind of fucking game? We get calls from three goddamn senators and I don't know how many other assholes with clout. Washington's on fire. We were told to get out here on the double because you and Trotman were meeting to—"

The man was angry, shouting loud enough to push back the dawn and drop us all into darkness.

One call to Mrs. Karakas, like Gaylord Ran Harley had figured. And one call to Lanford Greeve Paugh, giving him that second chance we all wish we had. I told him I had trouble, big trouble, all of it tied in with the Havilland assassination. And this was his opportunity to do *now* what he hadn't done *then*, to stand up. All he had to do was call some of his powerful friends and get them to lean on the Company hard, real hard, because my life and my ex-wife's life depended on it. If the CIA heard it from some big people that Trotman and I were meeting in Nevada regarding missing CIA papers, hopefully they would come out here to see us.

If those documents ever appeared in the newspapers, said Paugh's powerful friends, heads would roll. All of this, plus my flight number, had been what I counted on to draw somebody, *anybody*, out here in the desert. I'd won my gamble. This time.

Harley was breathing deep.

"Roy," he said, greeting Lupus.

"Harley. What the hell's going on here? What—"

Lamont walked over to me, shaking his head from side to side, adding one of his stingy grins. I nodded back in greeting. We added nothing else to our hellos. Now wasn't the time.

Harley's handsome face wasn't so composed anymore. He was fighting to get his brain in gear. He frowned, eyes staring up at the dawn.

"Harley," yelled Lupus, jabbing a finger at the good-looking man, "if you're in on this, if you've fucked up this time, nobody, but nobody's going to save your ass. I've got top priority on getting our property back. Anybody gets in my way, gets hurt. That's from the top.'' The neat little man was shook up. Whoever had given him the word to get traveling this morning must have really taken a chunk out of his behind.

Lupus' face was a bright red. Veins jumped from his neck. Trotman must have been Topic A around Langley. Lupus had seven men backing him up right now, three of them with shotguns. None of Harley's men had shotguns. My kind of odds.

I had my arms around Loni, who was still shaking, her face streaked with tears. Reaching over, I took my notes from Harley.

''Lupus, I'm going back to my car.''

''Harker, you ain't goin' anywhere. You're staying—''

''To the car, Lupus. I'm cold, I'm tired. So's Loni. We'll wait there for you.''

''Harker, those papers—''

''My notes. And you're not touching them.''

''Harker?!''

''You can scream your ass off, I don't give a shit. I say you're not touching them.''

''Oh?'' Arrogance dripped from his neat mouth.

''Yeah, *oh*. First, your muscling me out of D.C. was part of my plan. Don't try it here. You do, and I'll not only tell that story—which I might do anyway—but when your people learn that your leaning on me caused Kalter's death, one of your own agents—''

''Wait a minute.'' Roy Lupus stepped closer for us to hug and kiss. ''Kalter—?''

''Yeah, Kalter. He worked for Harley here. Harley suckered me to the airport. When I wouldn't go along with what he asked, he tried to kill me. He got Kalter instead. Now I don't expect Harley to admit shit. But Lamont here saw him at the airport. And Regis Cooler, a New York PR man, set up the meeting. Check him out, if he's still living. Working for Harley and DeBlase can be dangerous. You fuck me over, Lupus, and I'll do a story that will ruin your whole day, especially if some people with clout in D.C. read that you set up your own agents for killing. That's how the story's gonna come out, believe me.''

Loni felt warm next to me. In the cool dawn, I smelled faint traces of her expensive perfume. I hated Harley for trying to kill her. I hated Patrick Maxian for using her to get at me. It was good to feel like my old self again. Hostile and mean.

"Harker, I have to see those notes." Lupus was almost gentle.

"You don't. All you have to do is to make sure I don't have any CIA documents here, right?"

"Yeah."

"I'll hold them up quickly. Don't blink, 'cause you'll miss it. You won't find any of your stuff here. Will that cool you out? It had better."

"Yeah, that'll be OK." He sighed. Life is compromise, after all.

We played show-and-tell on the highway, with Lupus squinting at my papers as I held up each page. He kept nodding with relief as each page came up minus any official-looking stamp. The stuff I was showing him was my notes, and a copy of my unfinished rough on the assassination. I didn't hold it up long enough for him to read that much of it. He was only looking at the head of each page anyway.

"Satisfied?"

He nodded.

"Good. Like I said, I'm going to my car. I'll wait for you. Ask Gaylord here about Kalter and airport meetings. Bet he's got some kind of answer, right, Gaylord?" I looked at the handsome man. He was glaring at me like he wanted to pull out my heart with a bottle opener. The man was good at hating. At the moment, so was I. Loni being here made me just as good at that game as Gaylord ever was.

I walked away from the highway, an arm around Loni. Let Harley tell Lupus about airport meetings, about why he had me and my ex-wife on a lonely, cool Nevada road early in the morning. I didn't want to hear it. I already knew why.

Behind me, I heard Lamont say, "I'll see them to the car."

When the three of us were sitting in my Chrysler, Lamont said, "What's happenin'?"

"Harley. Tried to kill me. Us."

Loni was trying to clean her face, using her finger and
the rear-view mirror.

"Why?" said Lamont.

"You wouldn't believe me if I told you."

"Let's see."

I told him.

Lamont believed me. White people, he said, were capable of anything.

34.

Two days later in the *New York World-Examiner* conference room, Jack Sommers fingered a small pile of bankbooks and letters. "This stuff, you've checked it with the Mexican banks?"

"Yeah," I said, pointing to it. "The bank has a branch here. The branch confirmed the type of passbook used. One of the officers called Mexico City for me. Records are still there on file. The CIA deposited money there for the Mafia to use in killing the premier of Cuba. This Mr. Voltaire you see on a couple of these letters is Harley's code name. He set up the money, all right. No two ways about it. I've confirmed his identity and code name."

Ruben Weiner aimed his pipe stem at me. "Those pictures, the convicts—"

I cut him off. "I had Ray Stance fly down to Mexico City with the tearsheets. Only one person at the bank remembers Roger Joel, the one who looks the most like Perry Joseph. But he remembers him. And there's a couple of Perry Joseph signatures on hand. Withdrawals."

"These guys," said Jack Sommers, flipping through a passbook. "Where are they?"

"Hiding." Walter Fragan and Miranda were in New Jersey, in a Cuban community. They were waiting for my story to be printed before contacting the CIA again. Miranda's code name was Cuchillo. Mr. Knife. The man who had brought prostitutes from Estevez to convicts in Texas. The man who had heard the convicts' names mentioned by Harley and his men more than once.

It was my business where Fragan and Miranda were hiding out.

Trotman. I still hadn't heard from him. And that secret CIA report on the assassination. Did he have it or didn't he? I'd written a damn good story. And that's why this conference was on, minus Patrick Maxian. He'd disappeared. His wife, his law firm, no one knew where he was. I had a feeling he might be at the bottom of Lake Mead, but I really didn't care. I'd spent the last two days right here at the *World-Examiner*, sleeping and working, getting that story down on paper.

I'd met Fragan and Miranda last night. After that, they'd taken off to wait for my story to hit print and increase their chances of living out the week. Trotman's report could have made the story perfect. The report about what kind of wounds Havilland really had, what kind of suspects really should have been considered assassins. Without that report, I had a good story but a less than total one.

Mrs. Evans was seated in her usual place, the head of the table. Jack Sommers, Ruben Weiner, Julius Ramey, and another attorney, one Baron Richardson, were all present. Richardson was small and had a flat head. He spent a lot of time pushing his glasses back up on his nose.

There was a knock on the door.

"Yes?" Jack Sommers roared loud enough to be heard in Newark. Mrs. Karakas came in with a folded copy of the *World-Examiner*. She handed it to me.

"Man dropped this off at my desk."

I took the folded paper. Big deal.

"Big. Big hands. Biggest hands—"

My heart skipped a beat. I unfolded the newspaper. It was there. Marked: CLASSIFIED TOP SECRET. Plain white paper. The CIA report on Victor Evan Havilland's assassination. Sixty pages.

I leaped out of the chair. Trotman. *Beautiful*. Fucking beautiful.

"Where is he, where—"

Mrs. Karakas frowned. "What are you getting so excited about? One truck driver, more or less—"

I sprinted across the room, yanked open the door, and ran down the hall. Trotman was gone.

Back in the room, Mrs. Karakas was saying, "Dressed like one of our truck drivers. Same uniform. Hands. God, they were frightening. Ugly."

I looked at the report. Fucking incredible. Victor Havilland *had been* one of several top-ranked politicians who had ordered CIA assassinations of foreign leaders. It was here in black and white, the killings and when they had occurred. Later, he'd changed his mind about doing it in the future, but it was too late as far as the Cuban premier was concerned.

Havilland was supposed to have backed a planned CIA-sponsored invasion of Cuba. He didn't. Because of this, the CIA was left hanging and it had cost them twenty agents, as well as over one hundred affiliated guerrillas. Somebody like Gaylord Ran Harley might take the death of twenty CIA agents hard, especially if they were his men.

There was something about more than one Perry Joseph and the fact that at least one Perry Joseph had been on the CIA payroll for eighteen months. It mentioned when he'd been recruited. The case officer he'd reported to had been Gaylord Ran Harley. There was more, a lot more.

But I had my story.

I passed it to Jack Sommers. He looked at the outside, frowned, looked at me, and opened the report. After waiting almost a full minute while Jack read it, Mrs. Evans said politely, "Jack?"

Without looking up, he closed the report and passed it

down to her. She read in silence for a few minutes. Then she closed it and passed it down toward me.

"Jack, when you've finished reading it, let everyone else in the room read it, too. Including Baron. When you've all read it, give it back to Harker. The story runs in all of tomorrow's editions. All. Harker, this is to be at least a five-part story. You've got some rewriting to do. Jack, you and Ruben work that out. Baron, plan on staying here with Harker for as long as it takes. I want you to clear whatever needs to be cleared. From what I can gather, there's not going to be that much of a problem. Harker, call your friends in. The Russian and the other one. We'll make arrangements to protect them until some official takes over. Tell them no pictures, so not to worry. Questions?"

"Yeah." I raised my hand. "I want to include the Vegas meeting in the story. I can't come out and say they talked about the killing. But two men from the New Orleans police department were at that meeting and on DeBlase's payroll. Just like Maxian. *That* bastard was on the board of directors of three companies belonging to DeBlase. How come nobody knew that?"

Mrs. Evans was sweet, and to the point. "It wasn't necessary for us to know"—she paused—"then."

"OK. Five-part story, huh? I might have to do more traveling. *After* the first one appears, not before. When it's public, I won't have to look over my shoulder."

"Travel where?" said jowly Jack Sommers.

"D.C., Mexico, Florida. Some of the same places. Got to make sure. Besides, I might get called in by the Justice Department."

"You will," murmured Baron Richardson, eye on the CIA report. "No problem. This, for example. When you're finished with it, I'll turn it in. Long as they don't find you with it, no problem. Far as DeBlase is concerned, you've documented everything about him pretty well. No problems."

"Harker?" Mrs. Evans stood up.

"Yeah?"

"Get to work." She paused and smiled. "Please?"

When all was said and done, the hand on the whip belonged to a sixty-plus, gray-haired lady.

That night I stood in the lobby of Loni's apartment house reading a note handed to me by the doorman.

> I missed you, and that bothered me. That's why I want to get away. When you were in trouble, you needed me and that was good. Now I may be learning to need you and that's not good. The truth is, I'm going away until I feel the way I did before you came back, before I started to miss you. Harker, I want my own life, I really do. Please understand.
>
> Loni

Nothing to say where she was or when she'd be back.

I read the note again. Then I kept my back to the doorman while I squeezed the teardrops from my eyes with my fingertips.

On the way out, I handed him tomorrow's newspaper, a copy of the *New York World-Examiner*. The one with my story on who had really killed Victor Evan Havilland ten years ago.

Two days later, I got a call from "Big Mac."

Trotman had killed himself. One in the mouth from a .45. He hadn't had help. It had all been his own idea. I knew why. When you've been a believer, and there's nothing left to believe in, then there's nothing left to live for.

I went into the nearest bar and ordered two beers, the kind I'd seen Trotman drink. One I swallowed in a hurry, as non-drinkers do. The other I left untouched. A tribute to a man who had really cared about something. Then I went to a telephone and used a credit card to send flowers to Mrs. Riley Sisson in Alexandria, Virginia.

I called Loni.

No answer. The recorder wasn't picking up. It never did when she wasn't in town.

Watch for

Dead and Paid For

next in the Harker File series
coming soon from Lynx